About the Author

This book was written in lockdown thinking I may be able to come up with a feasible story while reliving my teenage years vicariously, wishing they'd been as described. I'm now seventy-six, a widower, my husband (the dedicatee) having died in 2016 after forty-four years together. My home is in London where my current companion is an eighteen-year-old deaf cat, who is however, an excellent alarm clock, getting me up at four thirty a.m., to feed him before I go for a swim at the YMCA.

Kissing Frogs

Gerald L Milch

Kissing Frogs

Olympia Publishers
London

www.olympiapublishers.com
OLYMPIA PAPERBACK EDITION

A CIP catalogue record for this title is
available from the British Library.

ISBN: 978-1-80074-666-4

First Published in 2022

Olympia Publishers
Tallis House
2 Tallis Street
London
EC4Y 0AB

Printed in Great Britain

Dedication

In memory of Dugald MacIntyre MacInnes

Acknowledgements

Many thanks to all the friends who read the original and have encouraged me to complete the book wanting to know what the heroes get up to next with helpful comments on what is possible sexually and also about Scottish traditions. Also, thanks to friends who have provided translations and use of swearwords where needed. I'm sure I'd miss someone out if I tried to name them all.

Disclaimer

The use of living or dead authors', composers', lyricists' and performers' names and their published work in whatever format, is entirely without prejudice, and is merely meant to indicate the depth and breadth of fictional characters' knowledge and experience. Other than actual geographical locations or historical fact, the names of most characters and places are totally fictitious. They bear absolutely no resemblance to anyone living or dead. Any actual resemblance is purely coincidental. This is a work of fiction.

Chapter 1

It was a dark and stormy night when I partially lost my virginity. Apologies for the opening cliché, but it was all true as things turned out. Perhaps it would be as well to start from the beginning and provide some basic background. My name is Ethan Liddell, I'm seventeen, a little under six feet tall, brown hair and eyes and live with my parents in the town of Natick which is on the left bank of the Charles River. It is a suburb, in commuter terms, of the city of Boston, Massachusetts. I suppose locals would think of Natick as a desirable, leafy, fairly affluent place to live and sufficiently distant from the city to seem almost rural.

My parents are both teachers; my father is head of geography at a local high school and my mom teaches at an elementary school. For some reason they considered it better for me to attend schools closer to our home than the ones where they taught, and their careers confirmed that arrangement. It worked out very well I suppose and my education didn't seem to suffer as a result!

Elementary school was quite a pleasure and I made some wonderful friends, in particular Steph and Ed who live quite close by. Our little "gang" included a lovely girl called Caroline, but her dad eventually got a new job so she and her family moved away. Steph, Ed and I got on really well, so it was a relief when it was time to transfer to high school that the three of us went to the same one. On reflection, it may be that the reason we gelled so well was that we were almost the only single children in the school so we had our own siblings in each other.

At our first school we had all three been involved in plays in one capacity or another, so on transfer I looked forward to that continuing, but Ed had moved on to being more interested in soccer and Steph, rather to my surprise, took to soccer as well and was very happy that our high school offered girls' teams. This meant that our after-school activities rather separated us on many occasions, but we still got together frequently, enjoyed each other's company and were in and out of each other's homes all the time. It helped of course that our parents all got on and socialised together quite a lot.

I was definitely not a sports jock being, in retrospect, rather introverted except where drama was concerned when I was quite happy to be a part of any performance, but equally happy to participate in working backstage. My parents seemed content with this arrangement — neither was what you may call particularly demonstrative, but they were very supportive of what I did and always came to performances where I featured in any role big or small.

As the years passed, they were delighted when I got my driving licence and handed me their car (while buying themselves a new slightly smaller one), which was white and large enough for me to take Steph and Ed to school and also take them and be in the crowd to support them at any away soccer matches at other schools. Having my own vehicle also relieved our parents of the time-consuming journeys to drop us off or pick us up from school or wherever if the regular school bus were not available.

During the long summer vacations, we liked to go to Memorial Beach at Dug Pond on hot days, and it was on one of those days in July when, in late morning, having collected Steph and Ed, I drove us to the beach, and as we approached our usual spot, my eye was caught by a boy and girl stretched out on the sand. Both of them had what can only be described as incredible red hair and very fair skin, presumably brother and sister. The boy must have been about our age and the girl perhaps a couple of years younger. Both were wearing just navy-blue Speedos and sun glasses and there were bottles of suntan lotion to hand. They didn't seem unduly disturbed by our approach and that we settled almost next to them, perhaps only a couple of yards away. We settled in our usual places. I sat facing them, Ed facing me and Steph between us, they having stripped to their Speedos and applied some lotion. I just kept my t-shirt and shorts on because heat could bring me out in a rash. Normally, being so used to each other's company, initially there wasn't much conversation and we were happy to have our books, drinks, snacks around us and a small radio to provide some music, but playing very quietly so as not to disturb others.

I found it impossible for my eyes not to be drawn to the boy. To my mind he had a great body with clearly defined muscles, obviously a fit sports jock, and a well-filled budgie smuggler! I had to stop a smile on my face when I suddenly thought it must be a rather large budgie or even a cockatoo stuffed down there. I didn't know if he was aware of my interest, but at one point he turned his head to face me, his sunglasses not revealing if he was actually looking at me. I felt embarrassed to be caught staring so obviously and quickly buried my head in my book. When I did think to chance another look, I thought I saw a small smile creep across his face. Ed and Steph had been very quiet for a while but suddenly started chatting about something to do with soccer which rather excluded me, I didn't mind as it provided a bit of cover for my embarrassment. All of a sudden, the object of my admiration, stood up, took off his sunglasses to reveal a pair of brilliant piercing blue eyes which looked directly at me, he smiled slightly and spoke to the girl. He said quietly, but in clear English tones, "Ruth, I'm going in for a swim to cool off. Back soon."

He ran down the sand and plunged into the lake, striking out in a very adept front crawl. We all watched him go; that lovely body was the epitome of grace in my eyes. My friends looked at me for a few moments but nothing was said until Steph said, "I think it's time for some food."

This proved to be welcome distraction until a movement at the lake side caught my attention as the boy returned to get his towel. The water ran down his body and limbs emphasizing his contours, picking up the few hairs on his chest, arms and legs until they were towelled. He caught my eye again and responded with a broader smile which I found enchanting. He spread out the towel and stretched out on his back, replacing the sunglasses as before, but still lay with his head to one side so he seemed to be looking at me again with that definite slight smile back.

Steph and Ed continued with their quiet chat and gradually consumed their provisions. "Ethan, aren't you going to eat anything?" Ed asked.

"Yes. Of course."

So I managed to unwrap a sandwich and get some of it down but my mind was so full of our beach neighbour it was difficult to think of much else. His presence had really disturbed me as I'd never felt this way about anyone before. No one at school had ever interested me sexually, not even the generally well-built football, soccer or other sporty types. Actually, that isn't quite true, I'd had a crush on Jan for a couple of years. It was this that had convinced me that I must be gay. Jan was a very handsome, very blond boy who excelled at soccer and was likely to become the new academic year's soccer captain. It had crossed my mind that Jan was keen to get it together with Steph, but he always seemed to back off rather than approach her directly and she never said anything either. Ed and I were just really good friends who would do anything for each other, but after more than ten years of doing so much together, there was absolutely no sexual interest, and anyway, he was showing a distinct interest in a lovely girl called Rosita Martín.

As the realisation that I was gay had gathered, I came to heartily resent it. For the millionth time I asked myself why? why? why? why? why did it have to be me? It seemed so unfair that, while "life" might eventually turn out to be a total pile of shit in many ways for straight guys, their sexuality was a straight line from the appearance of the first pubic sprout to what I imagined would be the exhilaration of the first time they experienced an orgasmic explosion inside a female. Some fellow students had no problem in finding a girlfriend and a few seemed to have had several and I mean "*girl*friends" not friends who happen to be female (thank you Sheldon Cooper in *Big Bang Theory*!) and had that slightly smug self-confident air to show what men of the world they were. I considered myself a dreadful coward so didn't feel able to come out to anyone, despite my parents being very liberal minded, and thank goodness, not believers or church-goers, and I thought, highly unlikely to beat me or throw me on to the streets. But I was sure it would be a deep disappointment to them. I was an only child of two only children so there were no uncles, aunts or cousins. The school's Gay-Straight Alliance would've meant a too open declaration and I just couldn't face it. All I wanted was someone like me to *like* me and be prepared to explore possibilities.

Some nights as I lay in bed, I tried to dream up an ideal guy and what he would look like. My imagination covered his height, his build, his body hair, if any, the range of natural hair colours from ash blonde through the browns to solid black; more importantly the range of eye colours from almost washed-out pale blue to black; skin colours from the cold white of the undead to silky inky black. How full and kissable were his lips and where were they on my body? Fuck, fuck, fuck, fuck, fuuuuck. I wanted a boy with whom I could find out about that tentative first kiss which would slowly intensify to sheer unbridled passion as our hands felt each other's faces, bodies and… I knew enough that I wasn't going to go blind or have my hands covered in warts! Would my "endowment" be enough? Well, he'd have to accept what Mother Nature had thought sufficient. I wouldn't be able add anything to length or girth whatever I did! I wondered what his tongue would taste like. Tooth paste? His latest meal? Garlic? Pizza? The image of Jan usually emerged at the end and he would stand there, the sun making his hair even whiter than usual, his manly chest heaving, an enigmatic smile playing about his full, kissable lips as I would start to unbutton his shirt and then, having exhausted so many possibilities, I'd fall asleep eventually, really grateful to have good friends. Much of my depressing reading just seemed to say how lonely gay guys were. The only comfort (ha!) was knowing that I wasn't the only one.

As the minutes ticked by, there was another movement when both the boy and the girl got up and the boy said, the second part perhaps slightly louder than need be, "We'd better make a move if Mum's going to fetch us. We can always come back tomorrow at about the same time." They pulled on their navy-blue shorts and navy t-shirts with a logo which I was unable to read clearly, but may have been a school badge. With a slight nod of the head to me and still with the same slight smile, the pair of them, having gathered up all their beach paraphernalia, set off for the parking lot. They looked back once as if trying to memorise the exact spot. Ed and Steph had been concentrating on sending messages so, when they had finished and we noted that the beach had emptied as other users had gone off for lunch, we relaxed and enjoyed the rest of the afternoon having turned up the radio slightly. I just hoped that my interest had not been too obvious under my shorts!

Chapter 2

I haven't mentioned that, perhaps oddly for someone of my generation, I have absolutely no interest in popular music. My parents always had music playing at home, but it was usually classical, somewhere between Haydn and Britten but most often the 19th Century Romantics. At home there was a large collection of CDs and DVDs which pre-dated more up to date technology, but I was able to play both on my computer, if I wanted to put something on while doing my homework. Dad, being more up to date, had transferred most of his stuff onto his computer via iTunes so was able to select something with less bother. They were also keen, on stage musicals, German Lieder and French chansons. Dad was a competent pianist but when he tried to give me piano lessons, it proved to be beyond me, all those sharps and flats. But I learnt a lot of the lyrics by heart and used to sing along with some of the better-known songs and would even attempt a couple of arias, but definitely only in the privacy of my room where I was sure no one could hear me. Jonas Kaufman was my hero and one of my favourite opera arias was his performance of "La fleur que tu m'avais jetée" from *Carmen*, four and a half minutes of pure emotion and longing. A regular fantasy was me performing a selection of popular pieces to a wildly enthusiastic crowd, but I knew at heart that my voice, while I could hold a tune, didn't really have the heft to be heard across my bedroom, let alone a recital or concert hall. When the school drama productions required the cast to sing anything I was always very happy to participate.

Chapter 3

The next day turned out to be a repeat of the previous one, being wonderfully warm and sunny. So it was something of a surprise to find messages from both Steph and Ed to say that they wouldn't be able to go to the beach as previously arranged, but they both hoped I would have a lovely day without them. Just in case my hopes were realised, I made sure my morning shave was as good as possible. After breakfast I got my stuff ready, made a sandwich for lunch, grabbed a bottle of water and made for the door shouting out to my parents where I was going. My intention was to get to the beach when it opened to the public so that I might be there before anyone else, especially yesterday's pair.

At the beach I got one of the folding chairs we use on these occasions out of the trunk and settled in the usual spot. No one else was there, so I put on my headphones, plugged them into my retro-Walkman and sat back with a book, one of the prescribed pieces of literature we were supposed to cover during the vacation and waited expectantly and (if I'm honest) slightly nervously for them to appear. However, the warmth of the day and the strains of Tchaikovsky's *Evgeny Onegin* in my ears did make me lose concentration for a while, so it was only when a shadow crossing in front of me made me open my eyes, I found they had arrived and were preparing to lie down on the sand next to me. They were both wearing the same shorts and t-shirts as yesterday, and annoyingly, I still couldn't make out the white logo even when they stripped off to show the same Speedos. The boy took off his sunglasses, held out his hand, gave me a lovely smile, and said, "Hello. I'm Harry Brown and this is my sister Ruth."

Of course, I had to switch off the CD and ask him to repeat what he'd said before shaking his broad hand. "Hi. I'm Ethan Liddell."

"Are you here by yourself today?"

"Yes. My friends had something better to do today for some reason." His smile seemed to broaden a bit and revealed a beautiful even set of white teeth. Ruth looked up at me and smiled similarly. They were both very attractive. A thought came to me and I gushed "Would you like me to fetch a couple of beach chairs? They're in the car so it will only take a couple of minutes and you may find it more comfortable."

"Thank you. That would be very kind."

I jumped up and almost ran to the car, grabbed the chairs that Steph and Ed had used, and ran back. They had stood up ready for me and were applying some sun tan lotion, so after a few minutes they were done with covering themselves, with me wishing fervently that I was applying the lotion to that body. Whether he'd somehow divined my thoughts I don't know, but I was rewarded with a brilliant smile before they sat, and soon we were comfortably settled. I felt suddenly tongue-tied and didn't know how the take the conversation further, when Harry asked whether I went to school locally. I was relieved to be able to break the, for me, uncomfortable silence, by pointing out a somewhat tree-shielded building on the western shore and letting them know that that was John Eliot High School, my alma mater. Ruth asked about the clearly visible imposing building on the eastern side of the lake nearer us which I could tell them that that was Wilberforce High School where my father was Head of

Geography.

Of course, the inevitable question was why was I at a different school? So I explained that John Eliot was closer to home and that it was career progression that had finally got my dad his position. So I asked them about where they went to school. Conversation about school felt a bit easier, on home ground as it were. It transpired that both Harry and Ruth attended somewhere called Ruaridh (apparently pronounced Rory?) Urquhart's School in central Edinburgh and they were able to show me on their phones, pictures of the place. They explained that it was an independent school and it certainly looked like a magnificent baronial pile straight out of Sir Walter Scott, if perhaps a little small compared to John Eliot or Wilberforce High, which admittedly did have the advantage of being more modern and able to use big lakeside areas well away from the centre. They said that the Urquhart's school uniform required them to wear a lot of navy blue, hence the t-shirts and shorts. The thought of a school uniform in American schools, other than military establishments, was difficult to assimilate! When I made the mistake of commenting on their English accents, the smiles vanished briefly and I was told *very* firmly that they would have accepted being described as British, Scottish preferably, but *English* never! Perhaps, in other circumstances, they'd have crossed themselves at the very thought!

Between them, Harry and Ruth (they worked as a good team together) explained that their father was a history professor at a university in Edinburgh and their mother was a highly qualified doctor of medicine. They had an elder brother named Hamish who was a medical student in Edinburgh, but he had several more years of study to go before he would hopefully qualify. Their father had been offered the opportunity to come to Boston for two years to complete some research and do some lecturing. The timing was right for them to complete their school education in the USA, so that was why the family was now in Natick where the university had provided a spacious house for them as part of the deal. Their parents were still sorting everything out and were glad to have them out of the way for the day. I was told Hamish had been left to make a mess of their Edinburgh house, and according to them, Hamish was a notorious womaniser, so they imagined pairs of knickers hanging from every possible hook, piles of dirty laundry, unmade beds, no washing up done and lots of pizza boxes and other take-away junk! I was surprised to receive these revelations as we had only just met and they had no real idea who I was. However, I think they were exaggerating the point, as the scene they painted was far too much of a caricature of university student life.

Harry decided that he wanted to cool off in the lake, so I only had to bear the thankfully brief period without that face and body in front of me even though there was the delight of watching him run down to the water and see him return, dripping. I was aware of Ruth giving me a rather intense stare as Harry set off, but the moment she saw me watching her, the stare turned into another brilliant smile.

When he returned and had dried himself, he looked at his phone for the time and said that they should think about getting ready to go. The thought of them leaving so soon spurred me into unusually quick thinking, so I said, "Why don't you let your parents get on and not have to drop everything to fetch you. You can spend a bit more time here and I'll give you a lift home? Just let them know."

Harry and Ruth gave me lovely smiles of thanks. Harry got out his phone and said, "Mum, you don't have to come and collect us. We've made a new friend at the beach and he'll give us a lift." I could not hear what was said at the other end, but Harry then said, "No Mum, I don't think he's a serial killer or kidnapper, even though he thought we were English. That's been sorted, but he's just tidying away his axe and handcuffs and wiping Ruth's blood off his chin." Ruth let out a scream to help set the scene! (I quickly realised that they liked to dramatize for effect.) After a few more words at the other end, Harry turned to me and asked, "Mum wants to know if you'd you like to have lunch with us."

"That'd be really wonderful — I'd be delighted. Please thank her. I hope it won't be inconvenient."

"Mum, did you hear that? He's thrilled but we've got to bury the rest of Ruth first, so we'll be home at about one o'clock."

"I think you had better tell me where you live if this is going to work."

Harry and Ruth looked at each other as if they were not too sure and Ruth said, "Do you know Wampanoag Drive? I think it's about ten minutes car ride from here. It's a fairly new development from the look of the place and all the roads are named after local Native American tribes."

"Yes. I do know where you mean. Natick isn't that big a place."

Once Harry was completely dry and had stretched out in the sun again, giving my eyes much pleasure, but setting my insides churning, not to mention the stirring in my pants, the clock was showing twelve forty-five, so I managed to say that I thought we should make a move if we were to be on time. It didn't take much to get ourselves ready and to have everything ready to be packed in the trunk. As we walked to the car with our bits and pieces, Ruth held my hand and had a beatific smile.

"Okay. Who's going to ride shotgun?" I asked.

"Me, me, me," came Ruth's clear voice.

"Jump in then." Which she did.

Harry commented laughingly, "You're a sort of knight on a white charger then." Indicating the car, and sat right behind me which meant I had that face with that alluring smile and wonderful bright eyes in my rear view mirror the whole way. The only problem was the slight discomfort of driving with an erection.

Chapter 4

We arrived at Wampanoag Drive in less than ten minutes and I was able to park just outside the house as the car space was obviously taken up with the family's car. The house was set back from the road, was surrounded by neatly trimmed lawns and flower beds. It was one in a terrace of five or six as far as I could see, but due to a bend in the road, the far end wasn't visible so there may well have been more. The university's provision had been very generous.

Harry and Ruth grabbed their belongings from the trunk and they escorted me up to the house where Mrs Brown, a very attractive svelte woman, opened the front door with a warm smile of welcome. "Hello. Thank you so much for offering to bring this troublesome pair home. We're very grateful," she said as she indicated her husband who had come up behind her. "I'm Heather and this is my husband, Angus." Angus Brown was a tall well-built man with a neatly trimmed beard which seemed to have a reddish tinge, but Heather had the same wonderful vibrant red hair that her children had inherited.

"Thank you very much Mrs Bb… Heather," I managed to stammer out. "I'm Ethan Liddell."

"Please come in." And she led the way into a big bright house. "You two put your stuff away, wash your hands and come into the kitchen. Ethan, there's a bathroom just here off the kitchen if you want to wash your hands."

There were places set for five round a table in the kitchen

though there was a more formal dining room which I'd glimpsed as we had gone from the front door to the kitchen. Once everyone was ready, we sat, Ruth having asked me to sit next to her. Heather said that she hoped a poached salmon salad would be okay, which I told her would be a real treat as I'd only packed a sandwich. While we ate, Angus and Heather asked about my school because they were having to arrange suitable places for Harry and Ruth. I told them that John Eliot High was named after a Puritan who'd established links with the Native American tribe in the area. Known as "the apostle to the Indians", he'd translated the bible into the Algonquin language. (I wanted to add *"...and much good did it do them...!"* but I didn't know what their religious views were.) The school was co-educational and that the senior years were spent studying for the International Baccalaureate which is what I would be doing as I was about to enter the senior part of the school. It seemed from the nods that this would be a good idea for Harry too before he applied for a university place back in the UK, probably in Edinburgh.

It was all very relaxed, and as a result, I told them about my elementary school which had been named with startling originality, 'Springfield'. This got a chuckle, but I went on to say that each September the next lot of new students from there found it very funny that John Eliot's principal was called Skinner. Fortunately, I added, his first name wasn't Seymour, he was far too young to have been a Vietnam vet, and as far as I knew, he was married with children and didn't live with a domineering mother in a replica Bates' Motel. As the Browns were all familiar with the Simpsons, no further details were necessary. I was suddenly aware that I had taken over the conversation and apologised for being so voluble.

"Aye. It's a pleasure to listen to you," said Angus. He had a lovely deep voice and a much more discernible Scottish accent, though all of the Browns, I told them, slightly rolled their "r"s. For a moment I thought Harry was going to make a comment, but a quick look from his mother seemed to cause a rethink.

A thought suddenly struck me and I said, "In case you have any worries, please remember that *Grease* is forty years old and high schools aren't really like that. John Eliot is certainly not Rydell High in any respect — senior students don't all look at least twenty-nine years old and they are ethnically diverse!"

Angus laughed. "That's aye good to hear," he said and asked about my other interests so I explained about my deep love of music. It transpired that Angus and Heather were regular attendees at concerts in somewhere called the Usher Hall in Edinburgh, but had rarely persuaded any of the children to go with them. I was asked about going to hear the Boston Symphony, but had to confess sadly that I hadn't been to date nor to Tanglewood, the orchestra's summer home at the western end of Massachusetts. I tried to bring Harry and Ruth into it by saying that a good performance with a top flight conductor and soloists should have the audience, thrilled, excited, moved to tears or silence depending on the piece of music and that popular music would rarely, in my view, do anything like that. Perhaps a musical like *Carousel* with "You'll never walk alone" could do it, but I would recommend any newcomer to opera to see one by Puccini in particular. Angus and Heather smiled at the vehemence and passion, and I had to stop to apologise for taking over again. Angus said he wished some of his students would demonstrate such conviction and intensity, which I found rather flattering.

It seemed an appropriate time to take my leave, I thought, in case my parents were wondering where I'd got to., but before going, Harry asked me to exchange contact details so we could arrange further meetings once they'd fully moved in and perhaps go to the beach again or meet in town, perhaps with my friends too. He stage-whispered, that he may have to bring Ruth along, but we could just let her play with the traffic. This got the expected furious response, so I gathered her to me and gave her a hug. "I wouldn't dream of not including you."

She and Harry stuck out their tongues at each other. "So there!" They waved me goodbye as I drove off. The afternoon had been wonderful and being so close to Harry had been incredible. I hoped that I hadn't stared at him too much and given the game away!

Chapter 5

It was a only a few days later when I got a call from Harry to say that he and Ruth would be joining me and my friends at John Eliot and how much they were looking forward to it. He asked if we could all meet for coffee or a meal and would I please recommend somewhere. I told him that we'd be delighted and suggested our favourite cafe, the Urquell, in the Natick Mall which had some booths where we could be almost by ourselves away from "the madding crowd". I offered to come and collect them which was received with a loud "Yay" from Ruth who was listening in.

Steph and Ed had been most interested to find out how my day alone at the beach had gone. I filled them in about meeting our sunbathing neighbours again, our chat, giving them a lift home and lunch with the very Scottish parents, but didn't mention my almost permanent erection, which I'd hoped hadn't been too obvious! This was greeted with a few "Wows" and delight that I'd made some new friends. They'd exchanged a few, what looked like, knowing glances, but I took that as encouraging me to go on. They were very happy with the arrangement to meet at the cafe, and on that occasion, we agreed to make our own way there as I was picking up Harry and Ruth.

The Urquell Cafe was managed by a rather cute (to my eyes) young man called Tom, and while it was not really done to reserve a booth, as Ed, Steph and I were such regular customers, he kindly agreed to make sure that one was available. So, at the appointed hour, we sat round the table after introductions, with Ruth sitting right next to me again.

Conversation seemed very easy about school especially when Harry enquired about the soccer teams and whether he might be able to get involved. Steph felt that he should introduce himself to Jan at an early opportunity which would probably be the best idea as he, as the likely soccer captain, would have the ultimate say-so. There may have to be a trial to see how good a player he was, to assess which team may be the most appropriate. Harry asked about team outfits, and if successful, where would he get the necessary kit. He was wearing his navy-blue Ruaridh Urquhart's hoodie over the usual t-shirt. I noticed again how the close-fitting t-shirt emphasised his contours and tried to shuffle forward a little to hide my lap under the table. Ed explained about the school outfitters in the Mall, fairly close to the cafe and offered to show him where it was when we had finished.

Harry looked closely at Ed and asked, "Is your family by any chance Puerto Rican?"

"No, why do you ask?"

"It's just that a book about life in the US, that I read before leaving Scotland, has a character who's from a Puerto Rican family and has freckles like you. You'd be perfect casting." Without any embarrassment, he raised his hand to trace the freckles over Ed's nose and cheeks. I don't think Ed had expected anything as intimate as this to ever happen, so he didn't react at all to having his face stroked so gently and just smiled back at Harry.

"Obviously my family is Latino, but I've never heard of any Puerto Rican connection. I hope that doesn't disappoint you."

"No, but you'd be my first choice to play the role if I were ever to film it."

"What does the character do?"

"He's called Benito, Benito Alejo, Ben for short, a very handsome, engaging seventeen-year-old, but because of his not brilliant grades, has to attend a summer school. His main occupation away from school is making up a fantastic story about magic and dragons, but worlds away from Hogwarts, for which he does all the intricate drawings himself. Thanks to a very good friend he manages to get through summer school and eventually, after graduation, goes on to a community college, I think. His stories and drawings are found to be a great online hit so he becomes a success."

Ed complimented Harry on his convincing Spanish accent saying Ben's name which seemed to please him immensely. Ed wrote out his surname and then asked Harry to pronounce it. He made a bold attempt at "Vallejo-Benítez" and Ed awarded him an A- for being close enough. Harry, of course, having found that part of Ed's name was Benítez, considered it even more validatory.

I didn't say anything at the time, but I felt that there was something missing from that story, a crucial element to make it more complete. The full version was revealed to me rather later.

Chapter 6

At that moment a figure came up to our booth and said, "So this is where you are hiding. Dobré den, Štefánija."

"Dobré den, Jindřich," came the reply before they gave each other a big kiss. Jan's appearance surprised me, but I realised my thoughts had been so taken up that my friends' concerns had rather passed me by and they had got together after all. The fact that Steph's family name was Svoboda should have indicated to me more positively that her family, or a male ancestor at least, was Czech in origin as was Jindřich (universally known as Jan) Novák's. Despite having known her for over ten years, I'd never heard her speak Czech, even to her parents. Perhaps they were being polite in my presence and then only spoke English.

We shuffled around so Steph and Jan could sit next to each other and introduced Ruth and Harry. Soccer recruitment was raised so we heard again about the need for a brief trial as the school had several teams in each year. They talked about competition in the senior years between the soccer and football coaches to find the fittest and fastest to join their teams.

Harry said that he'd also played rugby at school, but having watched a few American football games, thought that all the padding required made it inferior to the real thing that was rugby. Jan asked if he had said as much yet to the likely football captain who would be Patrick Smith.

"Oh, Ruth and I have met Patrick," said Harry. "His father is the Dean of the History faculty where our father is to be based, and his parents kindly had us all over to their house for dinner. Patrick was very quiet and unsmiling throughout. As the Smiths live very close by and we'll all be going to John Eliot, it's been arranged that Patrick will drive us to school every morning but after-school activities make it unlikely he can drive us back."

"Your morning drive is going to be very interesting at a guess," came from Jan. "You'll have to keep us up to date".

"Ruth and I are determined to get a smile out of him and a laugh if possible. We're sure that under that stern outlook is a real pussy cat, very warm and cuddly." This was greeted with expressions of total disbelief from everyone. We've all known Patrick since we joined the school and he'd been very consistent across the years. He'd developed a reputation as a determined, very self-confident football player who marshalled his team very effectively through his personality without having to resort to threats or bad language.

Tom appeared to ask if we wanted any more drinks. "Ahoj! Tomáš," called out Jan and said something like, "Čai prosím."

Tom replied, "Ano, Jan." And went off, presumably to get what was ordered. He returned a few minutes later with some tea and a couple of lemon slices for Jan and glasses of a pinkish liquid called Malinovka, a refreshing Czech drink using raspberry juice and soda, for each of us.

Jan smiled at Tomáš. "Děkuji vam." It was really lovely. As under Massachusetts law none of us could be served alcohol, certainly outside our own homes, I'd never paid attention to the array of what I now saw to be a range of Czech beers and spirits behind the bar and realised that the cafe was named after the lager, Pilsner Urquell. I tried to remember the few Czech words I'd heard and promised myself to check them out with Steph when we were next alone.

Tom exchanged a few words with Jan and it seemed as if I was the subject of discussion. A little while later Jan said quietly that Tomáš was rather shy, but had asked him whether he thought I could be a possible boyfriend as he rather fancied me. I was totally taken aback by this as I hadn't come out or spoken about being gay to anyone. Ruth, unexpectedly, came to my rescue by grabbing my hands and declaring that I was *her* boyfriend at which everyone laughed. But that was the point at which the party broke up so, after the bill was paid, we all set off with a quiet, for them, Ruth and Harry coming with me for the ride home. Before we left the Urquell I had managed to say, sotto voce, to Tom that I was very flattered by his attention but my heart was engaged elsewhere.

Tom smiled ruefully and just shook my hand. "Perhaps some other time? Čau!" As he was right behind me Harry had obviously heard this exchange but didn't say anything.

On arrival at Wampanoag Drive, Ruth and Harry alighted, and we said, "Bye." I went home after putting the car radio on to find some suitable mood music. The turn of the conversation to my sexuality had really disturbed me and I wondered whether my "friends" had discussed me behind my back. At home I told my parents about the evening, other than the last part, and decided that I'd have an early night. However, getting to sleep was impossible and I tossed and turned for what felt like hours, but I must have slept at some point as it was light when Mom called to say that breakfast was on the table.

Chapter 7

It was a couple of days later when Harry called and asked if I would meet him at the Urquell because he wanted to talk. I said that it was probably Tom's night off, but he said that it was me he wanted to see. We arranged to meet after supper at about eight p.m., and oddly, he asked me not to bring the car as he felt like walking. When I arrived, Harry was just finishing a cup of coffee. He greeted me with one of his wonderful smiles, but instead of allowing me to sit down, he paid, grabbed my hand and led me out and along to a small park a couple of minutes away. He must have discovered this beforehand. As it was relatively late and the weather had turned with rain threatening, the place was devoid of anyone else. There was a sort of shelter with a bench where he sat, like Ruth had done, right next to me with our legs touching.

He came straight to the point. "I've had a couple of sleepless nights, Ethan, wondering who this person is to whom you've given your heart? Perhaps it's none of my business, but I thought and hoped we were closer than that." At that, he cupped my chin in his left hand and leant forward to brush my lips with his.

Our first kiss and my whole being felt galvanised. "Yes," I replied, "someone has stolen my heart and it is your business, because it's you." At that he seemed to light up and held my face in his hands while he really kissed me, tongue and all. There was just a slight taste of coffee! The ecstasy of the moment was slightly disturbed by the sound of rain starting to patter on the roof of the shelter, but we carried on kissing.

When we stopped for breath, Harry said, "I am gay, Ethan and I think you may be too." I nodded in acknowledgment of the truth.

"Have you had much experience?" I asked.

"Well, I have kissed a few frogs in the hope of finding a prince," came the reply.

"I haven't ever kissed or been kissed by any frog, but I think my prince is right here."

He grinned and kissed me on the mouth, the eyes, the nose until he looked me straight in the eyes only a couple of inches away and asked, "Are you saying what I think you're saying?" I nodded. The rain had now become torrential and there could be heard distant rolls of thunder.

After a couple of minutes gazing at each other, Harry suddenly got up pulling me up beside him and declared, "I think my house is nearer than yours, so shall we make a dash for there?"

I protested that we'd be drowned in seconds but of course this was waived away by Harry.

"It's only water and we're not going to dissolve." He took hold of my hand and we set off, inevitably getting soaked through in less than ten seconds. He was wearing flip flops which made moving much easier, but my sneakers seemed to instantly fill with water, and what with the sodden socks as well, getting moving was a squelchfest! However, we kept going and after about twenty minutes of pouring rain, with much louder thunder and flashes of lightning every few minutes, we arrived at Wampanoag Drive and got round to the back door of the house where the kitchen was. Through the window Heather and Ruth could be seen watching television. Harry opened the door and we entered to exclamations of horror at our bedraggled state.

Ruth beamed and said, "Hello Ethan." I was obviously too wet for her to approach to hold my hand again. Heather demanded that we stay right where we were and not go through the house and went to get towels. When she returned, the first command was for us to empty our pockets of everything.

"Ethan, please send a message to let your parents know where you are and that you'll be staying the night. I'll get you home in the morning after breakfast. Then strip off all your wet clothes." I was told to use the bathroom by the kitchen. Her tone sharpened then. "Alexander Henry, when you have got the worst off, please go and find something to wear and something for Ethan to wear."

"But Mum, you know I nev…" he tailed off seeing his mother's furious face. Harry was virtually naked by this stage, but obviously, I couldn't linger to see the bits that had been covered on the beach with his mother and sister waiting. So I shut myself in the bathroom, stripped off my shoes, socks and clothes and towelled myself dry. I heard Heather send Ruth to get some newspaper so that my sneakers could be stuffed to help them dry properly overnight.

From the bathroom I could hear that Harry had returned. Heather knocked on the bathroom door and said that she had put a chair by the door with some dry clothes for me and to put my wet things and the towel on the chair. On opening the door, I saw that Harry had brought me a Ruaridh Urquhart's t-shirt and shorts which really pleased me for some unaccountable reason. When completely dry and dressed, I put the wet and damp items on the chair as directed and emerged to find Harry in a similar outfit though his t-shirt may have had the rugby logo, while mine had the soccer (or in British terms) football one.

Heather had calmed down I felt but was obviously still angry with Harry for having got me in such a state. She asked if we wanted a hot drink before going to bed but neither of us wanted anything, so we were sent off with Harry being instructed to show me the spare room. I thanked her profusely for her kindness but she said it wasn't a problem — tomorrow would be the time for a suitable examination of what had occurred.

Chapter 8

As we went up the stairs, the storm could still be heard raging and the rain was really hitting the window panes hard. Harry said "Come in here for a moment." And ushered me into what was clearly his bedroom. "Now, where were we before we started our journey?" He gathered me into his arms and we stood there kissing deeply, tenderly and passionately in turn. His hands were under the t-shirt touching me everywhere and really turning me on. Suddenly he said, "Arms up," and whisked off the t-shirt and threw it in a corner. "At last, I've got you out of that bloody t-shirt you wear like a suit of armour all the time. Do you have any that aren't in battleship grey?"

"Do you have any that aren't in Urquhart navy blue?"

We laughed and kissed. "Touché." After a moment he took off his t-shirt and brought our bodies together before yanking off my shorts and then his own shorts. I was getting very wound up as his hands roamed over my nether regions fondling my cock and balls as well as squeezing my backside while moaning and kissing me in evident ecstasy. The anticipation of what was about to happen was almost nerve-wracking, but it was what I'd been wanting for what seemed like ages and he matched my ideal man to a tee except I'd never thought about a guy with *flaming red* hair! His mouth moved over my cheeks and chin before gradually going lower over my chest. He sucked, kissed and nipped at my nipples, and with his lips, pulled gently at the few hairs I had before continuing southwards. All the while he was playing with my ass cheeks, running his fingers up and down the cleft. When he arrived at my belly button, he pushed his tongue in which tickled a bit, but nuzzling in my pubes was much more so. He kissed and licked the top of my cock but instead of immediately sucking it he bent down a little further a proceeded to suck each of my balls in turn, running his tongue over them. I was clutching his hair by this time not really knowing whether I was supposed to be doing anything else. He paused and got up to kiss me and muttered how beautiful I was and everything he could have wished for. He manouvered me back on to the bed and then bent down to gently push back my foreskin with his lips before initially starting to fellate me and fondle my balls at the same time. He looked up briefly to say I should hold on to cumming for as long as I could, before resuming. My problem was that I was already about to explode and I couldn't stop what was about to happen. My hands were on his shoulders, my legs shaking and he could tell, I think, that I was very, very close. His mouth pushed down on my cock and that was the last of my resistance gone.

He swallowed and then stretched out on the bed next to me kissing me and playing with my genitals all the time. "Sorry, I couldn't hold on any longer."

"You were great and there's a long way to go yet. You're going to cum a couple of more times before I've finished with you tonight," came the reply. After a couple of minutes, he gently turned me over on to my stomach and started kissing my neck before gradually moving down my spine, though this was a little more quickly done than my chest. When he got to my ass, he kissed both cheeks all over before running his tongue down the cleft. His hands held the cheeks apart before his tongue got lower and lower and I suddenly felt it probing my anus. I think I gasped at feeling this happening. "This is 'rimming'," he whispered. "Are you happy to go on?"

"Oh yes, yes."

"Okay. I'm going to use some lubrication on my fingers first; this'll seem very cold initially so be prepared." I saw him reach across to a nightstand where he picked up a tube of gel and applied some to the middle finger of his right hand. Very gently he probed and gradually inserted his finger deeper and deeper. I was groaning with the pain initially as he started to move his finger in and out but it did feel good. "I'm going to insert another one. Are you still okay?"

"Oh yes," I panted, through teeth slightly gritted.

He pulled out very slowly, lubed up both fingers and started again. It felt truly wonderful. He didn't seem to mind my moaning and groaning which I supposed was to be expected from a virgin. "Are you ready for the next stage?" When I turned my head to look at him, I could see the concentration in his face. He gently withdrew his fingers and lubed his thick beautifully veined cock which I was seeing for the first time I realised. He moved to be closer and applied more lube before gradually inserting himself. At first it felt very tight and a bit painful but gradually by degrees he was able to get it all in. He stopped while I got used to the feel before, again, very slowly he began to move in and out and I began to enjoy the sensation, the rhythm of his body and gave myself up to him. He reached forward to grab both of my hands and the fierceness of his grip was amazing. I could hear his breaths getting shorter as he approached orgasm. He came with a great gasp and basically fell on me while kissing my neck and ears.

We were quiet for a few minutes while Harry's erection died down and he was able to just slide out of me.

"Why did your mother call you Alexander Henry?" I asked when we were still and he just held me close.

"Well, those are some of my names. I knew she was angry when she used them. If she'd used all of them, I would've known she was really incandescent."

"What are your other names then?"

"I won't tell you now to preserve some of my mystique. At home, Henrys are often called Harry or Hal (if you recall from Shakespeare) as they are here too, and Alexander is usually shortened to Sandy, but I definitely didn't want to be called 'Sandy Brown'. One of my great grandfathers was named Alexander Henry MacInnes-Brown I've been given to understand, but that was in the days when dinosaurs ruled the Earth. The greatest danger then was meeting a tyrannosaurus rex on the way to or from school! We've rather dropped the MacInnes bit of the name over the years to make life easier. Dad uses MacInnes-Brown to burnish his Scottish credentials, but his accent gives him away anyway. Mostly we use it to justify using the MacInnes tartan which is very attractive."

We chuckled as we lay in each other's arms until he reached down and found I was hard again. "So you're ready for another whirl are you?" And immediately repeated his lips and tongue descent down my chest, mistreating my nipples again and tried to get my whole scrotum in his mouth. He played with my cock before easing my foreskin with his hand this time before applying that so kissable mouth to my eager thrusting penis. This time I hoped to be able to exercise a little more control, but with one of his hands firmly but not tightly gripping my balls, my efforts were in vain as we could both sense when I was about to orgasm.

"You score another A+, Ethan," he said as he licked his lips appreciatively. I could sense that he was hard again and was moving to position himself to penetrate me, when he suggested that I apply the lube, which I was more than happy to do having not so far handled his cock and balls. His thick shaft was wonderful to touch finally, something I had lusted after since that first sighting of it albeit shrouded by his Speedos. I squeezed a pile of the gel onto my hands and gingerly at first applied it. He breathed in deeply, liking the feel and as I gradually applied pressure he started moaning slightly. I covered his cock and balls with the lube, pushed back his foreskin, tickled his balls and started to jerk him off more quickly. He gasped and asked me to stop as he was approaching climax too quickly, but I was determined to carry on whatever until, finally, he was unable to hold on any longer and his cum spurted over my chest. He emitted a loud gasp before again collapsing on top of me, kissing me hard as he did so. "You bastard." Was all he could utter.

When Harry had recovered, I gave him a lingering post-coital kiss before saying that it had been the first time that I'd really been able to get my hands on him and could take charge of matters. His piercing blue eyes stared into mine for half a minute before acknowledging I had been right and apologised for what he described as his "excess of zeal" (what a phrase!). He told me he'd been concerned at the way the evening had turned out at the Urquell and that Tomáš' apparent desire to have me as his boyfriend indicated that "the vultures were circling" so he had to do something very soon, preferably before school started, when he was convinced that I would be swept off my feet by some beauty or other. My sort of confession in the park that I was still a virgin had confirmed his determination to be my first experience. He'd been wondering how to get me into his bedroom, stripped and ready for him to "have his wicked way with me" (as he put it). (I briefly wondered what he'd been reading to come up with these phrases.)

Asking me to leave the car at home had been the first part of his barely formulated plan. The storm arriving had proved to be an incredible godsend which, of course, he could hardly have counted on. Harry said that, had he been a believer, he would have got down on his knees and thanked God for his beneficence! His immediate thought was that the storm presented an ideal opportunity to get me thoroughly drenched, and if he could get me to walk to Wampanoag Drive through the teeming rain, he knew his mother would have exactly the reaction she did — i.e. get me undressed and insist I stay the night.

Slowly and stickily, Harry rolled off me, grinned broadly and suggested a shower would be a good idea. "The en-suite shower is big enough for two and we could have fun soaping each other." I didn't need a second invitation to touch him intimately, and what a pleasure it was.

Needless to say, there was a lot of kissing as our soap-covered hands roamed over each other's chests, inevitably drifting southwards again. Harry moved round me to wrap his arms around me, kiss me on the neck and tweak my nipples. I could feel his erection against my cleft when he whispered, "Bend your knees slightly so I can get inside you again." He slowly inserted himself and then held my cock and balls in his hands. "Let's see if we can both cum at the same time as I want to watch you shoot." And he gently moved himself in and out while starting to jerk me off. I put my hands behind him clutching at his ass and pulling him closer so our bodies could move in unison. Gradually his movements speeded up and I could feel myself approaching climax and his breathing indicated he was too. "Are you close?" I nodded. "Say when." I was able to shout "Now." And two seconds later we shot our loads simultaneously.

When we had got our breath back, Harry said, "You were magnificent. It was beautiful to see." He grinned at me and wryly commented, "Whoever said men couldn't multitask?" He switched the shower back on and we finished washing ourselves. Once dry, Harry said we'd better change the bed and took a fresh sheet from the pile on a side table. He stripped the old sheet off and put it in the laundry basket and quickly made up the bed again. "I think we can sleep now," he said winningly. "You happy to be a spoon?" I smiled and nodded approval and we lay down in that configuration once Harry had switched off the light.

Chapter 9

I fell asleep very quickly even though I'd wanted to let the events of the evening parade through my mind, and try to store the memories. I woke to find Harry's genitals in my face and him sucking gently on my balls rolling them around his mouth. "Good morning," I offered, and having taken the hint, proceeded to imitate the action at the other end of the bed. There was a mumbled greeting in response as he carried on, pausing only to nuzzle in my pubic hair again before starting to lick my dick and then, with his lips, push down my foreskin and commence to slowly suck. With such encouragement as a model, I imitated his every action and got very responsive moans as I got to work with a will (or a willie?). At one point Harry writhed ecstatically as my tongue evidently caught what he later called his "tickle spot" and which, much later, I discovered is called the frenulum. All penises have it but is much more ticklish for some than others. He tried unsuccessfully to find mine. The puckered rose of his anus was so close, so I gently probed with my finger and got a response when he seemed to press back onto it, but I felt it was a positive move of welcome rather than rejection. We both climaxed within a few seconds of each other before Harry changed ends to lie beside me and was going to kiss me, but I said he tasted wonderful and I wanted to keep the taste for as long as possible. "You're creamy, a bit sweet and very smooth. It should be bottled." His reply was he would've been worried if I'd said his cum was lumpy! but there was plenty more and I was welcome to get more samples at any time.

We both laughed and settled back for a long cuddle while I just kept my tongue moving round my mouth to make sure I had every drop. "Of course, I should have remembered, that was your first time at fellatio. You did seem to enjoy it and I enjoyed your enjoyment!" I could only nod in agreement. "By the way, the next time we do this I want you to be in me to complete the circle."

"What does that mean?"

"I think that, so far, you only partially lost your virginity last night. You need to complete the circle, but can we do it in your bedroom please, whether or not there's a storm?"

"Harry, I'm not out at home and I'm only out to you really."

"Not true. You're out to my family too," he said. "Just before I started to go through your wake-up procedure, Mum came in with your dry clothes and shoes." I sat up horrified as we hadn't bothered to cover ourselves before sleeping.

"What? Your mom has seen me naked?"

"Yes. Ethan, what's the problem? She's a medic and has probably seen hundreds of naked people, possibly many hundreds of naked people in her career and you were looking so beautiful, lying there so totally naturally with all your... erm... assets on display. That pose couldn't have been any more alluring."

"I'm not sure I'm bothered about what she's seen as a professional, I'm her son's... um... um..."

A tug on my cock. "Boyfriend?" A devastating smile from Harry.

My consternation was halted by a knock on the door. "Can I come in please?" came Ruth's voice. I grabbed the sheet to cover myself as best I could while Harry just stretched out naked as he was.

"Come in Ruth," he called out. She entered, went up to Harry to give him a kiss. "Good morning." And waved dismissively at his gently proffered bits.

"Please put it all away. I'm your sister, you don't have to impress me, and you don't. Good morning, Ethan." She came round to my side of the bed and kissed me too. She smiled up at me before announcing, "Mum says breakfast will be ready in ten minutes. You're not to be late whispering sweet nothings — or anything else!" she added pointedly.

"Ruth, piss off," ordered Harry. She flounced out but gave me a big wink and a grin as she left. "Ruth's a wonderful sister, I love her dearly, and as you see, we've no secrets from one another, but we'd better do as we've been told I suppose." Harry pulled the sheet off me, grabbed my penis and led me to the shower. "We can spend a minute soaping each other if you're ready now? Unfortunately, we can't linger, however tempting, or mum will get cross again. There's a spare toothbrush if you want."

Chapter 10

On time, we presented ourselves, washed and dressed, in the kitchen. "Ethan, would you like some porridge?" My face must have looked blank. "Not something you've had before? It's basically just boiled oats and you can then add milk if you want. Most Scots add a pinch of salt. It will certainly give you the energy to keep you going the rest of the morning."

Harry, from his bowl, intervened to say that only the heathen English added sugar, but then admitted that some people in Scotland did put honey or even maple syrup these days on their porridge.

"Thank you, Mrs B… Heather, I'd love some porridge and milk."

"Would you like some scrambled eggs on toast to follow?"

"Sounds fantastic. Thank you very much." Ruth sat next to me tucking in to her porridge so I was able to see how she dealt with it.

Angus arrived with his laptop. "Hello Ethan. It's aye good to see you again." And sat down while Heather put a bowl of porridge in front of him. He got up and fetched a bottle of whisky (the label said Teachers) and poured a small measure on the porridge. He noticed my look and asked if I would like a dram?

"Thank you, Angus. I've never drunk any whisky but perhaps it's not something I should have at breakfast."

He chuckled. "Aye, perhaps it's not a good idea at that."

"Would you like tea or coffee?" asked Heather.

"Tea please. Do you have any lemon so I could have it Czech-style? Ow!"

The sharp kick to my shin was followed by Harry hissing, "You cockteaser!"

"Cockteaser? Are you a cockteaser Ethan? And can I have Czech-style tea too please?" Ruth grinned at me.

"I didn't know that I was until just now," I replied rubbing my shin. Heather and Angus looked rather bemused at this, but evidently decided not to ask for any details. However, Angus having finished his porridge decided it was perhaps a good time to get on with reading through *The Guardian* online in peace. He quickly told me it was the only English newspaper worth reading as virtually all the rest of the English press was horribly right-wing, and in his opinion, just propaganda sheets for the current government. He also had to get on preparing lectures for the new term and then retreated rapidly. "Please excuse me."

"What have you started now, Harry?" Heather was obviously still not too happy. "You know this 'new' word will be known all over Edinburgh in a few minutes."

Harry chimed in with, "Those trainee witches that Ruth calls her school friends that I've met, are not innocent little angels by any means. I'm sure most of them have seen a few cocks already and will have exp…"

"Harry, that's enough."

"They've probably chopped up a few for their cauldrons before now too," Harry muttered sotto voce trying to have the last word.

"Alexander Henry, listen to your mother," I put in. After a brief pause, they all started laughing and Heather dished up the eggs on toast which was really delicious.

As we tucked in, Heather asked, "Ethan, what tea would you

like?" And opened a cupboard to show a range of coloured tins of various teas. "If you want to have lemon rather than milk, could I suggest Earl Grey?"

"That sounds lovely but I've never had it before." To my amazement, instead of fishing out a couple of tea bags from one of the tins, she proceeded to put out cups and saucers, spoons, sugar bowl, a plate for the lemon slices, tea strainer (as I soon saw) and a tea pot, which was initially warmed with some boiling water before being emptied and several spoons of loose-leaf tea put in before boiling water poured in. To top this display, she put a woolly cover over the pot.

She smiled at me having seen my astonished face. "In this house, Ethan, we don't use teabags. It's part of our tradition. You'll have to come for afternoon tea one day and have some homemade scones too. Angus, do you want some tea? she called out.

"Aye, please dear. I'll be there in a sec."

When we had our cups filled Heather said, "Well, are we going to get an explanation of your language? Actually, on reflection I think I'd prefer to remain ignorant of what brought it on." So we sat in silence for a moment sipping the tea.

"This does have an unusual flavour. It's very nice and refreshing," I said. "Do you drink it very often?"

"The taste is oil of bergamot. We have it when we fancy a change from Assam or Darjeeling which is what we usually have in the afternoons. Ethan, as time is marching on, I think it may be a good idea to get you home before your parents think you've been kidnapped."

"You're the most unlikely version of Ebenezer Balfour of Shaws one could hope to meet," I replied with a grin.

"Are you a Stevenson fan then?"

"Oh yes. I've read most if not all of his novels though *Catriona* I thought was a rather silly girl and needed a sound slap round the face."

Heather chuckled at that and it seemed to a good moment at which to leave! Angus bade me farewell and said he looked forward to seeing me again soon. Ruth and Harry asked if they could come along for the ride to see where I lived. As we got ready, Harry raced upstairs and came back with the Urquhart's t-shirt I'd worn ever so briefly the previous night and asked if I wanted it. "Thank you, yes please." I could smell his scent and after-shave on it. "I'll never wash it." We all piled into the car with me as shotgun to give directions. It didn't seem to take long to get back home though, during the ride, I thought nervously about coming out to my parents, what could I say and how I would face whatever music ensued. I think Harry understood what was going through my mind as he squeezed my shoulders by way of support. Heather saw this and I think realised why.

Chapter 11

The car stopped at the door and Mom appeared to greet Heather who had got out. "Thank you so much for looking after Ethan last night."

"It was our pleasure. I'm Heather MacInnes-Brown and those miscreants in the back are my children Harry and Ruth."

"Monica Liddell and this is my husband Jonathan," she said as he came up behind her. "Would you all like to come in for a moment for coffee?"

"I'll take a 'raincheck' (is that correct?) if you don't mind and we'll visit soon. We haven't been in Natick very long and there's still stuff we need to sort out. My husband, Angus, is rather tied up with preparing his lectures so inevitably most of it falls to me." She came round the car to give me a hug and said, "Ethan, you're always welcome at our home. We look forward to seeing a lot more of you." And gave me a wicked wink. She whispered "Good luck." Before getting back in the car. They all waved as the car sped away with Harry's face looking back through the rear window. Of course, her last remark had made me blush furiously as I followed Mom and Dad indoors.

My parents were obviously curious about last night and why I hadn't taken the car when the weather forecast hadn't been good. I didn't know what to say other than to suggest they sit down before stammering, "Mom, Dad, I think I'm gay — no, I don't think it, I know it." I closed my eyes waiting for a tirade but there was only silence.

They both got up to hug me and Dad said, "At last. Thank you for telling us." My eyes were still closed. "Were you actually expecting us to shout at you or threaten to throw you out?" I opened one eye and then the other. "Ethan, you're our one and only son and we love you too much to ever think there's anything wrong with you being something over which you have no choice. We're teachers and part of our role, as we see it, is to have regard to all aspects of a child's upbringing."

"What did you mean by 'at last'?"

Dad sighed before saying, "Well, we've had our suspicions for some time, but we just thought we should wait for you to tell us in your own time, whenever you thought it was appropriate."

Mom asked, "Has this anything to do with Harry, who seems to be your only new acquaintance in ages?"

"Yes, it has." I gave them a brief outline of the events of the past couple of days from what had meant to be the celebration at the cafe of Harry and Ruth joining John Eliot, Tom's comment, Harry's reaction and how I came to be spending the night at the Browns.

Mom asked, "Without wanting any details, did you spend the night with Harry?"

"Yes." She hugged me closely when, for some inexplicable reason, I suddenly burst into tears.

When my sobs had subsided, Mom handed me a couple of tissues to dry my eyes and blow my nose. "Is there anything else you want to tell us?"

"I don't want to be an abandoned frog." Before a few more snuffles.

"What does that mean please?" I told them about Harry's comment that he'd kissed a few frogs seeking a prince and my response that I'd found mine.

Dad sat next to me, took both of my hands in his, sighed and said, "Ethan, you're only seventeen. You don't know what the future holds and your first love may possibly not be your only or last love. Sexual passion may fade, friends and lovers may drift apart. It's no one's fault, it's life. You probably don't want or need to know this, but neither your mother nor I were virgins when we found each other and fell in love all those years ago, and we're still in love, that hasn't changed with the years. We've watched you grow up to be a kind, thoughtful, generous, handsome, very bright young man, but perhaps a little innocent, too innocent possibly. You may not have noticed our perhaps too subtle attempts to alert you to our suspicions when you were encouraged to read the Armistead Maupin *Tales of the City* series. Your mom and I had thought you would send us Michael Tolliver's famous/infamous 'Letter to Mama' before now."

"Thank you for being so fantastically understanding. Sometimes it's all been so confusing as if everyone else is on the right road map but I've got the wrong sheet, it's upside down, I've been given the wrong map reference and a faulty compass."

Mom hugged me again. "Just remember that we love you as you are and don't want you any different."

"Thanks, Mom. Harry may have at least sorted out my map and given me a working compass. I think I should really say something to Ed and Steph."

"Do you want to invite them here?"

"If you don't mind, I'd prefer to be somewhere neutral."

"Okay. By the way, your grandparents, all of them, were happy for your mother and I to sleep together in their homes before we were married, your great-grandparents probably would have been less so. In our turn, if you want to invite Harry here, whether or not it's for overnight, please do so and don't feel in the slightest bit embarrassed. Dad paused briefly before saying, "Ethan, in preparation for this day, we want you to have this, but you'll have to buy any replacements." Dad handed over a bag from a local pharmacist; it contained a couple of tubes of lubricant and a selection of condoms.

Needless to say, I started crying again and hugged them both before rushing to my room to send messages. The first were to Steph and Ed asking them if they were free because I had something to tell them, and then one to Harry to tell him that my parents were okay with me being gay and I'd be more than happy if he wanted to complete the process of deflowering me in my bedroom whether storm-tossed or not!

Steph and Ed were ready when I stopped outside their homes and we drove into Natick and parked as usual in the Mall car park. Rather than go to the Urquell cafe, I led the way to the small park nearby, to the bench where Harry had first kissed me. Other than our initial greeting, I'd been silent so they must've realised this was important to me. We sat before I said, "I have to tell you that I'm gay."

It took a moment before Ed smiled and said, "We know or, rather, we knew. Steph and I have been wondering when you were going to say anything since that first day at the beach when you saw Harry and Ruth. Ethan, you have a wonderfully expressive face and we could see you were quite overcome at the sight of him."

Steph followed up with, "Your expression, when they got up to go, was a veritable picture of badly dashed hopes like Prince Charming looking at Cinderella's coach disappearing into the night, but immediately lit up like the prince finding the glass slipper when Harry said they'd be back the next day and said it loud enough to make sure you heard. Ed and I immediately messaged each other to agree that we would make excuses to not come with you the next day to make sure the ground was clear for romance to blossom. So has it?"

"Yes, it has and it was on this bench that Harry made his move," I replied before giving them the same brief outline of events that I'd given my parents.

"Good for Harry," came from Ed. "And so, you've now come out to your parents who, as we would have expected from them, reacted as we've done, without it coming as a surprise. We've known you for over ten years Ethan. You're such a wonderful, lovely guy, we're amazed it's taken anyone this long to make an approach but… um…" He hesitated. "…Forgive me for asking, but how sore is your culo?"

"Ed, que te follen! You necessita una buena patada en el culo, so if I had proper shoes on rather than sneakers, I'd kick your culo so hard you'd be knocking on the door of the International Space Station." Ed's astonished face almost made me laugh, but I managed to keep a straight face. "As it is I'll just have to use my hands to…" And he was off, running to the far side of the park. He slowly crept back looking sheepish and apologetic.

Steph, hiding a smile, waved to get my attention. "I think I can guess what that all meant. Culo is…?" and pointed. I nodded. "Would you like me to hold him while you give him the spanking he deserves?"

I shook my head but gave him what I hoped was my evil curse look. "I wouldn't want to harm anything that Rosita holds dear."

"Truly, haven't you ever noticed Tom's expression whenever he sees you at the Urquell? He really fancies you and doesn't make much of a secret about it. In case you hadn't realised it, he's a senior at Wilberforce High and does shifts at the cafe to earn some pocket money — your dad probably knows him well. He's not on duty at the moment, so shall we have an undisturbed coffee there now that we're all clear."

"Thank you both for being such good friends. How could I cope without you?", and when Ed was back in range, I hugged them both tightly and explained that I'd heard him and his fellow Latino soccer players swear and curse so often about their opposition, it had been relatively easy to pick up a few words and one of them had been happy to teach me some as well.

When I got home feeling slightly bothered that everyone seemingly knew about me but me, I was delighted to see a message from Harry who was thrilled that my coming out had been totally the opposite of what I had feared. He was looking forward to our next meeting followed by an emoji of a flower with missing petals!

Chapter 12

My parents were enjoying a cup of tea (teabags!) when I joined them. They smiled when I told them that Ed's and Steph's reaction to the news that I was gay had matched theirs. It did cross my mind to ask Dad about Tom but thought better of it for the moment.

Dad then said, "By the way, Ethan, do you remember telling us about Harry's question to Ed about being Puerto Rican and his freckles? Well, we thought about what book he could have been thinking about and realised he meant *What if it's us* by Becky Albertalli and Adam Silvera and there's a copy in the bookcase if you want to read it and keep up with Harry's imaginary film production."

"Fantastic. That's great Dad."

"Your mom and I very much agree that Ed really would be very good casting." And they both laughed. "There're a few other books there by both of them writing separately and some by Bill Konigsberg and David Levithan as well as a couple by British authors such as Justin Myers and Simon James Green. Between them they cover a wide spectrum of gay matters including parental and student homophobia, suicide, blackmail, jealousy, death of loved ones, intense emotions but also love, sincerity, integrity, loyalty, selflessness, and essentially, friendship. Of course, most if not all of those can be applied to all relationships but that's life. You could do worse by reading a few. Some have leading characters who are older, in their mid-thirties, but the need for successful, and hopefully lasting, relationships is eternal — it's rare for human beings to do without." He got up and found *What if it's us* and said, "Why don't you make a start and see if you can tease poor Ed too?"

"Good idea. Thanks. I'll go to my room and read until dinner if that's okay?" Actually, I lay on my bed and fell asleep within a couple of minutes.

When I woke up, I saw that there were several messages on my phone. There was the expected one from Harry, but also one from Heather who had obviously got the number from him. She said that the house should be ready in a couple of days and would like me and my parents to be among the first visitors. She said it may be a good moment as the summer vacation would end after Labor Day (so she understood), about a week away, and then school and post-school activities would probably take precedence on our time. She suggested the Saturday before the holiday and would I please ask my parents (a) if we were free and (b) if there were anything that they didn't, couldn't or wouldn't eat so she could cater accordingly. I freshened up and went to see Mom and Dad with the invitation.

Mom said to say yes, they'd be delighted to be there, and would be more than happy with anything that was provided but could she please let us know what time we were expected. Having passed that on, I read Harry's message. He and Ruth would like to see me and wondered about the following day and perhaps Steph and Ed could join us too. A message from Ed had proposed something similar and said that his girlfriend, Rosita, who had given him a bad time apparently for having missed out on the Urquell party(?) (as he put it) would like to be there too. I replied to both and copied to Steph (to be forwarded to Jan) to suggest we return to the "scene of the crime" and meet at the

Urquell at around two p.m.

Everyone seemed happy with that and the rest of the evening passed quietly with Mom, Dad and me reading, until dinner. I'd started on *What if it's us* and was soon totally absorbed in the world of Arthur and Ben and NYC and whether they were going to meet again after their first encounter. It was a real page turner so, when Mom called me to say dinner was ready, I took the book with me to the table. Mom and Dad seemed very amused that I was so taken with it and I could see why Harry and my parents thought Ed fitted the bill to play Ben. He really would be perfect except he wasn't gay!

Chapter 13

So the following afternoon I picked up Harry and Ruth, and with the whole gang managed to crowd into one of the Urquell's booths. Rosita was introduced to Ruth and Harry. She was a vivacious brunette and very enamoured of Ed. She said she was sorry to have missed our previous get together, but she had had to be at a family gathering; Ed had told her all about it however and about the aftermath! Tom hovered while we sorted out who was having what drink and there was a slight pause while we waited for someone to say something.

The silence was broken by Steph asking Ruth if she had received her first timetable. Ruth said she had and her first lesson would be with a Ms Berenson. We agreed that it would be a good start as Ms Berenson was a firm but fair teacher who had taught all of us. Steph hoped she'd easily make friends with the other students and suggested she may like to befriend a girl called Rusalka Ostrava. Apparently her parents were rather Romantic, hence the first name, but as a result, at every full moon she was teased mercilessly. It didn't help that she was an excellent swimmer, which was how she knew her, both of them being in the school team.

"Can you help out here, Ethan, as you know what I'm talking about?"

"Okay. *Rusalka* is the subject of Dvořák's most well-known opera. The basic tale is like that of *The Little Mermaid* so you'll know what happens, but there's a tragic difference. She's a naiad or water nymph who falls in love with a handsome prince." I let my eyes drift up to Harry's face. "A very handsome prince who liked to come to Rusalka's pool, deep in the forest, where he could swim naked. As he swam through her welcoming embrace all he could ever sense was a slight ripple in the water along his body. Poor Rusalka wanted much, much more than that and decided, against all advice, to find the local sorceress to cast a spell to make her human. She sings to the moon, a beautiful aria, which I think all sopranos have in their repertoire, and pleads with the silver moon to shine on him, to shine on him wherever he may be and take her love to him." I hadn't taken my eyes off Harry and had used gestures to indicate the rippling of the water and the plea to the moon, when I was suddenly aware of the silence round the table and the cafe's sound system burst into life playing the very aria. "That's it, the aria…" I tailed off. "Have I been set up?" I asked rather crossly.

Steph hugged me tightly and said, "If only you could have seen the rapture on your face and the emotion in your speech as you explained it." Rosita hugged me as well and kissed me on both cheeks.

Harry mouthed, "Thank you." Then leant across Ruth, got me to my feet and kissed me full on the lips which got a cheer from the others.

Ruth wanted to know what else happened in the opera. "Well, the price for becoming a woman was to forfeit her lovely voice. Of course, as she cannot speak, she cannot communicate, (I suppose no one thought of 'Charades' in fairy tales), so she seems cold and passionless. She is betrayed by the prince on their supposed wedding day. She returns to the pool where the prince comes to find her to ask for forgiveness, but because of the betrayal, the spell is broken — she cannot go back to being a naiad nor is she a woman — she is forever a damned wandering spirit. All she can offer is to kiss him when he'll die. He says that would be preferable to being a tormented soul, so she takes him in her arms and kisses him very tenderly before his lifeless body slips to the ground and she slowly descends back into the depths of the pool. Dvořák's music is sublime. The actual opera has a lot more going on, but that's the main gist. I'd love to see it in an opera house, not just on a DVD."

Jan opined, "I think after your account, we'd all like to see it with you."

Tom appeared with more drinks and told me that the "Song to the moon" was the most requested number on the cafe's system; all the Czech customers seemed to know it.

I turned to Steph and asked, "Was this all a set up?"

"No, it just worked out that way, but Tomáš overheard most of the conversation and realised he could play a role by putting the aria on the sound system."

"Hmm. I still think I should try for revenge. Tom, do you know anything about Štefánija I could use?"

"Sorry, no. She is my Libuše, queen of Bohemia." And the next moment I could hear he'd changed the music to the opening bardic harps of Smetana's "Má Vlast".

To change the subject, I turned to Harry to say "I've been reading *What if it's us*, my parents have a copy, and I quite agree about Ed."

"What's that?" came from Ed.

"You being perfect casting for the role of the freckled Puerto Rican, Benito Alejo." And in imitation of Harry, gently let my fingers trace the pattern on his nose and cheeks.

"Oh, Madre de diós! not that again please. Why did you have to raise it?" He was very cross and started muttering and I thought he was about to have a real fit of temper.

I caught a couple of syllables and challenged him "Did you call me a pen...?"

"No. I'm sorry. I shouldn't use those words, certainly not to you, ever, and anyway, how do you know any Spanish swear words?"

"Ed, as I've already told you, I've watched the soccer team many times and heard you and the other Latino players using the phrase quite often, so I asked one of your team mates. So I do know those words. Actually, I think I'm the one who should apologise for teasing you quite unnecessarily. Are we good?" Ed nodded.

Rosita whispered very quietly in my ear so no one could hear "Was he about to say 'Pendejo cabrón'?"

"Yes."

"Well, Eduardo Vallejo-Benítez, I thought you were a nice, well-brought-up boy I could take home to my parents." Ed briefly looked a bit crestfallen until she grinned at him to show she was teasing him in her own way. It was great to see them kiss and make up. They decided to call it a day and that rather broke up the party.

On the way out I thanked Tom again for the aria. He was happy to have done it but added that my friend and I were welcome to have an intimate chat when he was off duty when we could fill each other in on preferred opera performances. Harry was most amused at this and the others laughed too, possibly mostly at my deep blush.

Chapter 14

When we arrived at Wampanoag Drive, I asked Harry if he would like to come back to my place. Before he could reply, Ruth said she could take a hint and would let their mother know where he was, kissed us both and got out of the car. We looked at each other, kissed lingeringly before I put the car in gear and set off. When we got home, I opened the front door and shouted "We're here." With a slight emphasis on the "we".

My parents evidently got the message and just shouted "Okay," back in acknowledgement.

I led the way upstairs to my room. Harry slipped off our hoodies before we kissed again, more passionately this time. He raised my arms, pulled up my grey t-shirt ("tut tut") and took it off before another kiss and running his tongue down my throat. He moved on to my nipples which he licked, kissed and nipped while undoing my jeans and loosening them and my boxers so that they could slip down easily. His mouth moved down to where he had cupped my balls and gently took each in his mouth rolling his tongue round them as if he had never seen or felt them before. He held my stiff cock, kissed the top, pushed down my foreskin and gave the glans a lick and a kiss. As if speaking to a friendly dog, he said, "Now you behave like your master, Ethan, wants, okay?" And shook it like it was nodding agreement. "Shoes and socks." While I took them off, Harry removed his and then his t-shirt, jeans and underwear. He realised my nervousness and kissed and hugged me very close which allowed us to feel each other's erections between our naked bodies.

"Are you okay to go on?" I nodded, so he tugged me towards the bed where he lay on his stomach and asked me to apply the lube which he had seen on the nightstand. "Use a big dollop to start with." There was a sharp intake of breath as the cold gel was applied. "Now put some on your middle finger and slowly insert it." He gasped as I pushed in but urged me to keep going. Harry's head craned back and I could see he was biting his lower lip, but I kissed him as my finger went in further. "Now in and out but use more lube." His moans sounded alarming but I carried on steadily. He said it felt really good and then asked me to curl my finger slightly which brought even more harrowing noises. He slid his body round so he could grab my face and kissed me fiercely before asking me to remove the finger but then, with more lube, use two fingers. He took a deep breath before nodding that I should continue.

So, very gingerly, I started to push in despite the groans and Harry seeming to chew the pillow! "Should I stop?"

"Oh no, no, it's wonderful. I think I'm now ready for you." Very slowly again, I pulled my fingers out. He shoved me on to my back and knelt over me. He put a lot more lube on to my cock before gently lowering himself onto it, guiding me into him. I worried whether the tightness was to be expected but Harry heaved some deep breaths before grinning at me and pushing down until I was all in. After a few moments he started to move up and down which felt absolutely amazing, so much better than jerking off using my imagination., and looking up at his wonderful body, I did not know whether it was my imagination, or the light or the tension or whatever, but the muscles seemed to have better definition than ever, his veins like whipcords. He leant forward to kiss me so I was able to squeeze his beautiful taut ass and then grab his waist before starting to move my hips up and down too until we quickly found a rhythm.

Harry arched his back, his head thrown back with closed eyes as more noises and grunts from both of us came thick and fast, until I realised I was about to orgasm. "Harry…" He realised what was about to occur and said while panting, "Try to stay in me when you've cum, don't pull out."

"Okay." And then…

As our breathing became more regular, Harry said he wanted to try something which would require us to carefully change position so that he was under me. "Hello Missionary Liddell," he muttered, after we finally achieved the manoeuvre.

"What does that make you?"

He raised his voice an octave and simpered, "Oh sir, sir, I'm just a weak and feeble supplicant awaiting so willingly your next fuck, sir." And then in his normal voice. "This does feel soooo good. Do you realise that that fuck was so intense that I came all over your chest?"

"What a waste!"

He laughed, but then tensed to prevent me sliding out. "What I want now is for you to have an erection so I can feel you grow inside me before you fuck me again, missionary style this time."

"I see. You may have to wait a little while, so why don't we just have a tongue sandwich until then or we could even pray, my weak and feeble supplicant!"

"Well, Ethan, your deflowering is now complete, the last petal has fallen away, so will you stay a Beast or join the beautiful people?" I replied that I had found my princely Beauty and just surrendered to his encircling arms.

We lay quietly for some minutes kissing each other's eyes, noses, cheeks and lips when I did sense a stirring and Harry, obviously, was aware of it too. The kissing gradually became more and more urgent as my cock strained to expand and then it was possible to very slowly start moving in and out again, Harry found his rhythm too. I got hold of his head while he then tried to play with my nipples but we were too glued by his cum for him to do much as we both panted, moaned and groaned as I built steadily towards climax. Our lips were firmly attached as we speeded up a little and I tried to hold on as long as I could before finally letting go with a great gasp. When we had recovered a bit and our breathing again became more normal, we grinned at each other at the success of the manoeuvre. We kissed, then separated as I gently withdrew and we lay side by side facing each other. "Does your shower fit two?" came from Harry.

"I don't know as you're the only person to ever ask. We could try." We grabbed our towels and went to the bathroom and found that it might be a bit of a squeeze, but it was feasible and there was just enough space to allow us to soap each other. After getting ourselves wet, I stood behind Harry and applied soap to his arms and back first and revelled in touching the biceps, triceps and other muscles. My hands gradually moved down and made the most of feeling his lovely firm ass. I used my finger to soap his anus which drew appreciative sounds before soaping his chest, again loving the feel of his pecs and abs and so down to his genitals.

His beautiful cock and balls felt really good and Harry obviously liked what I was doing as he stiffened under my ministrations. "You evidently like doing this given the amount of detailed attention you're giving to these bits."

"They're your best feature. Perhaps as your missionary I should have them chopped off and use them as a paperweight."

Harry turned round, kissed me and said, "It's your turn, so

twirl." He then started on my back and soaped me vigorously which made me tingle all over. When he got to my ass, he really made sure my asshole was well soaped and then his soapy fingers pushed in and I realised his intention was to screw me again. He got a lot of lather on his now erect cock and pulled me tight against himself. "Bend your knees slightly." He slowly inserted while holding me round the waist with one arm and my cock and balls with the other hand. His mouth was on my neck trying to get my head to turn enough to allow him to kiss me while he thrust. It was even better than the last time and I was surprised to discover that I was hard again which of course meant that Harry was able to masturbate me as before. It was a fantastic exhilarating sensation as we both climaxed a couple of seconds apart.

"I always expect my weak and feeble supplicants to multitask, even the male ones, and you do pass muster — just," I said which made him laugh. We finished showering properly and dried ourselves before returning to my bedroom.

"By the way," Harry said quietly and rather shamefacedly "I've been very wrong not to have used condoms from the off and asked you to do so too."

"Well, it would be fantastic to rewind and do it all again but unless you've got a magic wand…?" We just kissed.

Mom was obviously aware that, after the shower had finally stopped, we were probably getting dried and dressed, because she knocked and asked, "Do you boys want some dinner, because it will be on the table whenever you're ready?"

"Thanks, Mom. We'll be down in a few minutes."

Chapter 15

After a few more kisses and cuddles we went down to the kitchen to find the table laid including wine glasses and Mom about to dish up. "I hope you'll be happy with lasagne and a salad," she said.

"Sounds and smells mouth-watering," replied Harry. I suddenly recalled my manners and introduced Harry properly. Mom and Dad told him to call them Monica and Jonathan. Dad beamed at us and asked if we would like a glass of wine as a sort of celebration and winked at me. Of course I blushed, but Harry laughed and said he would be more than happy to raise a glass to whatever Dad had in mind. Dad had found a bottle of what he described as his and Mom's favourite red wine which turned out to be Montepulciano d'Abruzzo and poured each of us a decent glassful. He raised his glass and toasted Harry and me and deep friendship. Both of us thanked him, raised our glasses, and drank to friendship.

Mom was a really good cook, so to my mind, the lasagne was brilliant as usual and for several minutes there was no sound as we ate and sipped the delicious wine. I think Harry thought the same as he certainly got through the pasta like there was no tomorrow. I'd been surprised by Dad offering us wine as it was only at dinner parties when Steph's and Ed's parents came round that alcohol was available, though not to us children. It crossed my mind that now he knew that I'd had sex, I was old enough to indulge what had seemed an adults' only pleasure before. What would be offered the next time Steph and Ed came round, possibly with Jan and Rosita in tow? Would the Svoboda and Vallejo-Benítez parents do the same?

My thoughts were interrupted when Mom asked if we were done. "There's dessert if you want. I made tiramisu to round off the meal and/or there is fruit as well."

"Brilliant," enthused Harry. "Do you need help in clearing the plates and washing up?"

"That's very sweet of you, Harry, but my slave dish washer usually takes care of it all." Mom chuckled. "I don't mean Ethan or Jonathan either." As she pointed to the machine in the kitchen behind her. However, Harry did gather up the plates and took them through. The dessert was wonderfully creamy, the coffee and Marsala flavours really came through the mascarpone and the cocoa was just right too. Mom had excelled herself. Obviously, my parents were very happy with Harry! We were offered another glass of wine which we gladly accepted and that finished off the bottle. Dad invited us to move to the more comfortable seats in the living room.

Harry looked round the room and said, "This is a wonderful home that you have here. The house the university has provided is very spacious and comfortable, there is even a piano there, but it's not really a home like this is." He had seen our slightly battered piano, when his eye was suddenly caught by the bookshelf and he exclaimed, "Bill Konigsberg, Adam Silvera and more Becky too!" He got up to look more closely at the titles on the spines. "I think I have most of those at home in Edinburgh. When Dad told us we were going to be in Natick, it was really thrilling because Bill's books about Rafe and Ben, are set here albeit in a fictional boys' private school. The town itself doesn't feature much, but just to be here feels great. Have you read them

Ethan?" I had to confess I hadn't. "I did write to Bill asking if there was going to be a third book because of all the unresolved plot lines at the end of *Honestly, Ben*. He very kindly replied but didn't mention anything about another sequel. What did you think of the books Jonathan?" Dad agreed that they were very well written and dealt clearly with issues facing teenage boys.

I wondered whether Harry was feeling the effects of the wine because he went on say he thought Ben was a bit of a wet dream with him being, "Six foot two with eyes of blue and built like a brick sh... erm... outhouse." My parents evidently thought this was very funny. Harry asked them if they had seen the film *Love, Simon* based on Becky Albertalli's *Simon vs the homo sapiens agenda* and declared that he thought the book to be much better. Mom agreed with him and said that the film portrayal of the school principal was probably the worst aspect and the final scene in the fairground was just a nonsense, but it had been a success in the cinema. Harry was getting very expansive now and talked about getting emotional and crying buckets at the end of Konigsberg's *The Porcupine of Truth* and Silvera's *They both die at the end*. It was a revelation to learn about Harry's softer side, so I grabbed his hand and got him to sit back down on the sofa before he went through the entire lot. Mom asked if his parents needed to know where he was. He explained that Ruth would have told them and they would be assured he was in safe hands.

I was suddenly aware of the music that had been playing in the background. I had been humming along when I realised Dad had been trying for mood music. "Dad, your good intentions about suitable musical accompaniment are about as subtle as a brick through the window. I thought I'd heard 'Fingal's Cave' when we were upstairs; we've had Mendelssohn's *Italian* symphony through dinner, segued into his *Scottish* symphony, and if I'm not mistaken, that will segue in to the *Midsummer Night's Dream* music when the evening ends."

"Don't worry, Jonathan," said Harry. "My knowledge of classical music is minimal so you could have put on Mongolian's *Serbo-Croat* symphony and I would have happily accepted it."

My parents laughed. "Thank you, Ethan for pointing it out. I was going to suggest that when you go to bed you put on Strauss' 'Dance of the Seven Veils' while you get undressed!"

"I think we may do just that now if you don't mind." We thanked them for the dinner, the wine, and made a move. I hugged Mom and Dad and got a kiss from each and Harry got a hug too.

Chapter 16

We got upstairs and started kissing again until Harry slurred, "What's 'Fingers Cave?' Were you talking about sex?"

"No. It doesn't matter. Let me show you what Mom and Dad gave me after telling them about being gay." And brought out the bag of lube and condoms.

Harry opened the bag and exclaimed, "Wow. There are some flavoured ones. Can I have a strawberry one please?"

"Of course." I found a blueberry one and waved the sachet and said, "This is a Ruaridh Urquhart's blueberry condom". So after putting on a performance of Strauss' "Dance", we slowly stripped each other as the music built, dropping our "veils" every minute or so, then took the condoms out of their wrapping. Then I put the strawberry one on Harry while he put the blueberry one on me. We both seemed to find this exciting in itself.

Harry said, "Well, missionary, I have a very ripe and juicy strawberry here, where would you like me to put it? Which orifice?"

"I have an Urquhart's blueberry equally ripe and juicy, but so as not to waste the flavouring, shall we just use our oral orifices?"

"Hmm hmm." And so, we went head to toe and sixty-nined. The flavour was just about there, but the feel and taste of Harry's lovely cock was definitely missing as well as any pre-cum. I'd obviously realised the purpose of the condom was to prevent possible transmission of STDs, HIV and AIDS, so a small consolation was that his unadorned naked balls were there to be fondled and tongued which got a responsive groan and a slight bucking of his torso before he answered in the same way. We brought each other to a climax and I immediately took off Harry's strawberry condom and sucked and licked his cock clean while he still throbbed a bit, savouring what I could of his cum as he lay back. It was a surprise that a couple of glasses of wine had had such an effect on him when I hadn't experienced anything similar. I removed the condom from my penis and went to the bathroom to wash, depositing both rubbers in the bin there. When I returned to my bedroom Harry was splendidly laid out and fast asleep, so I took a photograph of him before stretching out alongside him, having kissed his slightly open mouth.

When I woke up Harry was leaning on his elbow, his deep blue eyes staring at me with a smile on his face. "Good morning, blueberry," he said and gave me a long kiss.

"You remember that bit, do you?" I asked.

He seemed a little shamefaced. "Sorry. I don't know why just two glasses of plonk should do that. I also vaguely seem to recall mixing up 'Fingal's Cave', which I have heard of, with Fingers which is ridiculous."

"It really doesn't matter at all. It is so incredible having you naked on the bed with me in my bedroom, as I so wanted from the first moment I saw you on the beach."

He gave me a brilliant smile. "Did I go on too long about the books and make a fool of myself?"

"I think my parents realised that the wine had perhaps gone to your head, but you didn't say anything out of place. Perhaps the tiramisu had too much Marsala in your portion."

"That seems very unlikely, though it was truly delicious, not as delicious as you however." And he rolled on top of me, his mouth clamped to mine, tongues eagerly searching for each other while my arms were pinioned above my head. I didn't struggle. When we paused for breath he lifted his head, grinned broadly and then moved to start another longed-for tour of my body with his mouth and tongue while I responded likewise.

When we had finished our morning "'exercise" and were resting with our arms round each other, Harry noticed that there was something under the pillow and moved me slightly to reveal the Ruaridh Urquhart's t-shirt he had given me after our first night. "What's this?"

"It still has your distinctive smell, your body plus your musky after shave so I can smell it before going to sleep and when I wake up, I can then pretend you've spent the night with me." He kissed me tenderly and told me that that was the best compliment he'd ever received and then carried on kissing me until there was a noise from downstairs telling us that my parents were awake. I waited to see what mood music Dad was going to use to get us up. Would it be a fanfare or something like Grieg's "Morning" from *Peer Gynt*? In the end he went for "The Lark Ascending" by Vaughan Williams. When I told Harry what we could hear, he thought it was a great incentive for us to get up. I went to check on the bathroom and found that both parents had already showered, so this time, I grabbed Harry's cock and pulled him into the shower.

Chapter 17

So showered and dressed we presented ourselves in the kitchen. By this time VW's "Thomas Tallis Fantasia" was playing. My parents wished us good morning and Dad raised a eyebrow to ask Harry whether he'd slept well.

"Yes, thank you. I hope I didn't waffle on too much about books."

"Not at all. You seem to have read quite widely about young American gay experiences."

"Actually, I read voraciously just to have some idea of what Ruth and I might expect. She's read most of them too, including several stories about teenagers becoming drag queens. There was one where a professional told the hero how to tuck his genitals away which was enough to make me want to cross my legs and keep them crossed!"

Trying not to laugh, Mom intervened to ask what he would like for breakfast. "Whatever you normally have will be fine. Thank you."

So Mom gave us some juice, bowls of cereal, put some bread in the toaster and several bottles of various jams on the table. "Tea or coffee?"

"Tea please." A jug of milk appeared. I had told my parents about Heather's cupboard full of tins of different tea, but we just had our usual supermarket brand tea bags in the cup. Harry didn't seem to notice the difference and happily drank his teabag tea while schlurping his juice, eating his cereal and toast. I think Dad must have decided on a VW binge because after the "Thomas

Tallis Fantasia" came the "Greensleeves" one and then "The Wasps" overture. Fortunately, breakfast was finished before he could start on the wonderful rhapsodies, so I grabbed Harry's hand and announced we were going back upstairs to get ready for me to drive him home. Harry managed to splutter out his thanks for breakfast before we escaped from the kitchen to the VW-less safety of my bedroom though a few strains could still just be heard. "After all our kissing etc., it should be safe for you to use my toothbrush," I offered.

He smiled. "I think it can wait until I get home." Between us we changed the bedsheet and pillowcase, put the Urquhart's shirt back in its place and tidied up before Harry took me in his arms, kissed me gently and asked, "How do you feel now?"

"Do you mean now that my virginity is old news? Fantastic. Wonderful and it's all thanks to you." After a few more fond kisses we decided to make a move and descended to "See, the conquering hero comes" as Dad must have been keeping an ear open for our movements. "Thank you, Dad. Ha ha very funny!" Harry said his goodbyes and reminded my parents that they were due for afternoon tea next Saturday. We piled into the car and set off for Wampanoag Drive.

Over the next few days, I spent time trying to catch up on the summer reading programme before term started, but I made sure to finish *What if it's us* first. Arthur and Ben were wonderful creations though the ending wasn't quite what I thought would happen. Of course I also looked to see what other books my parents had which Harry had mentioned. The first one I found was *The Porcupine of Truth* by Adam Silvera which was totally absorbing. It was very easy to see why Harry had cried at the end.

Chapter 18

Saturday dawned and my parents and I set off in good time to be at the Browns for three p.m. Heather and Angus greeted us and ushered us through to the living room where Harry and Ruth were waiting. I got a kiss from both. Heather explained that a few of Angus' university colleagues had also been invited. The Smiths had had to cry off, but a couple from the French faculty would arrive shortly.

Angus asked my parents about their surname and whether there was any connection with Eric Liddell the Olympic athlete or any Scottish link. Dad said that he was unaware of any relationship with the runner, but that he supposed a distant ancestor may well have originated in Scotland and had possibly left at about the time of the Highland Clearances. This ancestor could easily have finished up somewhere in North America and eventually the family, in the form of Monica and himself, came to be in Natick as they tried to get jobs in the same place. The occasional showing of *Chariots of Fire* had inevitably given cause for enquiries about Eric Liddell and one cheeky student had asked if he were Eric's son. Bearing in mind the film portrayed the 1924 Games in Paris, Dad said he could at least have made it grandson or great-grandson! Another student had confused 1924 with 1974 which hadn't even been an Olympic year.

He went on to say, "The other Liddell who confused students was Alice Pleasance Liddell, the young muse for Lewis Carroll's books. So I do get the odd enquiry about my white rabbit and whether I play cards, chess or croquet."

Mom intervened to say, "When Ethan was in my womb, we didn't know what sex our child was going to be, so any discernible movement was described as 'Jabberwocky's on the move again!'." Chuckles all round, I just groaned inwardly.

Angus laughed, and said that some of his less savvy students, seemed to have no idea about historical periods. "Aye, I know there are a few grey hairs in my beard, but I have been asked if I'd known Mary Queen of Scots."

My father spotted the piano and asked if he could see it. Heather explained that as no one could play, it had been untouched since they'd moved in, but the university's Music faculty would send someone to tune it on a regular basis if they requested it. Dad ran his fingers over the keys and said that there was no need for any tuning at the moment and that it was enviable to have such an instrument available. He remarked that he occasionally accompanied me when I tried to sing some show songs or operatic arias. I hadn't ever said anything about this to Harry, so this revelation, very unfortunately timed in my view, came as a complete surprise. Of course our hosts being hospitable people invited me to sing something. I glared at Dad who looked the picture of innocence of course. "Come on Ethan. Your mother and I hear more than you think we do and your voice is better than you think. We've heard you singing the 'Pink Aeroplane' song recently so how about that?"

"Sorry about my father's ghastly sense of humour, he means 'La vie en rose' made famous by Édith Piaf. If you slightly change the emphasis, you get L'avion rose, the pink aeroplane." I took a deep breath. "Oh well, here we go."

The doorbell rang, and Harry rushed out to answer it. After

a minute he ushered in two elegantly dressed men of about fifty who stood at the door seemingly enraptured by my singing. At the end, they both applauded and Dad and I were profusely thanked by them and the Browns, while Mom looked fit to burst and I just blushed at the attention. Harry grinned and Ruth gave me a big kiss, when the newcomers came up to shake my hand and introduced themselves as Laurent Robespierre and his husband Yves Delarue. "Merveilleux, mon petit," said Laurent. "A beautiful rendition." He turned to Heather and Angus to offer their apologies for being late and then to me and Dad for having missed the opening. Yves said that they were *the* French faculty at the moment and that every year when their new students found out that he and Laurent were married, Laurent was immediately renamed "Adam". It had become a rather tedious joke over the years but they'd got used to it.

Heather announced that tea was ready and invited us to move to the dining room where there were plates of various sandwiches, cakes and cookies, and the table laid with crockery and cutlery all formally laid out. "Please help yourselves while I just fetch the teapot and put the scones on." A couple of minutes silence ensued while we looked to see what was in the sandwiches and put a few on our plates. Heather returned with the teapot and asked me if I wanted some lemon slices instead of milk. I caught Harry and Ruth trying not to laugh and said that milk would be fine, thank you. The milk jug was passed round and Heather filled everyone's cup.

"Do you know many French chansons, Ethan?" asked Laurent.

"A few. It's such a lovely language to sing in." He and Yves obviously liked my reply and so we chatted about some other Piaf songs, Tino Rossi singing "J'attendrai" and Yves Montand, especially the last's version of "Les feuilles mortes".

Dad asked Angus and Heather about how they'd voted in the Scottish independence referendum and on leaving the European Union. Angus said they'd agreed that, while an independent Scotland was an attractive idea, staying in the UK would be a better option economically, as would remaining in the EU be, but he foresaw problems with determined politicians who thought that Britain should, could and would survive outside a powerful trading bloc. I saw that Dad did not want to press them on their thoughts about whether the current government of the USA could be trusted.

Angus and Heather asked my father about his piano playing and the music that he and my mother liked. They discovered many likes in common and there were suggestions that they would consult the Symphony Hall season brochure to find a concert they would all enjoy, timetable permitting. Heather suddenly remembered the scones and rescued them just in time. We were offered jam and cream to put on in whichever order we thought fit. Apparently in the UK different counties had different traditions in this regard. She also said that, if we preferred, we could use butter rather than cream. The teapot was refilled and the afternoon passed very pleasantly. I saw that Harry was watching the two Frenchmen quite closely and gave me a conspiratorial wink at one point, but I wasn't too sure what he meant.

Laurent and Yves asked Angus and Heather about where they lived in Edinburgh. The address, which apparently was quite central, confirmed their clear idea of where that was as it was near some of the bars and a gay sauna they used to like to visit. It transpired that, when they lived in Paris, they'd visited the city on a number of occasions while following the French rugby team for the biennial VI Nations game in Edinburgh. They had usually stayed in a luxury hotel, the Balmoral, which was convenient because the bus that took them straight to Murrayfield rugby stadium went from a stop just outside. They missed those trips when they'd moved to America. These were just names to me.

In their turn Angus and Heather said they had gone to Paris sometimes for the France v Scotland games, but that was in the days of the V Nations before 2000 when they were just married and only had one child. Yves related how all the tartans livened up the streets of Paris when several thousand Scottish rugby fans arrived. He said it always seemed as if the Auld Alliance were back from the days of Mary Stuart when she was the Queen of France. Harry, of course then chimed in with, "My father knew her personally."

"Aye, thank you for that observation, Harry." As Angus shook his head seemingly in great sadness. "Be careful you don't meet the same fate!" As most of the sandwiches and scones had been eaten, the tea party came to its natural end and everyone shook hands, and with all the usual pleasantries about doing it all again etc., the Frenchmen took their leave.

My parents said they would go too and asked if I were ready. Reluctantly I said yes, kissed Ruth and Harry (who whispered, "Jabberwocky?") and told them I'd see them next week at school, shook Angus' and Heather's hands and said, "Thank you for a great afternoon." And so, we went home feeling rather full.

Chapter 19

The following day I was surprised to get a message from Harry asking if I were free to come round at about two p.m. as he had some questions about the school timetable and we could help finish off the few cakes and biscuits left over from yesterday. I replied that of course I would be there. On arrival, Harry said that his mother and Ruth had gone out to do some last-minute shopping and his father was still very busy with preparing his lectures.

We went into the kitchen where he'd made a pot of tea (no lemon slices!) and had the cakes and cookies out on a plate. His lesson timetable was waiting too, so we sat and I asked what the problem was. Harry sat very close to me, putting his arm round my shoulder, and without warning, stuck his tongue in my ear which tickled. He then whispered, "Come upstairs, I have something I want you to see." When we got to his bedroom, he shut the door and immediately started to undress me so, of course, I responded. When we were naked, he had a mischievous smile on his face and said in a mock, antiques show voice, "Mr Liddell, what do you think of this exhibit?"

"Am I allowed to handle this obviously priceless item if I'm very careful Mr MacInnes-Brown?"

"Most certainly."

"Are these baubles integral to the piece?" I asked, picking them up very delicately.

"Oh, very much so, yes."

"Hmmm, well, this may be an early twenty-first century piece, perhaps of British or even Scottish manufacture but without any tattoo or other identifying mark. Ah! I see this part of it retracts, and oh, there's a spot of automatic polish which I'll just lick off." Harry shuddered ecstatically as the pre-cum was removed with a kiss and said that he thought a very close inspection was needed, that a bit of spit and polish would allow a full blossoming, but perhaps an immediate oral examination would be best. I simply had to agree, so we gave each other a very thorough oral examination, questioning every possible aspect! When we were done and the answers had come thick and fast, it was wonderful to have that taste again and to be lying in his arms on the bed, with occasional hands wandering over chests and asses, while exchanging lingering kisses.

Harry asked whether I had been aware of the Frenchmen's evident interest in me which was why he had winked at me. "That song evidently really got to them and I could see they just wanted to strip you, and between them, fuck you silly. Didn't your parents say anything because I thought they were so obvious?"

I shook my head feeling that I couldn't believe what he'd just said. However, all other thoughts disappeared when there was another stirring and Harry wondered whether, as a pre-school exercise, we shouldn't have a more probing examination to make sure we had taken in everything necessary. We agreed that was an excellent idea so…

Afterwards we had a quick shower and were dressed and back in the kitchen to be ready for when Heather and Ruth got home. Harry made a fresh pot of tea, and before we could tuck in to any of the food, he asked if I would sing him a song. "You have a lovely voice and I'd like something just for me." This was a complete surprise as obviously I hadn't prepared anything. I asked if he would be happy with another French song. He smiled and said, "Yes and don't worry, there's just me and no Adam and Yves to rape you with their eyes."

"Okay. I'll have to hum or la-la the non-vocal bits, but one I think you'll like is one your grandparents would have known in the 1960s. A great hit at the time for Françoise Hardy, 'Tous les garçons et les filles'." I took a breath and sang. At the reprise I stopped to tell him that the English version, not a translation though, was called "Find me a boy" and sang that. Because I was concentrating on singing and looking at Harry, I didn't hear the door open behind me.

When the song was finished Ruth flung her arms round me. "Hello Ethan," she cried and gave me a hug. "That was fantastic."

"This is a lovely surprise, Ethan, you really do have a good voice," said Heather. "When did you get here?"

"About two o'clock. Harry wanted to ask about the timetable."

"Oh, yes? And that has taken you until now?"

Harry intervened, "Well we did have tea, cake and biscuits and this is the second pot. I wanted to ask about some of the teachers that we'll both have."

"Hmm, hmm. Did you ask your father if he wanted any tea?"

"Sorry, we were very absorbed."

"Yes, I'll bet." As I felt myself blushing under the questioning, I'm sure Heather and Ruth knew exactly how we had spent the afternoon. Heather called out, "Angus, do you want some tea dear?"

"Aye. Yes please. Be there in a moment," came the reply followed by a slightly dishevelled Angus, hair uncombed, shirt only partly buttoned revealing a magnificent expanse of hairy chest. I doubted that my father would look the same! "Hi there

Ethan, the song was great, a pleasure to hear it in both versions." Angus chuckled and ruffled my hair. "Aye, I see you're here for second helpings from the look of the crumbs on that plate." Heather of course immediately put out a few Jaffa cakes, shortbreads and chocolate digestives which Angus started to munch. I wondered whether he had been so intent on getting his lecture preparation done, he'd missed lunch if not breakfast as well.

"Well Harry, I think you're all set for the semester, the first lesson is English with Bill Bailey and I'm in the same class. As I told you, he usually produces the school play so it'll be interesting to see what he intends for next semester. There'll be a list on the notice board to sign for those interested in performing and/or helping backstage and he can then try to find a play to use those people. Usually there are more girls than boys wanting to participate which immediately presents a problem, as you may imagine."

Angus said, "Ethan, why don't you suggest that he looks at changing the gender of some or all the characters. Before we left Edinburgh, there was a grand production of *The Taming of the Shrew* by the Royal Shakespeare Company where *all* the roles were reversed so Petruchia came to Padua to seek a husband. We're sure the audience found it very revelatory, particularly on domestic abuse! Mr Bailey may be grateful for the chance to do something different."

"Thank you very much, Angus. It's a wonderful idea." And with that, I said my goodbyes, kissed Harry and Ruth and drove home.

Chapter 20

HARRY

The next couple of days before term started gave me space to think about my relationship with Ethan. He was exactly what I'd wanted and needed. The few sex encounters I'd had in Edinburgh had been very pleasant, if not downright enjoyable in one particular case, but only one of the boys had left me wanting to know them better, the others not at all. I'd actually persuaded a couple of them, quite separately, that we were taking each other's virginity, but I'd happily given mine, the previous year.

It had been a warm summer day during the Edinburgh Festival. I was just ambling through Princes Street Gardens in a t-shirt and shorts, when a very good-looking young man gave me a really lovely beaming smile. Of course I smiled back, and he immediately came across to chat. He was French and spoke only a little English, but between that and my school French, it was established that he was a student in Paris and just coming to the end of his holiday. He told me that he had seen me wandering along a little way away and had been attracted by my hair! In France, he said, most red hair came out of a bottle but mine was obviously natural. In my turn, I was attracted to his lovely eyes and mouth and couldn't help staring. He obviously got the message, because he raised his eyebrows and asked if I would like to come to his hotel which was close by in Charlotte Square.

En route we exchanged names; he was called Richard-Alain.

All the childhood warnings about "strange men" vanished like magic as we strolled, weaving our way through the tourist crowds. When we got to his room we paused and looked at each other. "Will this be your first?" I nodded and wondered whether it was that obvious. He smiled again, pulled me gently into his arms and kissed me tenderly. "Please don't worry, we will only do what you are happy with." He undressed me, which didn't take long, but I was quivering all the time. When I was naked, he gazed admiringly at my body, stroked my hair, and pushed his fingers through my red pubes. "Fantastic," he murmured. His clothes came off and his slim muscular body with a patch of dark hair on his chest was delightful to look at. He then started to kiss me, gradually moving down my body which was something I'd only imagined happening in dreams.

My shoulders, arms, hands were all subjected to his kisses and tongue, raising goose bumps as he progressed. My nipples got special treatment as his tongue got to work on them before he traced the muscles of my abdomen and ran a circle round my belly button. He nuzzled my pubes and worked round to my balls which he sucked and rolled around his tongue one by one. He kissed along my cock before sampling the precum while pushing my foreskin down and taking it all in his mouth. It was so exciting that I almost came immediately but managed not to. However, it didn't take long before I was pumping cum down his throat. He put his arms around me and said, "Now, you." I was about to start by imitating what he had done, but he laughed and pushed me onto my knees in front of his waving cock. I fondled his balls and licked his penis up and down using my lips to push his foreskin down and got busy. From his noises he was really enjoying this and kept running his fingers through my hair, and as he neared climax, holding my head in place as I sucked. When he came, the spurt hitting the back of my mouth surprised me but he held me while I swallowed and let the throb of his cock subside in my mouth.

We lay in each other's arms until he stirred and reached round to touch my arse and move his fingers to examine my anus. "Would you like to...?" he whispered.

"Oh yes."

He reached for a tube of lubricant, and while I watched him, he squeezed some gel onto his cock and spread it thickly up and down the shaft before squeezing more onto his fingers, then pushed my thighs apart and I gasped as the cold gel was applied to my arsehole and his finger was gently but firmly pushed up. "Are you still okay with this, Harry?" I nodded, so his finger probed before he pulled it out and then inserted two presumably to accustom me to the sensation. After a couple of minutes, they were withdrawn and he proceeded to gingerly penetrate me. It felt very tight as he got further into me but eventually, he was all in and I really was quite comfortable, but then he began to move, incredibly slowly at first, but got faster as I moved with him. His lips were on mine most of the time, but as he came closer to orgasm, our breathing didn't allow it. When I felt him cum, he collapsed on me and pressed his lips on mine quite forcibly this time.

Once he'd recovered and his breathing had returned to near normal, Richard-Alain turned to me and asked if I would like to... "You'll have to show me what to do." He put a lot of gel on my cock, and as he applied it, the thrill of what was about to happen, my masturbatory dreams coming true was almost too much. I saw him apply more gel to his arsehole which I saw for the first time, like a puckered rose, and to his fingers which he pushed in.

He grabbed my hand and said, "Now you." So I put some gel on my fingers and followed his guidance. When he was ready, he wriggled down the bed to be in a better position, spread his thighs and put me on top of him before he got hold of my cock and brought it to where I could penetrate him. The tightness made me wonder if I was doing something wrong but Richard-Alain's noises told me otherwise and I pushed in to the hilt. After a few moments rest, both of us started slowly moving, gradually more rhythmically until, after too short a time, I got to orgasm. The whole experience was exhilarating. We had a wonderful post-coital kiss before I apologised for not having been able to hold on for longer.

Richard-Alain could not have been more gracious. "This was your first time, n'est-ce pas? I am honoured to have been your partner." He said we should shower as I could certainly not go home without one. It was very tempting to have more sex in the shower as we soaped other with particular attention to each other's genitals, but the clock told me that time was passing and I should get home soon to avoid too much questioning. Richard-Alain said he had to return to Paris the next day to attend to his studies which is why he was so determined to "meet" a Scotsman on his last day. With many fond kisses we said goodbye.

Then the image of handsome Duncan suddenly came to mind. The weather was wild that weekend, and inevitably, there was a home rugby match to play against one of the other Edinburgh schools. Soon after the start most of the players were completely mud-spattered, the pitch was a quagmire, but we were all hardy Scotsmen, the descendants of Robert the Bruce, so of course we ploughed on! About half way through the first half there was a pause while some rule infringement was dealt with, when I saw close to me through the rain, my opposite number, who despite muddy heaving chest, matted hair and everything, looked incredibly desirable and sexy. He noticed my stare, raised his eyebrows questioningly and grinned. I nodded imperceptibly (I hoped) and grinned back. The whistle blew and we were off again.

At some point he managed to run past me, breathily murmured, "Car park after." And was away down the field. After the match I made sure to shower thoroughly before getting ready to meet this vision and there he was, even better without the muddy adornment. The rain had thankfully stopped during the second half. "Duncan Robertson."

"Harry MacInnes-Brown."

"The car's over here." And he led the way. In the car we exchanged minimal details so I learned he was 19 and in the final year of school. "My parents are away this evening so, if that's okay with you, we'll go home."

"Wonderful." As we drove, he put a big hand on my thigh and slowly moved it up to my crotch and gently squeezed.

"Have you done much?"

"I've had my moments."

"Well, I hope you're going to last longer than that!"

His home was one of the apartments in Roseburn overlooking Murrayfield and was very comfortably furnished. He ushered me into his bedroom before we kissed at last and then… After a really satisfactory (from my point of view at least) mutual suck and fuck, he made us a cup of tea before wanting to chat. "Won't your parents worry about you?"

"No, it's a regular thing to go out after a match, so I won't be missed unless you're planning a kidnap," I said hopefully.

He grinned. "Unfortunately, that will have to be another time. I was surprised to get your signal during the match, but I'm happy, it seems to be so rare, although there must be at least a couple of gays in any group of thirty."

"Yes, that was us!" We giggled.

"Are you out at home?"

"Yes, are you?"

"Sort of. I think my parents know but we just don't talk about it. They may be disappointed that I'm not bringing girls back all the time, but I can't change who I am."

"I think my parents are mostly concerned about my happiness and that I don't get involved with the seamier side of life, not whether I'll meet that 'someone'. I'm only seventeen and I want to do something with my wild oats first. I would guess that you've sown some oats though from what we've just done."

He grinned and told me that once he had turned eighteen and could legally visit Edinburgh's gay bars, life had definitely become much easier and the car was a real boon. He gently fondled my cock before saying that one of his pickups had been a doctor at the Royal Infirmary's Genito-Urinary Department, who had told him about the frenulum, which was highly erogenous for most men, a sort of tickle spot.

"Well, you certainly found mine and you knew your way round my body. I just copied you and hoped you would enjoy it all as much as I did — you're a good teacher."

He laughed, then kissed me and held me closely. "I did. You're a good pupil and I can check on how much you've learned and retained when our schools have the return fixture." I was delighted to be told he wanted a return match. By chance the return fixture was only three weeks away so we happily agreed to a date. Bingo!

Chapter 21

The other "adventures" were mere fumblings in the dark, compared to Connor. He was a year above me at school. Connor pursued me on and off for some time before I finally agreed to what he called a sleepover. His home was in one of the grottier parts of Edinburgh (they do exist) and when I arrived there was no attempt at seduction, my clothes (and his) were pulled off followed by just a brutal kiss forcing his tongue into my mouth while he put some lubrication on his hand and vigorously masturbated me until I came. With more lube and my cum, he coated his sizeable cock and my arsehole, turned me round, pushed me face down onto the bed and fucked me. He was insatiable. I can't recall how many times he fucked me that night, but he varied it, once with my legs over his shoulders and once having me straddling him while pushing up and forcing me down onto him. His preference seemed to be having me face down while he pounded me on the grounds that I had a fantastic firm arse which was a pleasure to bounce up and down on. Eventually even he tired and then wanted me to fuck him. His sweaty body by then wasn't particularly inviting, but I did as commanded. It was during the second fuck I realised he'd fallen asleep! There was no breakfast on offer in the morning or the chance of a shower, that had to wait until I got home.

Being seventeen and stupid I actually had a second "sleepover" with Connor when he wanted to see how often we could sixty-nine. I managed three before feeling exhausted but of course Connor could manage more than that. While I sucked, he fingered my arse and tried to see how many well-lubricated fingers he could insert. It was difficult to concentrate on getting him to cum when he pushed a third finger into me which really hurt but fortunately, he did shoot because he then said, "Next time, Harry, I'll get my whole fist up you."

I decided that he'd done enough and told him that wouldn't be happening. His reaction was to stare at me coldly and say rather bitterly and sarcastically, "Harry, you're no fucking fun at all. Just go. Now."

"But it's three a.m."

"So?" I got dressed and left. Needless to say, there were no taxis in that part of Edinburgh at that time of night, or at any time as far as I could tell, so it was a long trek home before I could have a shower and crawl into bed, sadly regretting I had been such a bloody stupid fool for allowing myself to be so badly used just for Connor's gratification.

Connor had told me something of his life in the brief intervals between fucks. Puberty had found him rather earlier than for most boys so, well before he was fourteen, he had started meeting men for sex. They could be any age, size, shape, colour, as long as they had a cock and an arse and wanted to use them or have them used or both. Needless to say, the gay Edimbourgoisie was ready and eager to welcome a young teenager into their midst. He enjoyed it very much especially when it was a group who all wanted to fuck him and be sucked by him. He told me that, at the prospect of a teenager in their bed, some older men couldn't wait to get him and themselves naked and he thought that a stroke or heart attack might carry one of them off at any time. Connor's cruel sadistic smile as he said this made me feel that he would've relished that. Connor completely ignored me at school after that, and fortunately, it was only a couple of weeks later, that Dad told us about the opportunity to go to Natick, Massachusetts, USA.

Chapter 22

It was that chance encounter at the beach shortly after we had arrived in Natick, when this incredibly handsome boy and his friends sat down next to us and his transparent look of innocent wonder, it wasn't lust as I had thought at first, that immediately drew me to him. He seemed to exude a longing which I could certainly reciprocate. I could sense his wanting to reach out, which is why I thought a couple of smiles might draw him to do or say something, but it was only when Ruth and I had to make a move that his face showed disappointment so clearly and then changed back to delight when I said loudly enough that we'd be back the next day, that I felt really encouraged. It was obvious to me that Ethan's friends had noticed his eyes constantly following my every shift of position, so their absence the following day wasn't surprising at all! It was very good of them to give Ethan the clear opportunity to make the necessary contact.

Ruth had cottoned on very quickly what was afoot. We didn't and don't have any secrets from each other. I'd told her previously of my sexual adventures, the "frogs" who I'd kissed and… The only reference to Connor had been that he had turned from a frog into a poisonous toad which fortunately didn't lead to any questions, but I was sure David Attenborough's and Chris Packham's spirits would've been appalled at such a nonsensical confusion of amphibians!

Ethan appealed to her as well and I knew that, in other circumstances, she would've been thrilled to have him as a boyfriend, not just because of his looks, but as we got to know him, his innocence, kindness, generosity, intelligence and captivating smile and he sings too! I reflected on whether it had been a good idea to confess to "kissing frogs", but it would've been a fraud to claim to be as completely innocent as he evidently was. I couldn't believe that no one had tried to relieve him of that innocence, but perhaps that was what had been his protection, like those blasted battleship grey t-shirts he was seemingly so addicted to.

I was very, very happy to have been his first and be what he really seemed to want and need as he was definitely what I wanted and needed. The passion behind his kisses was so unselfish, unlike the experience with Connor, that I felt myself melting each time and responded accordingly. I loved his lovemaking, but I suddenly thought about the "L" word and did I mean it? Ethan's intense gazing into my eyes told me that he loved me and that should really be enough. With a broad smile to myself, I settled into the pillow and fell asleep hoping to dream of him and his kisses. I did want our relationship to last a long time, perhaps as long as the next two years before we returned to Edinburgh.

Chapter 23

The first day of term and Ruth and I were ready for Patrick to drive us to school. We had discussed how we were going to get dour Patrick to laugh or at least smile, but without anything definite to go on, it seemed best to see how the drive went. Patrick Smith was very handsome with a superb physique for a seventeen-year-old, and it showed in the tailored short-sleeved shirts revealing his powerful arms as well as his tight pants which emphasized his muscular thighs not to mention the straining material round his crotch. Definitely wet dream material! He was bang on time, so after waving Mum and Dad goodbye, we clambered into the car with me as shotgun and Ruth behind.

"Good morning," we said in unison. "How are you?"

"Okay thanks. You both prepared for the first day in a new school?" We said that we were because, by chance, we had met some other students from John Eliot and become friends. Patrick, of course, wanted to know who they were so we listed Ethan, Ed, Rosita, Steph and Jan. "Good contacts. Are you planning on meeting them this morning?"

"Yes, in the car park. Ethan said he would take Ruth to her first class with a Miss or Mrs Berenson." Patrick nodded.

After a pause he said, "So you're gay?"

"Have my parents been talking?"

"Uh huh."

"Does that worry you?"

"No, not at all, I'm 110% straight."

"I'm sorry to disagree with you on our first date."

"This isn't a date!" he protested.

"Sorry, I forgot that in America that word has different connotations than it would at home. This first drive then, but to be pedantic, you can't be more than 100% anything. You'll never pass maths at that rate."

Patrick grudgingly agreed, "Okay. 100% straight and it's math."

"In the UK it's a plural, and no human being is perfect, even you Patrick. You must have a flaw."

"Okay then, just for this drive, I'm 99.9999% straight."

"Well, thank you that definitely gives me hope even if it's only 0.0001%."

Patrick actually chuckled. "You're certainly persistent."

I assumed a look of total innocence and asked, "As a football player, are you good at handling balls?" The innocence was ruined by Ruth's shriek of laughter as Patrick nearly stalled.

He kept a straight face however. "Are you trying to flirt with me?"

"Oh Patrick, if you only knew what I have in mind for you."

"Thank God we're at school as I really don't want to know." He pulled into the John Eliot car park and stopped in what seemingly was his usual spot. "Here's Sam come to rescue me," he said as he got out and kissed a stunningly beautiful girl. We were introduced and he reminded us that he would see us the next day before giving us a big smile and a wave before walking towards the main entrance with his arm round Sam. Patrick was suddenly conscious that Ruth and I were watching him, because he pulled the back of his jacket down as if to try and cover his very inviting arse but it wasn't long enough!

At that moment Ethan, Ed and Steph arrived having parked

just a couple of spaces away. "Did we see Patrick actually smile? What did you do?"

"Oh, I just teased him about wanting to get him into bed without quite saying that." They all laughed. "Fat chance," was their considered view.

Ruth had grabbed Ethan's hand and gave him a quick kiss, when he said, "I'll see you lot in Bill Bailey's class, save me a seat please, while I deliver this parcel to Miss Berenson." Ruth was obviously excited and I think pleased that her new classmates would see her arriving with such a very handsome escort.

Chapter 24

ETHAN

I took Ruth to her classroom and was warmly greeted by Miss Berenson. "Hello Ethan. Good to see you again."

"Good morning, Miss B. This is Ruth Brown who I think you should be expecting. She's just come from Edinburgh to join the school so I can leave her in your safe hands."

"Thank you, Ethan." I kissed the top of Ruth's head and told her we'd meet later while Miss Berenson steered her to an empty desk and introduced her to her neighbours. "This is Rusalka and this is Oksana. I'm sure they'll tell you all you need to know at the break."

The rest of the day passed in a bit of a whirl. Mr Bailey (he was properly called William but no one ever used it, the short form being much easier) had put up the lists for would-be actors and backstage personnel to sign and I put my name down on both as usual. Jan, Ed and Harry were due to meet the soccer squad at some point and Steph would meet hers, or perhaps it was the swimming team, to plan the term's activities. It looked as if all our after-school programmes were going to be very full.

We met up at lunch and managed to sit at the same table, but I knew from experience that wouldn't last very long as we would probably chat to those with similar interests. Patrick and the football crowd rather dominated the dining hall at one end and Jan and the soccer lot at the other. The food at school wasn't too bad, if a little stodgy for my taste, so I preferred to bring my own sandwich and sit with a book or a script if I were in a play.

The next couple of weeks passed quickly. Patrick drove Harry and Ruth in every morning, while I brought Ed and Steph. Depending on what was planned, I took whoever was free after school back to their home though, at times, when rehearsals demanded, that proved impossible.

Bill was quite enthusiastic when I told him about Angus' suggestion about changing gender in *The Taming of the Shrew*. He had certainly heard about it from friends in London, but he had been more intrigued by a production, also in London, where Oberon and Titania exchanged roles and lines in *A Midsummer Night's Dream* although he would be obliged to adapt it for a proscenium stage. He considered the play a great possibility, given the list of possible actors. The other advantage, he claimed, was that it was one of Shakespeare's shortest plays!

He had decided to hold auditions so, along with the couple of dozen other would-be actors, Ruth and I went after school to the school's auditorium. Bill and another colleague from the English department knew most of the older students and their acting abilities, but in order to be fair on the younger ones and newcomers from the senior years, and to avoid any suggestion of bias, we all had to be seen. We were told that an announcement would be made in a few days' time and a list posted on the Departmental notice board.

The following week I found that I had been cast as Oberon/Theseus, a girl who I'd never really noticed before, a rather shapely blonde called Michaela Stratstone would be Titania/Hippolyta, Hudson Greenberg, a reliable comedian was cast as Bottom, and Randall Robinson as Puck. Bill was delighted to find that, because of the number of people who wanted to be in the cast, he was able to use a wonderful ethnic range for the young lovers, Rude Mechanicals and fairies. Rehearsals would begin the following Monday. Michaela and I seemed to hit it off and agreed to meet regularly outside of normal rehearsals to go through our lines. Ruth had decided to join the drama group before term started (to keep an eye on me?) and was cast as one of the four fairies who now served Oberon rather than Titania. She would be Pease-blossom.

The first rehearsal was a read through with all the cast. I think Bill may have been thinking about what possible textual cuts could be made. He also had to make a decision about whether to preserve the Theseus and Hippolyta roles as written — i.e. as King and consort — or to change them in line with Titania and Oberon — i.e. Queen and consort. Only a read through using both would sort out this dilemma before he could decide. I felt that there was a distinct tension in the atmosphere, perhaps because of the change of gender in two of the main characters, but there were bursts of laughter at some of the lines. Poor Hudson had naturally large ears, so when we were ostensibly in my fairy bower, the line "...*and kiss thy fair large ears, my gentle joy*" inevitably got him blushing and the cast giggling. However, only a little later when I had to turn to him and say, very lovingly, the immortal line "...*I have a venturous fairy that shall fetch thee new nuts...*", there was pandemonium and the reading came to a total halt until everyone recovered. Even Bill was laughing so that line was definitely not going to be cut!

Needless to say, that got out and round the school very quickly, so Hudson had to endure being teased about needing new "nuts" for quite a while, but when the relationship between Harry and me became known, there were the inevitable comments about me having attendant fairies and whether Harry was one of them! I was just hopeful that this would soon pass, but as the saying goes, "there's no such thing as bad publicity", it could be construed as advance notices, and the show may get good audiences as a result — there would be only three performances in the lead up to Christmas.

Chapter 25

Harry had quickly established himself in the soccer first team captained by Jan and had Ed as a teammate as well. They had a couple of practice sessions a week and a match against local school teams most weekends. Steph's team also had a couple of practices a week and a match at the alternate weekends to the boys. How she fitted it all in with the swimming team and meeting Jan I'll never know.

When we didn't have a rehearsal, it was possible for Ruth and me to support whichever team was playing at home, despite the occasional bad weather. Turnout for these matches varied enormously depending on how well the teams were doing in the local league, but the finals wouldn't be until next year. So we went armed with flasks of coffee to keep us going on a few rather dismal Saturdays and cheered the John Eliot team as loudly as we could. They always knew if we were there, largely because Ruth's hair could be seen across any soccer field. The school notice board was a most helpful aid in following Patrick's football team's successes. He obviously did a magnificent job, because it was very rare that any loss was reported.

Ruth always kept me informed about the banter between Patrick and Harry on their drives to school, with Patrick apparently matching Harry's teases effortlessly and with great good humour; he was certainly smiling and laughing a lot more. Ruth was convinced that Patrick was deliberately wearing tighter and tighter pants to excite Harry, but I didn't think there had been much attempt to disguise his endowment in the first place. If Mother Nature had ever intended to dish things out equally, a few Massachusetts men had definitely been short-changed!

Ruth, being a very intelligent, attractive girl, seemed to have gathered a lively group from her class mates around her as well as joining me in the play. Her classroom neighbours, Rusalka and Oksana in particular, became very good friends. Inevitably she had been asked about me and whether I was her boyfriend, but fortunately she'd been non-committal and not said that actually I was her brother's boyfriend. The more observant soon discerned the truth. Ruth had actually persuaded one of the boys in her class to join the drama group because, as she said, "I think he may be gay but he doesn't know it yet." Jocelyn was a slim, slightly effeminate boy and was happy to be cast as one of the fairies along with another younger more butch looking boy, so Bill could at least have male and female fairies.

Each of the initial rehearsals involved blocking so we would know where and when to move on the set that Bill had arranged. Of course, with the finalised script the cast was told to try and learn our lines as soon as possible, but initially, we would go through it twice a week with books in hand. Bill said that the number of rehearsals would gradually increase as the performance dates got closer and a couple more Saturdays might require our attendance too. This never went down well. Michaela and I spent quite a few lunchtimes going through our lines where our characters met and I think we developed a good relationship.

Chapter 26

Ruth and I were sitting in the dining hall with our lunch, and the script, when Hudson and Randall asked if they could join us. "Of course." I knew they were both gay and was fairly sure they were interested, especially since my relationship with Harry had become common knowledge. They were both leading members of the school's Gay-Straight Alliance and I wondered if they were on a recruiting drive. They denied this but said Harry and I would always be welcome.

Hudson said he was surprised to see me with the script as I already knew my lines. I replied that Bill had asked the cast to let him have any ideas for raising the comedic element. This was a first because he'd never sought any help about a production in the past that I was aware of. Randall said they'd had to leave that rehearsal early and had missed it. As I had been cast as Oberon, and Hudson Bottom, he said, rather shyly, he was looking forward to rehearsing our kiss and promptly blushed. I thought he blushed almost as easily as I did.

A couple of tables away Harry sat with the soccer crowd enjoying lunch and the usual noisy banter that that group always seemed to indulge in. Harry looked round and saw Ruth and me with the other actors and may have noticed Hudson in particular, looking rather longingly at me, something which I normally just tried to ignore as I certainly wasn't interested, even though, I suppose, he was quite attractive in his way.

Harry got up and joined our table, having I think possibly

overheard Hudson, and held my hand. "Who's kissing who?" he asked, so I introduced Hudson and Randall and explained that we were all in the play. Harry grinned and said, "Wow, your life is straight off a bookshelf, isn't it?" He turned to the two and asked if they were lovers. They seemed rather shocked at the suggestion and it looked as if they'd never even thought of the possibility. Harry went on to say, in that case, they should read a book called *Camp* by L C Rosen where the heroes were Del (short for Randall) and Hudson. Del was determined to have Hudson as a boyfriend having lusted after him for a few years. They'd regularly attended the same summer camp for teenagers but he was too theatrically camp, and physically, he was not like Hudson's usual summer conquests, Hudson being the camp's pin-up, being butch and sports oriented. He grinned at Hudson, who was the better built of the two, and winked at him. Hudson promptly blushed again. "As far as the kiss is concerned," Harry said, "why doesn't Oberon just grab Bottom's head?" Here he took hold of Hudson and brought him so close they almost touched noses. "And give him one… of… your… kisses… that… take… the… breath… away." Pausing between the words, almost whispering them. "But don't tell Bill until the rehearsal." He let go of Hudson, turned to an open-mouthed Randall, and in the same whisper continued, "And see if Oberon, while still under the influence of the juice." And ran a finger lightly round Randall's lip. "Could also give Puck a fuck."

With that he gave me a very quick kiss on the nose, and Ruth on the top of her head and went back to his table. We all watched him go and I said, "Now you see what he does to me." Ruth giggled and hugged me.

The next thing I heard was a plainly angry Harry saying to another soccer player, "What did you call me? If you have anything to say, Stuart, say it to my face and don't be such a bloody coward." The dining hall fell mostly quiet.

Stuart, who was by no means a lightweight and a couple of inches taller than Harry, got up and said, "You're a fucking queer."

"So what? Being gay is not contagious or infectious. No one will catch anything so why are you so concerned? Listen, Stuart, a person's sexuality." He glanced down the table at the team. "Their skin colour, race, height, gender, family, parents are all matters where you don't have any choice, you just have to live with it. You, Stuart, on the other hand, do have a choice. You could wash thoroughly and brush your teeth because you stink."

At this Stuart repeated more angrily, "You fucking queer." And took a swing but this was easily blocked.

"You said that already. Violence isn't ever an answer, but as your mouth is so full of filth, perhaps you should fill it with something more wholesome." At this he picked up Stuart's barely touched meal and thrust it into his face. Stuart spluttered and took another swing. Harry wasn't quick enough this time and Stuart's punch hit him very hard on the face. He staggered back but unfortunately his leg got caught up in the table supports and he fell heavily, badly twisting his leg in the process. He groaned, "My leg. I think it's broken."

Jan immediately called the emergency number, a teacher ran to get the principal, and inevitably, a crowd gathered, some taking photographs for some sick reason. Harry was obviously in considerable pain and managed to look round, see Ruth, tears streaming, and me, his face contorted with pain before passing out.

Principal Skinner arrived and took charge, telling all the students to keep clear and those who had finished their meal to go, and others to return to their tables. In the meantime, Stuart had crumpled into his seat sobbing quietly. Principal Skinner looked at Harry and said to me, "It's probably a blessed relief that he's fainted and it doesn't look like a compound fracture." Jan told him he had telephoned for the paramedics who should arrive very shortly. "Thank you, Jan." He looked sadly at Stuart. "Please take Stuart to the bathroom so he can clean himself up and then bring him to my office."

The paramedics arrived and had to gingerly extricate Harry from the table supports before putting him on a stretcher. They told the principal he would be taken to Natick General Urgent Care. Mr Skinner thanked them and then turned to Ruth and said he would let her parents know what and where and said she and I should go with the paramedics so that Harry would see familiar faces when he came round. I noticed that a boy was solicitously helping Ruth and handing her tissues to wipe her eyes and blow her nose. As I got up, I felt a hand squeezing my shoulder. It was Hudson with my script and jacket. He said that he and Randall would let Bill know what had happened in case I couldn't get to rehearsal. I thanked him and ran after the paramedics.

It was a bit later that I heard, via Jan in confidence, that Stuart had an appalling home life, which mostly explained his self-neglect, with parents who had no interest in him or his welfare and were heavily into alcohol and drug abuse. Most of the soccer team had known Stuart for several years and knew about what he'd had to tolerate at home and so hadn't commented, but Harry, being new, wouldn't have had any notion. Everything had built up and the confrontation with Harry had finally brought matters to a head. This had all come out in the principal's office where Stuart had sobbed uncontrollably for quite a while. Having had no response from Stuart's parents,

Principal Skinner and the school's welfare officer had made a few calls to the to the local social services team as it was hoped to find Stuart somewhere more suitable to live. In the end, one of the soccer team's moms, who knew Stuart and his parents, offered Stuart a room in their house.

Chapter 27

In the ambulance Harry had still not come round. Ruth was very tearful, but to try and distract her, I asked who the boy with the tissues was. She managed to say that he was in her class and a member of the soccer squad. Apparently he was called Marcantonio Romanesco and had tried several times to ask her out but she wasn't interested. Most of the girls had been subjected to pestering by the boys, but fifteen-year-olds were out of the question when there were much more attractive possibilities like me (?) and the other seventeen- and eighteen-year-olds in the school and other local schools too.

A few boys had tried it on with younger girls and she was concerned that some of them may have succumbed to the attention and flattery into losing their virginity which, she was certain, would be a matter of great regret. Those boys were just trying to notch up as many conquests as possible so they could show off. While young Marcantonio, she conceded, was quite handsome, she thought he was rather too cocksure (here she even managed a giggle at the word) for his own good. She gazed up at me, gave me a hug and sighed. "It's such a shame you're gay. My brother's very lucky." Ruth looked back at Harry, who stirred and tried to open his eyes, but it was clear that Stuart's blow was going to result in a truly nasty black eye. He grimaced at the pain, but the ambulance had arrived at the hospital and he was quickly transferred into its embrace where Heather and Angus were already waiting.

Once Harry had had his leg X-rayed, it was found he'd suffered a non-displaced fracture (and of course a promisingly colourful black eye, not to mention a rather bruised ego!) so, to allow for a full recovery, he would have to rest and wear a plaster cast for about six weeks. The first two weeks would be spent in hospital where he could be kept an eye on. Needless to say the prospect of such a period of inactivity wasn't well received.

However, matters definitely looked up when he found that the nurse, who was assigned to look after him, hand out pain killers etc. and give him bed baths, was an incredibly handsome blonde young man called Alexander Macpherson, who also had to make sure there were no bed sores — i.e. check his ass! Harry, of course, flirted wildly and was very conscious that, while the bed baths were taking place, his crown jewels were conspicuously displayed to advantage under the harsh ceiling lights of the hospital room, but Nurse Macpherson's were totally hidden beneath the folds of his loose uniform with no indication of any bulge, no "X" to mark the spot as it were.

It seemed to me that the nurse was more cheerful when Steph, Sam and Rosita, in some combination, turned up to visit (mostly to ogle Nurse Macpherson it should be admitted!), but of course, this was just another spur for Harry to make greater efforts to get his hands on Nurse Macpherson or even just a glimpse. He even complained, in my presence, that Nurse had seen what he had to offer and that was being ignored but he, Harry, had not even seen, let alone anything else, of Nurse Macpherson's, he was sure, sparkling treasures.

Nurse Macpherson quietly just accepted Harry's adoring nonsense, (he must have had much more and worse attention elsewhere) and smiled through it all. "Do you really want me to lose my job, Harry? There are very strict protocols about staff-patient contact which you want me to breach."

The two weeks passed, and once he was deemed to have got over the worst, and of course, had his own doctor at home to look after him, he was allowed to leave the hospital supported by a crutch when Heather came to collect him. Nurse Macpherson came to see them off and said, "Goodbye Dr MacInnes-Brown and" — rather pointedly — "good luck!" Just before he finally left the hospital, Harry asked if he could have a goodbye kiss. "Okay, just one." And he leant forward to kiss him on the forehead but Harry seized his chance, grabbed the nurse on either side of his head and kissed him full on the lips. After a few seconds resistance, Nurse Macpherson seemed to realise the futility of trying to stop Harry, and through force majeure, let himself be kissed. When they parted, he grinned and said, "Goodbye Harry. I'll have to tell my wife all about you."

Chapter 28

While Harry was in the hospital life briefly returned to normal (or pre-Harry anyway) to some extent and it was possible to meet Steph and Ed in the Urquell for a quiet cup or two. When we were seated one day, I saw Steph looking at me very carefully and was evidently building up to say whatever was occupying her thoughts.

"Well, Steph, spill. You've obviously got something on your mind and I don't think I'll like it."

"Oh, it's not that bad. It's just that I overheard some of the senior girls chatting in the bathroom, as girls do, and you were the subject."

"Me? But girls haven't ever shown any interest."

"Hear me out, Ethan. It was nothing bitchy but it appears that you've become a matter of interest since your… erm… association with Harry has become known. The girls think you're very good-looking, charming, polite etc., and please don't take this the wrong way, probably now have enough sexual experience not to make a fool of yourself. There were a couple of comments about a few senior boys which I really cannot repeat to either of you two."

"But I'm not a sports jock who always seem to have girls hanging round."

"Ethan, not all girls want to have a dumb, muscle-bound ox in tow. You're obviously intelligent, cultured, well-spoken, and from your frequent giggling sessions with Michaela, not averse to female company, Ruth notwithstanding. Similar tales from

Sam and Rosita who have told me they've heard the same. And don't forget, Ethan, it works both ways. You may not have shown any or enough interest."

Through all of this Ed had been grinning like an idiot. I dreaded what smartass comment he was going to make, but he didn't say anything, just put his arm round my shoulder and gave me a bit of a hug. "Courage, mon brave," he eventually came out with in his awful French accent.

Steph continued, "Don't be surprised to suddenly find you have a few more friends of the feminine persuasion when we're back in school."

"You do know, of course, that Michaela and I have big parts..." Ed burst out laughing and Steph had to try and stifle a laugh. "Don't be disgusting, the pair of you. I was going to say, *in the play*, so we have to get together to rehearse our lines. But I can't deny she is very attractive and great fun to know. Anyway, she does have a boyfriend, I gather, some evangelical creep. What do they say about Harry?"

"Harry just exudes sexual self-confidence. He could give most of the straight boys a run for their money and leave them standing. A couple of the girls think that they could show him a very good time and 'convert' him but think you have too much of a hold because you're so innocent. By the way, apparently that little speech to Stuart about not being infectious or contagious made some younger students heave a sigh of relief once they'd looked up the words in a dictionary!"

"I see. Well, thank you for the advice, Steph."

We drank up and I drove them home. There was a lot to think about. However, back at school there were some big smiles and greetings from a few girls but no suggestions or even hints about meeting. Phew!

Chapter 29

HARRY

Back at home, I allowed my mother to give me a regular bed bath until a waterproof cast protector was found which allowed me to shower without assistance. Occasionally I found keeping my balance a bit of a problem, but on the whole, I was able to keep myself thoroughly washed and shaved. I was also bought some sweat pants so I could come downstairs if we had company. However, one day Mum came into my room with a fresh cup of tea. I asked her for a hug, said, "I love you, Mum." And started crying which astonished her as I was not really the crying type.

"What on earth's the matter?" And she held me close while I just sobbed into her shoulder.

Eventually, when I'd pulled myself together a bit, she held me by the shoulders and looked into my eyes and asked, "Well? This must be important."

"I'm worried about Ethan and I don't want to lose him."

"What put this notion into your head?" "

"When we first met him, Ruth and I were struck by his innocence and it was that and his… his…"

"Oblivious?"

"Yes, that's the word. He seemed oblivious to what was going on and it seemed that'd protected him from what I described as the vultures that were circling to relieve him of that innocence. Luckily, I was the first vulture to land and you know the story about the heaven-sent storm and how I knew what your reaction would be if I got him home drenched through."

"Hmm, hmm."

"He was more than willing to be seduced, but now the vultures, or rather the ones that I know about, are getting too close for comfort. There's Tom in the cafe."

"He is very cute."

"Yes, well, then there are those French lechers (he'd be dead after a night with them), and since our relationship became known at school, there's a couple of gay boys who are in the drama group and looking predatory. I think I've managed to divert them onto each other for the moment, but they'll be back. One of them, Hudson, is playing Bottom and is itching for the moment when Oberon and Bottom kiss and he can really go for it."

"I do understand, Harry, I do, but you're both seventeen and you have sown a few wild oats to date."

"Has Ruth been talking?"

"Yes, but you're not as discreet as you think, so your father and I have been very aware of your recent past. I seem to recall that lovely boy who came round to help with 'school projects', and however long he stayed and whatever the project, it always seemed to require that you both showered before he went home! I could go on. Harry, darling boy, Ethan has sown one wild oat, but for him, he's reaped an entire farm's yield with you. Haven't you seen him looking at you? He even sings songs to you and for you alone. You're so fortunate to have that. When I think about your father's singing, where he sounds like a set of bagpipes left out in the rain for a couple of years, listening to him murder *Flower of Scotland* at Murrayfield and Parc des Princes where that poor wee plant has lost every petal well before the end of the first verse, I pretended we weren't together. Your father and I have watched him at meals and the simple longing and devotion in his face is remarkable and touching. Ethan would probably die for you Harry, if you asked.

"In our younger days, your father had that expression when he looked at me, so I knew he had to become my husband. It hasn't changed that much either though he wonders how I have lumbered him with three children — don't you dare say a word, I can read you like a book and I am your mother! Harry, Ethan's feelings for you are incredible. Your father and I are concerned about how the Liddells would cope with his heartbreak if you do something really stupid to cause a parting. Nature must be allowed to do her work. Your behaviour, your flirting for example, may have already planted tiny, tiny seeds in Ethan's mind so please don't water them incessantly. Have I made myself clear?"

"Yes, Mum." And the tears started flowing again while she hugged me.

"Harry, when your father and I were young and started going out, we had a number of gay and lesbian friends. Yes, we did, so don't look at me like that. It was Edinburgh after all, and it would have been strange *not* to have had LGBTQ friends. We were all too aware of people's relationships, gay and straight, that had ups and downs, tears, heartaches, heartbreaks, and even we had some minor tremors, partly because of the different nature of our studies, but we worked at resolving them. As a doctor you meet all sorts of people and have to treat them equally regardless of what they are like as human beings. We're very happy that Hamish seems to have taken that to heart in his medical training. In a very small way that's reflected in his gay friends."

"Do you mean the 'beast and the priest'?"

"Yes, Gordon and Alasdair, though sometimes I wonder about the future of the Scottish medical profession, if those two, graduate. At least Alasdair, with that lovely Orcadian lilt, is understandable, but when Gordon gets excited or drunk, that Aberdonian accent is only fit for his fellow Aberdonians I fear. Hamish is happy to go to gay bars with them and then leaves them to it, whatever 'it' may be, and goes to see Helen who, by the way, is looking more beautiful than ever. Has Hamish sent you a recent photo of her? If not, I think I've got one if you want to see it. How are you now darling?" Mum cuddled me and kissed me on the tip of my nose. I beamed at her, hugged her, and thanked her for being such a comfort and so understanding. All too soon her words came to taunt me.

Chapter 30

ETHAN

Heather found herself having to make many cups of tea for all the visitors who wanted to see the invalid. The Urquell gang plus Patrick and Sam were probably the most regular, but none could come every day because of schoolwork, homework, soccer and football practice, and for me, rehearsals. Patrick, in particular, was very solicitous but found Harry, even in this state, didn't give up on his flirting. Patrick took this in very good part, even when he told us that Harry had said, "If I were not temporarily incapacitated, I would rip off those too tight pants and fuck you till your eyes popped out." We all laughed, none more so than Sam.

Patrick continued that he had replied, "Not till Hell freezes over."

But inevitably Harry had to have the last word and grinned before replying, "In that case I'll just keep you warm, wrapped in my arms." And blew him a kiss.

On one occasion I arrived to find Jan and a few of the soccer team all writing their names on the cast before getting back on the team bus. The last to sign was one of the youngest who found that there wasn't much room left and he had a long name. Being Harry of course, and in all-male company, he hadn't bothered to cover himself, so his lower body and legs were visible. As the boy wrote at the top of the cast where there was a little space left, his concentration meant he had his mouth open and ran his tongue round his lips, but it was noticeable that his gaze fell frequently on Harry's fully exposed cock. When he finished, he looked up to find Harry smiling at him and imitating him by running his tongue around his lips, rather provocatively I thought. The boy grinned and got up to go, but not before giving Harry a rather cheeky wave and a wink as he went out. Before he too left, Jan advised Harry to take care because, in his opinion, that boy, Marcantonio Romanesco, could be trouble. "Oh, so that's who he is. The one who's bothering my sister. I never got round to knowing his name."

Sometimes Harry felt rather tired because of the visitors, so he dozed while I did some homework. There were a couple of occasions when he wanted sex, so we blew each other which seemed to perk him up and his resulting bright eyes caused Heather to shake her head in wonder.

Ruth, of course, was his daily visitor, and I understood, regaled him with how rehearsals were going, as well as tales of Marcantonio's unwanted attentions. He also tired because he had to keep up with his schoolwork. The teachers at John Eliot made sure that a regular list of assignments arrived at Wampanoag Drive with completion dates. Fortunately, his parents helped out with tutoring in the sciences and history where they could, and my father volunteered to tutor geography, which Harry was very grateful for as he knew that Dad didn't have much spare time.

Chapter 31

Towards the end of October, I found that I had a spare evening with my homework done and no rehearsal that day. I didn't want to bother Harry, who I felt needed a break from all the attention and a proper rest, and Steph and Ed both had soccer practice. As the weather was fine, the skies clear, a walk seemed the best idea, so I donned my earphones, and with music playing, I set off without any plan or destination in mind. Perhaps inevitably my steps took me into the town centre and the Mall. As I approached the Urquell I could hear a lot of noise like a big party and found that the cafe was hosting a celebration for the centenary of the founding of the Czechoslovak Republic on 28 October 1918 and apparently still very much celebrated in Czechia and Slovakia. Red, white and blue flags were all over the place and tri-colour balloons floated above the crowd. Tomáš saw me through the window and beckoned me in. He told me that virtually all the small Czech and Slovak community in Natick had turned up except, he said rather bitterly, his mother and stepfather.

I saw Steph's parents and Jan's, waved at them and they waved back with beer glasses in their hands. Tom manouvered me into our usual booth which happily was unoccupied. "Can I get you something, Ethan?"

"For a change, could I please have a hot chocolate?"

"Of course, I'll be back in a couple of minutes." When he returned, he brought the drink and a small glass with a clear liquid. "This is on the house," he declared.

"Thank you very much but what is this please?" Indicating the glass.

"Just for you, slivovitz, the best we have, made by Rudolf Jelínek of Prague." He grinned and said, "Pay no attention to what those Poles, Slovaks or other Slavs say, Czech slivovitz is the best. It's plum brandy but you should drink that little measure in one go." Well, with that advice from a Czech, I did so and was grateful to be sitting down as that firewater hit my throat and I thought I'd never breathe again!

"What proof is that?" Once I recovered and had a big gulp of the chocolate.

Tom chuckled. "Never mind about that, but the aftertaste when the plum comes through is fantastic." I just felt happy to have survived!

Tom disappeared to deal with customers while I slowly sipped the chocolate and hoped that no one would have seen an underage drinker in the cafe. I was certainly not prepared for him to come back with another measure of slivovitz for me and one for himself, but he was most insistent that we two should toast the Republic's centenary. Thinking that suicide is a once in a lifetime occasion, we clinked glasses, and after instruction on pronunciation from Tom, said, "Naz drovie." And drained the glass. Tom said to just sit there to recover because he was about to end his shift and someone else would handle the rest of the evening. The rapidly cooling remains of the chocolate helped me regain some semblance of normality and Tom, having changed out of the red, white and blue flag design cafe apron, ushered me out into the fresh air which was very welcome. "Why don't you come back to my place for a talk? It's something we haven't really ever done."

"Okay, but is it far?"

"No, just a few minutes." Actually, it was about ten minutes, but I was in a little bit of a haze!

Tom lived in small block of apartments all of which seemed to be studios. He opened the main door and led me to one of the ground floor front doors which he unlocked and let me go in ahead. He locked the door, closed the curtains, stood in front of me, and without warning, leant forward and kissed me on the lips. He was so gentle that I responded and kissed him back. We parted and stared at each other for ten seconds before launching into a hungry, passionate embrace, tongues searching everywhere.

Tom pulled me into the room and tenderly started to undress me with many kisses as each item of clothing was discarded. Every part of my body was subject to more kisses as he managed to divest himself until we were both naked. I was surprised to see that his chest was beautifully hairy, particularly about his pectorals with a very definite trail down the middle of his chest and then spreading out from his belly button into a thicker bush of pubes. I let my fingers run through his chest hair slightly tugging at the same time which made him smile. "It's real, not a wig," he whispered in my ear. We laughed and he then decided to move matters along by more kissing as he moved down my body, concentrating on my nipples before looking up at me and taking my paltry few chest hairs in his lips, smiling, letting go and moving to my pubes which he nuzzled before licking my balls then, taking my cock in his mouth, very gently began to suck. It was all so delicately done, it was extremely arousing and it was all I could do not to cum immediately. Of course, as I got close to orgasm, I had to grab his head and more or less oblige him to move faster and faster until I had to release him and let the cum flow. I hoped our noises couldn't be heard by the neighbours as we hadn't exactly been very quiet.

As my erection softened, he turned me around and proceeded to lick and kiss my ass before running his tongue down the cleft to my anus and trying to stick his tongue firmly into it. Tom stood up letting his cock prod my ass before whispering, "No, not this way round. I want to have my mouth on yours or look into your eyes as I fuck you." He turned me round again and making me move backwards got me onto the bed. From a bedside drawer he got out a tube of lube and a pack of condoms and opened one of the sachets. I watched him put it on and then apply the lube to me and then to his sheathed shaft. He parted my legs and again very gently pushed into me. I had put my hands on that lovely hairy chest as he lowered himself but had to move them as Tom wanted to kiss me. He held my hands in his as our rhythm got together and as his climax gathered, he managed to hold that kiss with our tongues together when he did cum.

Because of the condom, I hadn't expected to feel anything of his ejaculation as I had done with Harry, but I certainly did. When Tom let go of my hands and had withdrawn his cock, I quickly bent down to remove the condom and proceeded to lick him clean, tasting his cum. This seemed to amuse him enormously and he lay back watching me with a great grin. Tom's taste was very nice but not quite the same as Harry's, but I couldn't say exactly what the difference was. "No aftertaste of plums," I muttered and we both chuckled. Then we lay in each other's arms just kissing while I played with his chest hair.

"Thank you, Ethan. You cannot know how long I have wanted to… um… er…"

"Tomáš, I did get the slightest, tiniest hint when you asked via Jan if I would consider being your boyfriend! But that, I'm afraid, was the spur for Harry to make a move, so you did do me a great favour. If it's any consolation, you're only the second person to screw me and I've loved every second of every minute, despite it being, shall we say, a one-sided conversation."

"Well, you can come back to let me have your 'point of view' at any convenient time."

"Many thanks, I'll take you up on that. However, I'm sorry, but I must go home now — tomorrow is a school day. Thank you for the slivovitz by the way. Naz drovie, Tomáš."

Chapter 32

The following Saturday Harry wanted me to spend the night with him and there was no parental objection. After supper I stretched out alongside him but on the non-plaster side. We cuddled while I told him about the session with Tomáš which he found very beguiling, particularly the bit about the chest hair. "Sorry I'm a bit deficient in that department, but if I catch you making eyes at my brother, who is hairy like Dad, I'll never fuck you again."

"Harry, I know you say that no human being is perfect, but for me, you're as close as it gets and I wouldn't change you in any way. Occasionally I try to count your chest hairs, but you're never still for long enough."

We chuckled. "One of the things I love about you most, Ethan, is that you accept me as I am, warts and all."

"What warts?"

"We're not going into that now and even a full bottle of Jelly's slivovitz won't get me to say anything. So, how did Tom treat you?"

"As if I were a precious piece of porcelain or crystal."

"I wouldn't have expected anything else, even though he's guilty of corrupting a minor by plying him with highly alcoholic drinks in a public place. I think he should be punished, but in his absence, you'll have to do instead." Harry looked at me and his piercing blue eyes gleamed with mischief (or was it evil?) and said, "Okay, cowboy, get on top of this bucking bronco and prepare for a wild ride."

"Aren't you mixing metaphors here?"

"Who cares? Come on, get aboard."

"What about your leg?"

"It's not my leg that needs the exercise!" So I straddled him while he reached for the lube and a condom. He rolled it on and then applied the lube to me and his cock before carefully penetrating me and then starting to really move up and down, (bucking while fucking you could say) while gripping my waist firmly and with my hands on his shoulders so that I wouldn't slide off. Our eyes were fixed on each other the whole while as he concentrated hard on making sure that this would be the most active sex we'd had for a while. Again, his breathing told me that he was nearing orgasm and then... When I felt his ejaculation, that wave of exhilaration which followed was fantastic.

Harry gradually subsided while I sat astride him. I raised an eyebrow and started to count his chest hairs again.

He grinned and muttered, "Bastard." But then put his hands on my ass and slowly pulled me towards his head where his mouth and tongue were waiting to envelop my stiffening cock and then proceeded to suck furiously as if to draw out every atom of spunk I could possibly produce. It didn't take very long of course before I couldn't stop myself from cumming. Harry continued to lick and kiss but nothing else was forthcoming! He eventually released me from his grip so I could slide back alongside him and he said he couldn't let Tomáš be the only one to have enjoyed the pleasure of my body that week. Initially that thought was very flattering and I cherished it, until a less worthy thought crossed my mind about dogs and lamp-posts!

Chapter 33

Rehearsals proceeded apace and Bill seemed very pleased with the cast. Everyone had learnt their lines, so the time was spent making sure that we learnt the moves, particularly the four young lovers who had to make sure that the rapid entrances and exits were immaculately timed with almost farce-like precision. The Rude Mechanicals also had to be drilled to perform the play within the play with unerring accuracy and Hudson was turning out a wonderful performance which was sure to be a hit with the audiences, especially the ones for the senior school and the public one. What the junior school would make of it all was inevitably an unknown. Everyone was informed that tickets for the public performance would be on sale after Thanksgiving but we could place our orders one week earlier. Ruth and I looked at each other and had to send messages to the gang immediately to see whether they and their parents wanted to come and so secure enough seats.

Bill's ideas for the costumes raised a few eyebrows. He wanted all the fairies in very close-fitting outfits, the boys' costumes open from shoulders to the waist, so bare chests and large codpieces! The girls', obviously had to be much less revealing and no codpieces (ha ha). The humans would wear their ordinary clothes and the Rude Mechanicals rough workmen's outfits. A theatrical costumier in Boston was able to provide most including a superb ass's head.

For the final palace scene, he originally wanted us in evening clothes, but there was a timing problem, so he settled on simple white shifts which chimed nicely with everyone going to bed. I wanted to find out what music Bill had eventually decided to use. I knew he had mused about the familiar Mendelssohn and the less well-known reworking of it for a film by Korngold, but in the end, he dispensed with it entirely, using only the short Paul Dukas "Fanfare" from *La Péri* as a sort of leitmotiv for the Athenian court scenes, which was a great way to indicate a lowering of the auditorium lights to open each performance.

Bill's request to raise the comedy had led me to ask how suggestive we were allowed to be because it seemed that gestures could totally change the meaning of some innocuous lines. The scenes between Bottom and Oberon leant themselves beautifully as Hudson and I were able to demonstrate. We had rehearsed them separately and tried to make them as camp as possible which made the four fairies laugh a lot. I caressed Bottom's ass as we exited towards the bower *"...lamenting some enforced chastity..."* and continued later with *"...while I thy amiable cheeks do* (slight pause) *coy...".* My hand was cupped around Bottom's genital area at the *"nuts"* line, and at the end of the scene, as I commanded him to *"Sleep thou and I will wind thee in my arms...",* I came up behind him and thrust my codpiece into him while undoing his shirt and running my hand around his chest and starting to yank down his pants with the other hand. Bottom reacted accordingly and his mouth was a round "O" before turning and kissing me passionately as we sank out of sight into the bower while I let my finger run down his cleft. Hudson was fantastic and I was delighted to discover that he had a hairy chest, not as much as Tom, but very nice! These antics reduced Bill and the cast to lots of laughter as the gay sexual potential was exposed. Hudson really threw himself into it and I felt he wanted the kiss to continue longer than strictly necessary. Hudson kept up the campery without any problem and while relating *"Bottom's dream"* clutched at his balls while tenderly and appreciatively feeling his bottom as he exited which we were sure would go down well too. Bill thoroughly approved of it all.

He'd thought about using the Mendelssohn setting of "Ye spotted snakes" but the song mentioned *"...our fairy queen..."* and also used *"...our lovely lady..."* and so had to persuade a music teacher to arrange a simple melody with slightly different words that the four fairies could perform. Ruth and the other three had several sessions to learn it and were really good.

At the end of the song, in this version, while Titania delivered her lines, she got two elves to carry off the "sentinel" played by Jocelyn. Shakespeare, we'd noted, gives no stage direction on this. The elves were two fifteen-year-olds who would be naked except for very short pants with codpieces. Much to Ruth's displeasure, one of these elves was Marcantonio, but he and the other elf did look the part and were delighted to have the chance to show off their trim bodies. Bill instructed Jocelyn to allow himself to be carried off while emitting squeaks of horror, and as he left the stage, to let out a big sigh of erotic pleasure. In rehearsal, Marcantonio grabbed Jocelyn's legs and pretended to chew on his codpiece as they departed. Bill was pleased with the overall result as Jocelyn turned out to be most convincing at vocalising erotic pleasure!

Chapter 34

Harry had an X-ray at the hospital which indicated that the fracture was healing well and he was told that the plaster would come off at the end of November. However, he was not to return to soccer immediately, and should just take gentle exercise for a week or so. In the end he was delighted that the plaster was to be removed the day before the Thanksgiving break.

Thanksgiving usually involved my parents, Steph's and Ed's getting together for a slightly(!) alcoholic meal with all the usual turkey and trimmings. This year it was the Svobodas turn to host and they had proposed that the MacInnes-Browns should join them which they were delighted to accept. To avoid complicating catering matters, and as our little group had rather increased in size, we decided to have our own Thanksgiving.

I asked Tom if the Urquell would let us reserve a table for us three, Jan, Rosita, Harry and Ruth, and if they were available, Patrick and Sam. Tom confirmed there was no problem and Patrick and Sam said they would be delighted to get away from their parents too. Tom asked if we wanted the traditional American dinner or would we like a Czech version which would be cibulaćka (onion soup), vepřo knedlo zelo (roast pork, sauerkraut and dumplings) and valašský frgál (sweet cake). No one was a vegetarian, so everyone agreed very happily to the suggested menu which sounded absolutely delicious. Obviously, none of us could legally drink alcohol, so Tom also came up with a possible Czech-made drink called Kofola, which looked like Coke or Pepsi, but had about a third less sugar, and to get us through the evening, a much bigger load of caffeine! Harry, being free of the plaster and just needing the crutch for support, was particularly pleased to be getting out, and I think, wanting to give Tom another once-over!

The tickets for the public performance on the Saturday evening were going like the proverbial hot cakes. Ruth and I managed to secure seats for our parents, and because of our urgent messages, Steph, Jan, Ed, Rosita, Patrick and Sam did so as well. I did contact Tom but he had to do a shift that evening as he explained that the build-up to Christmas was always extremely busy and it would be difficult to change with any of the other staff. He did ask though, whether in the period between the performances and the Christmas break, I might come to give him a private performance! Hmmmm.

Rehearsals increased in number as the performance dates got closer and fitting in our homework didn't allow any time for socialising if our year group was going to progress. So the short Thanksgiving break was very welcome and our meal at the Urquell, and from reports, the meal at the Svobodas, went very well. Everyone enjoyed the Czech dishes and the different flavours including the caraway in the sauerkraut.

Tom told us that the Urquell cafe's management had wanted to give each of us (except Ruth of course) as good customers, bottles of the eponymous lager but were dissuaded. I suppose we could've taken them home for later consumption, but we didn't think of it! Because of the number, we were seated in the main part of the cafe rather than in one of the booths, so I noticed that some other diners were having glasses of slivovitz as digestifs and smiled knowingly at Tom when he caught my eye, but understandably, he just blanked me. Harry, of course, noticed this, but thank goodness, didn't make any remark, only raised an eyebrow at me with a slight smile.

Chapter 35

Michaela had proved to be magnificent as Hippolyta/Titania. She had learnt her lines very quickly and put the rest of us to shame as she was script-free for many rehearsals, but we did catch up eventually much to Bill's relief. She had a natural air of command and delivered her lines with authority. I felt that our scenes at either end of the play, the Athenian palace bits, worked particularly well, though we did have a very quick change right at the end where we only had a few lines from Puck to get out of our white shifts and reappear as Titania and Oberon for the last time, make our last speeches and slowly exit leaving Puck to end the play. Bill, Michaela and I had different thoughts about whether we should gesture our reconciliation with a kiss as we left the stage. In the end Bill decided to leave it to us, so Michaela and I agreed to a tender kiss, centre stage, to make the point.

I was in bed, clutching Harry's Urquhart t-shirt, when I realised I couldn't move, my hands and feet were held by totally naked elves, and I saw that one of them was Marcantonio Romanesco and then all of them were Marcantonio. They disappeared to be replaced by Harry and Tomáš holding me on either side. Then Michaela in her Titania dress advanced, waving her wand which she pointed at me and was about to strike me when it became a giant phallus and then… and then… I woke up. It was so very vivid, it took quite a while before I fell asleep again, but if I dreamt anything else, no detail stayed.

After consulting the cast and everyone involved, Bill

persuaded us all to agree to add a matinee performance on the Saturday afternoon for disabled (or, as he put it, differently-abled) children not in school, and those folk stuck in care homes or otherwise alone, and their carers. He thought it would bring a little joy as Christmas approached. It was thought to be a tremendous idea and everyone agreed although it would be fairly tiring.

Harry found it rather frustrating that he had to continue to rest his leg despite being out of the plaster. The hospital doctors had said that, if he felt strong enough, he could play in the final soccer match of the term, but if he experienced any pain whatsoever, he'd to indicate to the referee and team coach that he had to leave the pitch immediately. I did commiserate with him and stood while he had his hands on my shoulders swinging his damaged leg to get the muscles back in working order. The physiotherapist had given him a number of exercises to do and he did them every day very diligently.

The result of all this was that he tried to not use the crutch when back at school. I felt the best moment of his return to school was when Stuart, rather sheepishly, approached him, held out his hand and said sincerely, "I'm so sorry, Harry, for what I said, it was totally out of order. I do realise you were quite right and have taken it all on board."

Harry took his hand and pulled him in for a big hug, and with one of his radiant smiles, replied, "Stuart, I must apologise for what I said to you. I hadn't known about your circumstances, so it was unforgivable."

Stuart smiled too. "I look forward to seeing you back on the pitch, Harry. You're needed on the team."

The hug was resumed before they released each other to go to their next classes when the bell rang. Harry did say very quietly to me, "His new home has definitely made a difference to his hygiene and he looks so much better, mentally and physically, if that's possible. Perhaps we might become friends — not intimate ones you understand."

Chapter 36

The next couple of weeks flashed by in a whirl of schoolwork and rehearsals leading up to the performances. The first one on Friday afternoon for the junior school went very well, though it wasn't clear whether they understood all of the subtleties, but some of the broader bits of comedy such as the confusion of the four lovers was greeted with lots of cheers.

The performance for the senior school was very different. I think that the eternal (or infernal) grapevine had warned most of our fellow students (and probably the staff) of what was to come, so there was an air of expectation, not to say tension, much like that first reading. Every possible misinterpretation that could be discerned was seized upon with whoops, catcalls and shouts. Michaela's commanding presence as Titania was received with temporary silence, but the lovers, the Rude Mechanicals, the fairies, Puck and Oberon were greeted with a lot of noise. As the plot developed, and when everyone could see that Bottom and Oberon were going to settle in the flowery bower at the back of the set with a lascivious kiss as the four fairies looked on, the noise was incredible. Partly, I think, this was because most of them knew that Hudson and I were gay. Bill had decided that that scene should be where there was a natural interval. The curtains closed to thunderous applause, whoops, whistles and catcalls, and no doubt, some very indelicate comments on what happened next!

The second half was equally riotous. Puck's opening line

"My master with a monster is in love…" got a tremendous cheer and various noises from the audience. Apparently, Harry got many slaps on the back from the soccer team which he graciously acknowledged with a grin. Matters quietened down only a little while the lovers were sorted out, but then came the awakening of Oberon to the truth of how he'd spent the night and with whom or what! Fortunately, it's a brief scene but the audience reaction made it difficult to be heard.

For the next scene there had to be a brief pause for Michaela and I to put on the white shifts and a belt to go back to being Theseus and Hippolyta, so Bill had arranged for a repeat of the "Fanfare" which silenced the audience briefly. After the following court scene and we exited, Bottom had his big solo number. Hudson really milked it with a painful expression as he detailed his recollection of the night's events, clutching his genitals and tenderly rubbing his ass. He got a phenomenal reaction and eventually left the stage to tremendous shouts, whistles and applause. That really spurred on the other Rude Mechanicals to exaggerate the whole play within a play, so *Pyramus and Thisbe* got a rousing reception too. The play rather winds down after that, so the audience did too, but only to some extent! The final speeches had no interruptions, Michaela and I managed our final costume change and left the stage, as arranged, with a forgiving kiss to a few whoops from the audience. Then Puck's closing plea to applaud needed absolutely no such encouragement. The noise said it all and it continued right through the curtain calls, particularly Bottom's.

Bill was thrilled with the outcome, as he had been after the earlier performance, and was backstage to congratulate everyone, and I mean everyone, whether or not they had a line or worked very hard backstage. He hoped that the performances the next day would get a similar response. I thought that the next day's matinee, given the expected audience, would not react in the same way and the evening one for parents etc…?

There were so many messages about the play and the performances awaiting me at home, and because of reports at their homes, to my parents too, it was quite overwhelming. Needless to say, I read Harry's first. He told me that Ruth had got home in a state of great excitement. I knew that as I had driven them home and could barely get her, as shotgun, to sit still long enough to put on her seat belt. He'd kept fairly quiet, and other than a lengthy kiss for me and a big hug and kiss for Ruth and murmured congratulations when we emerged from the dressing rooms, let us gently subside in peace and calm as we all sat in the car, his hands gently massaging my tense shoulders and kissing my neck, until I felt able to start driving.

When home, Harry had let Ruth explode with details about the performance and the reception to Angus and Heather and just happily corroborated what she said, not wanting to steal any of her thunder. He told me she had been too energised to eat anything and wondered how she was ever going to get any sleep. He was full of praise for the entire cast, having never enjoyed a Shakespeare play quite as much and ended that he thought I had been especially fantastic, and for him, had been a total turn-on. He'd wanted so much to replace Bottom and have me fuck him in that flowery bower.

My parents had received many messages from friends whose offspring had been at one or other performance, but obviously, those who had senior students got very vivid accounts. They could see how exhausted I was by the time I got home, so just hugged me and offered congratulations for what had been a great success according to the messages, some of which they showed me. Mom eventually persuaded me to have some soup before suggesting that, despite the early hour, I should have a hot shower to relax and go to bed. I read a few messages when I got into bed particularly those from Steph, Ed, Jan and Patrick all of which were incredibly complimentary, and basically, echoed Harry's comment about it having been the best Shakespeare performance they had ever seen. Of course, rather uncharitably, it did cross my mind that they may not have actually seen any other Shakespeare play.

Chapter 37

Fortunately, I did fall asleep quite quickly, and when I awoke, couldn't recall any dream whatsoever. Being a Saturday, of course, Mom and Dad let me luxuriate in bed until I felt compelled to get up, shower and get dressed before having just a very light brunch and set off for the matinee. Mom and Dad hugged and kissed me and were sufficiently au fait to wish me "Hals und Beinbruch" (a broken neck and leg) before the performances! They were really looking forward to the evening.

I'd arranged to collect Ruth on the way but had to pause while Angus, Heather and Harry subjected Ruth and me to a similar routine instead of just saying good luck. Harry asked if he could come to school with me as a soccer practice had been arranged, so I said, "Do you have to ask?" He grabbed his kit bag and jumped in behind me, so I got more kissing and massaging all the way.

When I pulled into the school car park, we were all amazed to see a number of buses, cars and ambulances already delivering members of the audience. As we approached the main entrance there was a brightly coloured bus disgorging its occupants. An elderly man wearing a rainbow striped tie looked at us, smiled broadly and asked whether we were in the play.

I smiled back and replied, "Yes, sir, this is Pease-blossom, one of the fairies, and I'm going to be Oberon, king of the fairies and my boyfriend is playing soccer this afternoon."

He laughed out loud before shouting into the bus, "Hey,

girls, get those sad asses out of there, the king of the fairies is here." Which got a lot of whoops and whistles. "Son, how old are you?"

"I'm seventeen".

"Ohhh! If only I were sixty years younger, but I'm sure we at the Natick Stonewall Home will be rooting for you." He turned to Harry. "I'm sure most of us (there are girls here too) would like to see you... playing soccer as well. A fairy soccer player, wonders will never cease." And gave Harry an appraising look up and down as if he could visualise him naked. "Say, are you from round here?"

"No sir, I'm from Scotland."

"Edinburgh?"

"Yes, do you know it?"

"A really beautiful city with that castle, the gardens, the churches and that dog... er... er..."

"Greyfriars Bobby?" offered Harry.

"Yeah, that's the name and that black spiky tomb thing?"

"The Scott Monument in Princes Street?"

"Yeah. Ahhh." He sighed heavily. "The last time I was there, it was the mid-1970s, I guess. I was married then — poor soul, she's long dead now and should have done a lot better than me, no kids thank goodness — but one day she wanted to go shopping, God knows what for, so I went exploring and finished up in a long narrow street with loads of bars."

"Do you recall the name? Was it Rose Street?"

"That sure sounds familiar, but it's a long time ago. I went in one and got talking to a man with similar hair colour to you but..." He looked closely at Harry. "...Much hairier than you."

Ruth grabbed my hand and Harry gripped her shoulder.

"He took me back to his room at the university. I can't tell

146

you what he was studying, but he sure as hell 'studied' me. I had such a sore ass by the time I met up with my wife later."

"Do you remember his name at all?"

"No one gave last names in those days, son, but he did mutter something about the bloody English being better off. I gathered that being gay was just about okay in England but not in Scotland. I think he said his name was Sandy but it was over fifty years ago."

The other men and women were getting off the bus, all shapes, sizes and colours, but a few were still fairly trim, and checking us out.

Slightly reluctantly I said, "Sorry, but we must go to get ready otherwise there won't be any play for you to see. We hope you'll enjoy it." We waved goodbye to lots more smiles, whoops and cheers from quite a number of them while Ruth and I made our way into school and Harry to the pitch.

Before we parted, we were chuckling at our encounter before Harry said, "Ruth, we must grill Mum and Dad about our granddads when we're home. Ethan, the audience reception may match yesterday's if you're lucky."

"I wonder if Bill has any connection with that home? We may have to investigate." Harry and I kissed rather forgetting we were still in public view and got a rousing cheer from the now assembled gay crowd who had watched us.

The performance was a great success, if the audience noise could be used as a measure. I think some of the jokes were missed, but even the children understood the young lovers' mix up and the painful gormlessness of the Rude Mechanicals. Titania's majestic poise silenced them temporarily — she was evidently a woman not to be trifled with! The Stonewall Home crowd made their presence very obvious and got particularly vocal when Oberon kissed Bottom as they sank into the bower. I tried to make the kiss even more lascivious, if that were possible, which took Hudson slightly by surprise, but he'd got the message and responded fervently to great cheers. The similar whoops, whistles and cat calls and general reception to his Bottom's Dream speech again meant there had to be slight pause before the play could continue.

After the curtain calls finally ended and the cast could relax, Bill came round to congratulate and thank everyone for their performance. He stopped by Hudson and me to ask whether something had bought about that slightly more emphatic kiss. I felt I had to own up and told him about meeting the Stonewall Home crowd beforehand and wanted to give them something special. Bill initially just laughed but then looked a bit thoughtful, and Hudson, for whom, obviously, this was news, grinned, gave me a hug and wanted a few more details about the Home. I wasn't able to say much, only repeat what Ruth, Harry and I had been told by the rainbow tie man.

Chapter 38

To avoid having any cast member getting out of costume and make-up before the evening show, Bill had organised sandwiches and drinks for which we were very thankful. While we chomped and drank there was almost complete silence until Harry suddenly appeared and came to where Ruth, Hudson, Randall and I were sitting. He didn't say anything, nodded hello to H & R and just put his arms round Ruth and me and held us close. When Bill reappeared, he asked him if he could stay backstage, well out of the way of course, for the next show.

Bill said that would be okay and asked, "How's the leg?"

"I was trying to get in some soccer practice, but it really wasn't comfortable and ached a bit, so I gave up, had a shower and came to see how things were going. From all the noise you had a really appreciative crowd. When they streamed out at the end, the excited chatter in the car park was amazing and showed just how much they'd enjoyed it all from the fanfare start to Puck's invitation to applaud." He grinned at Randall who grinned back. "And you really seemed to have pulled out all the stops, Hudson, from what I could hear." Hudson blushed at this praise from Harry, or I think we would've seen it had he not been wearing make-up! We lapsed into contented silence with Ruth's and my head on his shoulders.

Eventually we had to stir ourselves to get ready for the final show. As the set was very simple, the backstage crew didn't have much to do, just move the fake hedges and trees back into place for the opening while the actors repaired any make-up and adjusted their codpieces where applicable! I think Harry was going to say something as I moved mine slightly to be more comfortable, but thought better of it as he retreated to a far corner of the stage way out of sight of the audience who we could hear gathering. Bill had told us that it was a sell-out which just made me more nervous if anything. I didn't want to let anyone down and the butterflies seemed worse than ever.

The Dukas "Fanfare" blared out, the audience noise died, the drapes parted, Titania and Oberon with the Athenian court stepped out onto the stage. All I can remember about the rest of the performance was a bit of a blur. The audience reaction was exactly as we could all have wanted, they laughed in all the right places and in a few unexpected ones too, perhaps having got a Shakespearian joke or pun that we hadn't spotted. No one needed a prompt and we swept to the interval and that climactic kiss where Bottom and Oberon really gave it everything we could muster and the drapes closed to tumultuous applause and cheers. The second part went equally well and there were lots of laughs at Oberon's horrified reaction as his night with an "ass" was revealed.

Bottom felt really encouraged and gave the finest performance of his Dream which caused another slight pause until the reaction calmed down and allowed the play to continue. The audience didn't really stay quiet after that and raucous laughter met the drama of Pyramus and Thisbe which the Rude Mechanicals and Bottom played to the hilt. The final scenes, despite the very quick change for Titania and Oberon in the middle, went very smoothly, helped by a repeat of part of the "Fanfare" as the court departed for bed and then the fairies too, all rancour forgiven. Puck's exhortation to applaud as the drapes closed around him was greeted with an explosion of rapturous cheers, shouts and wild applause. The curtain calls were also incredible. When Titania and Oberon kissed each other, there was a big cheer, and when Oberon and Bottom had a kiss…!

Michaela and I hugged each other for a while until Bill came to congratulate us and gave us both a bear hug. "You both were magnificent," he told us with a big grin, "as you were too." And hugged Hudson and Randall. He went round all the rest of the cast and backstage crew when he was stopped by Michaela who presented him with a wonderful bouquet to which we had all contributed as our thanks to him. I think he almost wept as he started to shake a bit. We took that as our cue to get a move on to remove our make-up, get changed and go home.

Harry waited until Ruth and I had removed our make-up, or the bulk of it at least, before giving each of us a kiss and telling us how magnificent he thought we both had been. He considered that our performances were even better than the second one for the school and grinned at us in the mirrors before saying to Ruth that he would see her outside with their parents who would take them home. "Ethan, I'll tell your parents you'll be out shortly. I'm sure they're waiting for you too." He whispered very quietly in my ear that watching me kissing Hudson had been quite a turn on again, before sticking his tongue in my ear (I never worked out why he liked doing that) and going out to the auditorium foyer where many of the cast's family members and friends were apparently waiting.

The backstage crew did a fantastic job of clearing the stage while we were in the dressing rooms, leaving us to put our costumes in the right boxes to go back to the costumier. I must have been very slow because most of the cast seemed to disappear before I was ready to go home. Ruth patiently waited for me so we could go together. As a result, when we got to the foyer there were only our parents, Harry and a couple of others waiting for the slowcoaches. Mom and Dad hugged and kissed me and I thought Mom was going to cry, while Heather and Angus did the same for Ruth. Angus grabbed my hand for a very manly shake and Heather hugged me. Ruth got the reverse treatment from my parents. Nothing much was said — I'm not sure that anything was needed.

When we got home, Dad did tell me how much he and Mom had enjoyed it all, how proud of me they were and thought my performance was phenomenal which was incredibly good to hear. They both thought we should celebrate, so Dad got out a bottle of sparkling wine (which I later saw was actual champagne!) which had been chilling in the refrigerator. We each had a couple of glasses before I felt myself falling asleep. I managed to get upstairs, undressed, into bed and was asleep the moment my head hit the pillow.

Chapter 39

HARRY

Ruth and I decided to wait until lunch before asking about our grandfathers to allow Dad to have got through the *Observer* newspaper online uninterrupted. When the meal was under way, Ruth kicked me to get started, so I asked if and when our granddads had been students. Dad said that his father, Dugald Stuart, had been at Glasgow University in the 1960s and on graduation had married Barbara, a beautiful redhead, like father like son and laughed, kissing Mum. He told us that they'd lived in Hillington, Glasgow, and he'd been born in 1973, just like your mother. His father had worked for the city authority for twenty-five years before retiring from a senior position. Despite being totally overqualified, he'd applied for a job with the Orkney Islands Council and had somehow convinced them that he was the right candidate. His parents had for some time wanted to live in Stromness in Orkney where they had some distant relatives, hence his partiality to Highland Park single malt whisky! Every time he had a dram, he felt he was toasting their memory. Unfortunately, no one had realised that his parents were actually ill when they moved north, and so eventual actual retirement only lasted a couple of years before they died almost simultaneously. They were buried in Warbeth Cemetery just outside Stromness overlooking the sea towards Hoy.

"Talking about them urges me to have a dram now. Would

you like one too, dear, and you, Harry?"

Mum said, "Yes please." And I smiled and nodded my thanks. Dad got three tumblers and ice cubes before giving each of us a rather large dram of Orkney's best-known distillation!

"This is far too good to waste on porridge, a blend is aye fine for everyday drinking but not today," Dad averred.

After a few sips, mum told us that her father, named Hamish Andrew Scott, had started his medical studies in Edinburgh in the mid-60s, got married to Mary on qualifying. She said, "They were both redheads, if you were wondering. With parental help they bought the end of terrace house in Hillside Crescent where we now live. My mother was a music graduate and played a couple of instruments, but focused mainly on the piano. As your father's said, I was born in 1973. I was too young to know what happened then, but mother got pregnant again in 1975. Apparently, it was a difficult pregnancy this time, but it went to term and my brother, Hamish Dugald, was born only to die a few days later. As you might have expected, my parents, especially my mother, were devastated and it left an indelible scar. I'm not sure whether she ever really recovered. In retrospect, she went into a very long, drawn out decline, alleviated by patches of brighter moods, but eventually resulting in a terrible depression. It was one of the reasons that I became a doctor and wanted to specialise in gynaecology. I think in the end, after she saw me qualified and your father and I happily married, she just gave up. We arranged for her cremation, as she'd determined in her will, at Mortonhall. A year later, your brother was born, and perhaps you'll understand, that's why he's named Hamish Dugald, after his grandfathers and his late uncle. It was only after you, Harry, were born and obviously going to survive, that my father seemed to feel that he too could let go. He was also cremated as desired at Mortonhall. There's a small plaque in their memory."

By this time Ruth had tears streaming down her face so I took a couple of tissues to wipe her eyes and cuddled her until she quietened. We sipped our whiskies in silence until Dad brought us back to the present and asked, "Why this sudden interest in your grandparents and where they were students?"

Ruth and I looked at each other before I launched hesitantly into the tale of meeting the elderly gay man who, from his account, could have been a one-night stand with a grandfather. Mum and Dad drained their whiskies before bursting out laughing. Apparently, the possibility of Mum's father having a gay escapade while Grandma was having dreadful difficulties with pregnancy was simply unthinkable.

Mum said, "My father didn't ever have any really close male friends that I can remember, just medical colleagues, but this man saying the hairy red-haired student was called Sandy doesn't ring true. If this were a one-night stand and they were never going to meet again, why bother to give a false name, and my father wasn't hairy either. Are you sure this man wasn't just trying to get his hands into your pants?"

"I don't know, Mum, I suppose anything's possible."

At that moment my phone sounded and it was Ethan. "Hi, how are you? Are you still lazing in bed...? Hangover? How come...? Jonathan and Monica opened a bottle of champagne," I told my family. "And now what...? You're doing what...? Ethan, I'm surrounded by family. Give me a minute while I go to my room. I'll see you shortly," I said to Mum, Dad and Ruth and ran upstairs.

I locked the door, dropped my jeans and boxers and stretched out on the bed. "Okay, carry on, Ethan. You've got the Urquhart's t-shirt over your face pretending it's me because of the scent and you've got a photo of me naked…"

Ethan described how he was feeling himself and gradually moving his hands over his body, thinking of me playing with his nipples, balls, cock, and with lubed fingers, probing his anus before slowly starting to masturbate while thinking of me penetrating him. I was doing exactly the same while he talked and we found ourselves moaning, groaning and writhing, while the very heavy breathing of our assumed other selves gradually brought both of us to a wonderful orgasm. I gave my phone as passionate a kiss as I could, hearing that he was doing the same. It was almost as if I could see him, but it was only then that we switched on the cameras to gaze at each other and bring lips to the screen again. Without the visuals it had been much more exciting to imagine the other.

All of a sudden there was noise and Ethan said, "Sorry, Harry, but I must go to see my clamorous, adoring fans thronging the stage door. Actually, it's Steph and Ed who've invited themselves over and I'd forgotten they were due, but I just had to make contact with you. Are you okay?"

"I'm so so happy you did. See you tomorrow, lover, back to so-called normality at school. Hugs and kisses." Big sighs on both sides. I mopped myself with some tissues and got dressed before going back downstairs. Mum had made tea which was very welcome.

Dad looked at me quizzically and asked, "So Ethan wasn't quite as hungover as all that then?"

"No, Dad. He's fantastic. Steph and Ed arrived though, which disturbed the mood a bit."

Mum asked, "Would you like me to drive you over there?"

I laughed and hugged her. "No thanks, Mum. I think we've… er… said everything we needed to say."

Chapter 40

ETHAN

The phone sex was tremendous. Every contour of Harry's body was so clear in my mind that even the pretence of running my hands over my much less well-defined body instead felt close to the real thing, helped by the still faintly lingering smell of him on the Urquhart's t-shirt. I told myself to ask him what aftershave he used so I could sprinkle some on the t-shirt as an eternal reminder. There was a knock on the door and Mom, who knew better than to come in to a teenager's room, let me know what I already knew, that Steph and Ed were downstairs and tea and cake awaited. I hastily wiped myself with a few tissues, got dressed and feeling much less hungover now, (part of the Harry effect?) went to meet Steph and Ed.

Lots of hugs and kisses and messages of congratulation from their parents who, they said, had enjoyed the show, almost as much as the senior school had done, according to them. They were full of stories about the reactions of our fellow students and families. Apparently, Patrick had laughed through much of it much to the astonishment of his football colleagues who'd barely ever seen him smile and Jan and Rosita had had similar reactions from their parents.

Mom had, of course, cleared away the evidence of last night's indulgence but that didn't stop me from telling them about it, and the result, too much laughter. I told them about the crowd from the Stonewall Home and the rainbow tie man who'd tried to imply that he'd had a fling with one of Harry and Ruth's grandfathers forty-three years ago. This was news to my parents too, of course, so over tea and Mom's wonderful home-made walnut cake, we spent a few minutes wondering if this could possibly have been true.

"I'm sure Harry and Ruth will have asked Heather and Angus about it so we'll probably be told at some point," I said, "but I must chat to Bill tomorrow after English to see what his connection to the Home is." After they went, I sent a brief text to Harry consisting just of XXXXXs.

Monday morning. I'd slept well, and with any lingering traces of hangover finally gone, not to mention qualms about the play, I had a quick breakfast, picked up Steph and Ed and set off for school. Fortunately, my usual space in the car park was free but our arrival was the cause of many students waving and shouting at me. Patrick and Sam each gave me a hug as did Rosita and Jan before we met Harry and Ruth. Harry whispered, "Thanks for the message. I hope we can do it for real *very* soon."

Getting to the classroom via my locker was rather more of an obstacle race as many students wanted to say something about the play, mostly complimentary, lots were just high fives and broad smiles. As a result, I only just made it to Bill's class as the bell rang. A brief round of applause greeted me so I just acknowledged it with a slight bow and sat down. Bill beamed at me and started the lesson. I can't now remember a word of what was said, but when it was over, Harry and I went up to him and asked if he knew the Stonewall Home. Bill replied that he did because, as part of the home's programme of activities, he led a weekly discussion group there. It was totally voluntary and residents could attend or not as they felt. I asked if he'd led a discussion about the play and those taking part to encourage interest in coming to see it. There'd been no problem with that as residents were always wanting to get out of the home to see anything on offer, but when he'd explained about the role transfer and the resulting difference, there'd been quite a clamour for tickets. Harry chimed in with, did he know whether the Home had a calendar or pictures of Edinburgh? Bill had to think about it and said, yes, in the communal dining room there was such a calendar with a different view of the city's principal sights for each month. Harry then asked about the striped tie man.

Bill paused for a moment, looked at me and Harry, and then said, "Yes, I do know him very well. He's my father."

We were all silent until Harry sort of blurted out, "Is it possible that in 1975 he was in Edinburgh?"

"I doubt it. The only time he's been anywhere outside the States is when he was in the army in the '60s and briefly served in South Korea. He was lucky not to have been in Vietnam. Why do you ask?"

"When we met the Home's bus outside the school, he more or less claimed to have had casual sex with someone who had hair like mine, so it could have been with one of my grandfathers."

Bill groaned and put his head in his hands. "I'm so sorry, Harry. He's a bit of a fantasist and you gave him a golden opportunity to exercise his fertile, or perhaps I should say, furtive imagination. He's presented me with problems over the years but never anything involving my students. My partner and I have learned to cope."

Harry asked, "He said his wife was long dead but they had had no kids." This was met with silence for a minute. "Gee, thanks, Dad." And I thought he was going to cry.

I decided to change the subject, took a chance and asked, "Is your partner tall, dark haired with a neatly trimmed beard and sits alone in the middle of the front row at your productions?"

Bill stared at me for a few moments and then said with a gentle, and I thought, loving smile, "Yes, that's Geoffrey. We've been together for twenty years now, legally husband and husband since 2004. He somehow puts up with all my extracurricular activities such as the Home, the plays, and if either of you had ever bothered to attend, you'd know I'm the staff member who guides the school's Gay-Straight Alliance. I'd like to see you both there some time. Harry, your speech to poor Stuart about choices was a major discussion point, so your attendance would be a real boost and may even encourage a few more closets to be opened and rescue those snow-bound souls trapped back in Narnia."

We all laughed at that. Bill continued, "But I'm afraid you forgot the 'T' in LGBTQ, Harry. Some people want and can achieve changes to their condition at birth. They're transitioning to adopt permanently the outward or physical characteristics of the gender they would normally identify with, as opposed to those associated with their birth sex. Sorry about the lecture, (it's one that is well rehearsed as you've just heard!) but whether the pair of you actually come to a GSA meeting is up to you of course. The bell for the next lesson is about to ring, so you'd better run along." He gave us both a hug before getting his papers in order for his next lesson for which students were starting to arrive.

Harry said, "That was a good guess. Have you noticed him before?"

"Yes, but only at school plays. He's always alone and in the same seat, so he's rather a fixture, but I never associated him with Bill. Despite knowing Bill for a few years now, I never thought of him as gay, but you seem to have really awoken my gaydar. It was only after we got together that Hudson and Randall's gayness became very obvious to me. By the way, they took your advice about reading the L C Rosen books and have become an item. Hudson told me during a rehearsal."

Harry laughed. "Well, it appears I've done some good then, but you're my greatest achievement. I do love you."

Chapter 41

That evening Dad said, "We need to talk about something, but this must be in total confidence. Do you understand what I mean?"

"Yes, of course."

"Well, it's about Tomáš Beneš, your friend who works at the Urquell, and as you know, is one of the senior students at Wilberforce and in my class. He had a dreadful upbringing. His father died when he was quite young, and tragically, his mother took up with an abysmal man who was and is an habitual drunk and drug taker. When he discovered that Tomáš was gay he became very violent and beat the boy so severely he had to be hospitalised. Tomáš' mother was and is just in thrall to this brute. The school, the welfare officer and Natick Social Services decided that he had to be found somewhere else to live, and by great good fortune, an apartment was found for him. The only problem, of course, is that there's rent and other bills to pay which is why he works so hard at the cafe. He's very bright and the Wilberforce staff think he's more than capable of getting a good degree. We're searching for a university anywhere which offers a full scholarship which would cover all fees, accommodation and provide an allowance to keep him afloat financially, but that's proving difficult at the moment."

"Dad, why are you telling me all this?"

"Your mother and I want to invite him to come here for Christmas and thought it would be better coming from you." He paused to look into my eyes and asked, "Have you…?" I blushed but kept a steady gaze.

"Yes, Dad and I have been to his apartment."

He smiled and ruffled my hair. "Well, I think that will definitely help. Why don't you add that he can stay the night too?"

"With me?"

"Of course, but there is one condition — he must *not* bring any presents, which you must insist on."

"Thanks, Dad. I'll go and ask him now."

I drove down to the Mall. Tomáš was on duty, but thankfully, the cafe wasn't busy, so I was able to sit in our usual booth, and when I was sure no one could hear, I said, "Tom, would you like to spend Christmas Day with us?" His face lit up with pleasure. "I'll come to your place to pick you up at about 11.30 and… you can stay the night with me."

I thought he was about to burst into tears but he just put his hand behind my head and pulled me in for a gentle kiss which rapidly developed into a very passionate one. A noise at the counter made him stop while he looked after a customer. He returned to say he would be delighted and very grateful. I told him about the condition to which he just nodded and then beamed at me before giving me another lingering kiss. We gazed at each other for a few minutes before he said very quietly, "Thank you, Ethan, you don't know what a family Christmas means to me."

The last couple of weeks of term passed all too quickly. The usual crew discussed holiday plans. Ed was going to be away with his parents visiting a pair of grandparents somewhere in deepest Connecticut, Steph and Jan would be together with both sets of parents at the Svoboda house on Christmas Day, moving to the Novák house the day after, Patrick and Sam would be with their respective grandparents, both feeling a bit miserable at being apart. Rosita would be spending a few days with cousins but at least they lived in NYC! Harry and Ruth were the most pissed off because they were going to be at home, which would've been okay, except that Angus had decided to invite a few university colleagues who would otherwise be alone.

Chapter 42

The last inter-school soccer match of the term was a home game scheduled for the final full weekend before the Christmas break. Harry had been selected though Jan had told him that the referee and coach had been informed about his leg, and if he felt any discomfort, however slight, he was to indicate that he needed to leave the pitch immediately. Ruth and I were determined to cheer Harry and the team and would have got more people to come too, but of course, inevitably, it was a damn awful, bitterly cold day with rain or sleet promised, so John Eliot High was rather poorly represented as far as supporters were concerned. Ruth and I wrapped ourselves in as many layers as possible, and armed with flasks of coffee, we tried to find the most sheltered spot on the bleachers and waited for the kick-off. The teams ran on, Harry's hair being the sight we watched for. He saw us and waved and we waved back while he jumped up and down trying to keep warm. The match started and through the gathering gloom, despite the floodlights, we got glimpses of the action as the game moved up and down the field. As usual I wondered why the main play always seemed to be at the opposite end or side of the pitch to where I was sitting. After about twenty-five or so minutes we heard the whistle halting play and could see a rather disconsolate Harry limping slightly as he came towards Coach who sent on a substitute and sent Harry to have a hot shower and get dressed. He waved up at us rather despondently before disappearing.

Chapter 43

HARRY

I was really pissed off that I couldn't stay on the pitch any longer, but the pain was becoming too much to cope with and I felt that the team really needed a more able player if they were going to win this match. I made my way to the changing room, dropped my kit, grabbed my towel and headed to the shower. The warmth of the water did help to soothe the pain and discomfort, so after soaping myself and rinsing it off, I just stood there luxuriating in the warm flow, eyes closed. I suddenly felt what must have been a stiff cock prodding my arse. I switched off the shower to find Marcantonio, naked and erect standing behind me. "What are you doing here? You should be pitch side as a substitute."

"Coach said I was no longer needed so here I am and I wanted to talk to you."

"About what?"

"Us. I know you don't want me to pursue your sister, though she's very attractive, but if I can't have her, what about you and me? I am sixteen."

"I'd like to see evidence of it."

"The evidence is looking at you! Perhaps you might like a change from Ethan? A friend told me that he's been seen with that Czech guy from the Mall cafe. Is it a question of Czech-mate?"

I managed to control my temper as I was sure that if I hit him, however provoked, it would not look good, especially as there were no witnesses and goodness knows what he would claim. As calmly as I could muster, I replied, "I'm surprised to know that a little shit like you has a friend in the first place, but more importantly, in the second place, I know all about Ethan's Czech friend thank you and I can assure you that there is absolutely no question of you and me having any sex."

He smiled coldly. "Well, it's your loss. We could have had lots of fun. I've fucked Jocelyn and he was very grateful to have lost his virginity."

"What did the poor boy do to deserve that?" I sneered.

"He was available and keen to do it after I chewed on his codpiece in the play."

I let out a deep sigh, but before anything else could be said, the team clattered in as it must be half-time.

Coach took one look at Marcantonio and me, damp and naked as I was, and obviously, in my case at least, in a foul temper, fists clenched, and said, "Romanesco, why are you still here? As you're now warm and just about dry, you can put your kit back on and play the second half. I'll let the ref know. Don't argue with me boy, do what I say. Now."

Marcantonio scowled but didn't dare say anything in protest or do anything other than as instructed. Coach came to me and asked if my leg was okay.

I replied, staring at Marcantonio, "That pain was just about tolerable until an even worse one came to plague me."

Coach clasped me on the shoulder, in sympathy I suppose. He turned to the rest of the team who obviously had no idea of what was going on and said, "Josh, you've done quite enough today, scoring two wonderful goals, so I'm taking you off. Okay team, half-time's almost over, let's go." With much grumbling about the conditions, the changing room cleared.

I dried myself and started to get dressed. But I was still trying to calm myself and sat still, holding my head in my hands. The next thing I knew was the naked muscular form of Josh, having showered quickly, sat on the bench very close to me drying his hair with his towel. "What was all that about, Harry?"

I looked up into his handsome concerned face, with his clear blue eyes and decided to tell him everything.

Josh said that, like Ruth, his sister had also been subjected to Marcantonio's attentions. He thought that sooner or later he would go too far and be expelled.

All I could add was that, in view of what had passed between Marcantonio and me and the ill-temper, I'd had to stifle a comment about the size of his cock. I hadn't wanted to give him a complex about what he evidently thought his best feature. I had wanted to say that, if he had indeed penetrated Jocelyn, would the boy have noticed, though I had been told, in other circumstances, some time ago, that small cocks could be painful to accommodate.

Josh laughed out loud at that and I smiled too. "Are you concerned about size then?" he asked.

"No, not normally, but I couldn't help noticing what he had to offer when he said he was sixteen and it was evident. It's just another reason to tell Ruth to avoid him. I think she deserves better." Then we both laughed and grinned at each other.

Josh put a hand on my knee and said softly, "Well, Harry, if you and Ethan would like to expand your circle of 'friends', don't forget me." To my amazement he leant forward and kissed me on the lips. "And I would really like to find out whether Ethan fills his codpiece like I know you could do." And put his hand on my crotch before kissing me again, but holding it for longer and letting his tongue find mine. He got up, crossed the changing room to his locker giving me a beautiful view of his muscular buttocks moving rhythmically, got his phone out and brought it to me to put my number in his contacts.

I gave him mine to do the same. That gave me a full view of what he had to offer and he dwarfed poor Marcantonio! Feeling much better, I finished dressing, packed my kit bag, and as I left, grinned as I saw Josh's enviable, delectable cock and balls disappear into his boxers, said, "Merry Christmas." Which got a cheery laugh and a, "You too Harry. See you next year." A big wink and a blown kiss too. I would never have guessed. My gaydar was obviously knackered!

Chapter 44

ETHAN

Ruth and I were worrying about what had happened to Harry. It had been some time since he'd left the pitch, obviously in some pain. We'd sat, shivered, slurped coffee and tried to shout encouragement at the first half goals until the team had gone in at half-time and eventually reappeared to resume the match. Ruth pointed out that Marcantonio, who had followed Harry into the changing room, had come back out as a team member not as a substitute.

When he finally emerged, Harry said, "Sorry, but it's too cold to sit here. Can we please get in the car and go home? I'll explain on the way."

As we arrived at the car, another swept round us, halted and a senior student and soccer player, Josh Carpenter, I think, lowered his window to shout, "Merry Christmas, happy New Year." Blew us a couple of kisses and gave a cheery wave before driving off.

"Isn't he lovely?" said a captivated Ruth.

Harry and I could only sigh deeply, "Yeah."

Harry's account of what had occurred in the changing room rather left Ruth and I almost speechless. His detailed description of a naked Josh clearly appealed to Ruth, and knowing that he wanted to have sex with Harry and me, certainly got my imagination working (not to mention the inevitable movement in my pants) as to how a threesome could and would work in practice. I think we were all glad that Marcantonio had got what he deserved from Coach and that perhaps Ruth would not be bothered by him at least for the time being. I dropped them at Wampanoag Drive and drove slowly home.

Chapter 45

The last day of term dawned bright and sunny, if not that warm, which was a welcome change. The final few lessons passed very quickly and then we were free for the shortish break to everyone's relief, staff and students. Harry, Ruth and I had agreed that we would celebrate at the Urquell leaving the others to do whatever Christmas preparations they needed to do. So in mid-afternoon we just sat relaxing with cups of tea (with lemon!) and not really saying very much. Tom had welcomed us but we could see in his face that he was tired from all the late sessions he'd had to work because of the holiday rush, not to mention the schoolwork and homework he'd had to fit in somehow. In accordance with Dad's instructions, I'd not said a word about his family.

"Can we join you?" suddenly came a new voice and Josh Carpenter and his sister appeared in our booth, followed by a seemingly energised Tom, who hovered while we sorted ourselves out. Harry introduced Ruth and me while Josh introduced his sister Oksana who knew Ruth anyway as they were in the same class and great pals. Harry also introduced Josh to Tom saying he had mentioned him during their changing room chat. "So you're the Czech mate are you? I'm very pleased to meet you." And gave him a lovely smile. Tom blushed and asked what he and Oksana would like to drink. Josh looked at Oksana and asked for tea like us.

"I'm sorry if this is an intrusion, but it just seemed a good opportunity to get to know you better." The girls were chattering away about their class mates and Christmas plans, so Josh asked what Harry and I were doing or planning. Harry, rather disconsolately, said that they would be at home and would have to tolerate a few boring old farts from the university, colleagues of their father who would otherwise be alone. He did add that the French lechers who wanted nothing more than to "fuck me silly" would be there too. This really intrigued Josh who wanted more details. The business of Adam and Yves was explained, but what really interested Josh was the fact that I could sing.

He seemed to look at me in a new light. "So not just a pretty face then, to quote that old line," he said. Of course I blushed which just caused more laughter.

To change the subject, I asked Josh about Oksana's name. He smiled. "Yes, we're often asked about it. As you know, since about 1500, all Americans are basically immigrants, so presumably somewhere in the family background there's an East European or Russian woman who's passed her name down the generations. The biggest group apparently is German, but because of wars, disease, racial and religious discrimination, slavery, industrialisation, loss of farmland etc. you don't have to go back very far in anyone's family to find an ancestor or three who hail from somewhere across Europe, Asia or Africa, and the folk at Ellis Island weren't above changing names if they couldn't spell yours. I couldn't actually swear that my family's original name was Carpenter. Perhaps an ancestor arrived with one of those impossible Polish names, all c's, z's, y's, w's and those l's with a stroke through the upright, or even something like Kraptinovich or Kraptinsky and the immigration official couldn't be bothered and thought the nearest roughly English-sounding name was Carpenter. You only have to take note of the names in

173

any television broadcast or read a newspaper to guess, probably accurately, at someone's family origins."

He looked searchingly at me. "Anyway, you haven't told us your holiday plans, Ethan."

"Well, we've invited Tom to come for Christmas. My father knows him well as he is a senior at Wilberforce."

"And your father is…?"

"Head of the geography department." I hoped that would be the end of any questioning in case I said anything I shouldn't. Fortunately, Harry asked about the Carpenters' plans which amounted to just a quiet family time, though a pair of grandparents were expected on St Stephen's. My query about St Stephen just got Josh to enquire, with a slightly mocking smile, didn't I know the carol about "Good King Wenceslas" looking out on the feast of Stephen, especially as we were in a Czech cafe!

The conversation moved on to New Year's Eve, so Harry said his parents were throwing a big Hogmanay shindig and his elder brother was flying over from Edinburgh to be there. He got out his phone to find a photograph of Hamish to show to Josh and Oksana. Josh obviously approved of what he saw and even, I think, licked his lips.

"Sorry, not remotely available," said Harry. "Absolutely sure. He does have gay friends who are on the medical studies programme too, but his girlfriend, the beautiful Helen, is also."

Josh sighed and lowered his voice. "Shame. The family resemblance is incredible, apart from the hairiness, but I'm sure you'd be a more than adequate stand in. And I'd definitely like Ethan's company too as there's lots to discover about you both. My parents are going away for a few days with Oksana in the new year, so perhaps we could get together for, um, mutual exploration. I'll give you a call about the dates."

I had to then say, "Stop. I'm sorry, but while you're undeniably very attractive, this is the first time we've met after all. I don't know anything about you, other than you're a fellow student and you play soccer. Is that it, or is it 'all fur coat and no knickers'? How am I to know? It's just that I seem to have no control about my own life. I'm under pressure from my parents, from your parents, Harry, and now from you Josh, to perform in some way. I just need some time and space for me." I was breathing heavily and felt a bit tearful. There was silence.

Josh spoke first. "I'm really sorry you're feeling so pressured, Ethan, and that I've been so thoughtlessly heavy handed on our first proper meeting. Thank you very much for the compliment by the way, which I must fully reciprocate." He took hold of my hand and looked into my eyes before continuing, "You must take all the time you want to sort out your life, there's no urgency. But I'd like very much to be one of your friends and get to know you. I only have another six months at John Eliot and much of that will be taken up with exams or preparation for them, so please don't take too long. I'd like to take some solid memories with me wherever I then go. I don't know about a fur coat, but I do wear clothes usually. I can't promise anything about knickers though." Even I managed a brief laugh at that. Josh still had hold of my hand, so he was able to pull me to my feet, still looking me directly in the eyes, before leaning in to kiss me gently. I wanted to melt.

When he let me go, he gave a me a really lovely smile which just enhanced his attractiveness. After a moment he said, "Oksana, I think we'd better get going. Merry Christmas to you all." And he waved at Tom to get the bill. He said something to Tom at the cash desk who smiled radiantly at him and nodded, so

I think Josh was perhaps setting up another date. He and Oksana waved at us before leaving. Just as they went through the door, however, Josh looked back momentarily, and on reflection, I didn't know whether I had imagined it, but his expression was one of mingled desire, longing and lust aimed at me, but it was so fleeting. I wondered whether Harry had noticed but seemingly not, as Ruth and Harry wanted to know what I'd meant, so I told them about their mother's request for me to sing a couple of songs for the big crowd at Hogmanay, my sheer nervousness at the prospect and my father's resultant almost daily rehearsal schedule, so Josh's invitation for almost immediate presumed sex had been too much. As I related this, I began to wonder whether I was making too much of it all and was I overreacting, but there hadn't been any real break in demands since the play, and that had required everything I felt I had to give. The tears that had been building up just started flowing.

Ruth and Harry put their arms around me and stayed silent until I stopped and wiped my eyes. "Sorry about that, I should have more self-control." They continued to hug me until I stopped sniffling, smiled at them and said, "Come along. It's time to go." We paid, and I reminded Tom I'd collect him at about eleven thirty on Christmas morning.

Chapter 46

When I got home, Mom was there, her school term had also ended and she'd managed to do whatever had been necessary before thankfully getting away, as she put it. However, she took one look at me and asked if I'd been crying. I said yes and she sat me down on the sofa, put her arms round me and asked what was the matter. Of course I started crying again but she didn't question me any further. We were quiet until Dad eventually came home. Mom got up to tell him what had happened. He replaced her on the sofa and lifted my chin to ask what had happened to cause this.

Very hesitantly, through tears, I told him about feeling constantly pressured to do things for other people and not being in any sort of control. "Okay. No more rehearsals until the day before Hogmanay. You do know all the words and tunes, and your mother and I have every faith in you being able to deliver. We've told you before that we've heard you singing out in your room, so we know you can do it, and don't forget, you'll know everyone there, it's not a White House Command."

"Thank you, Dad. You and Mom are such a comfort."

"Now, who's this Josh you mentioned?"

I explained as best I could.

"He sounds a sensitive young man, and you say that Ruth and his sister are best friends and have faced up to the rampant Romanesco, as you described Harry's name for him." Dad chuckled. "Josh may well turn out to be a good friend and they're always people that you'll need about you. Unless you take a chance, you'll never find out. Ethan, you're seventeen going on eighteen, when you feel ready, grab your opportunities. There's no point in later regrets for lost ones."

Later that evening Harry and I exchanged messages. He said that he and Ruth had been very concerned about me, but I hope I convinced him that I was now feeling much better having talked things over with my parents. I even told him that the prospect of us meeting Josh, and hopefully, being friends with him, rather than just an occasion for sex, had looked brighter too. Harry laughed out loud when I added that Josh was a *very* attractive proposition! We wished each other and our families a merry Christmas and we looked forward to seeing each other at Hogmanay.

Chapter 47

Christmas Day was a bit grey and overcast though the weather forecast hoped for brighter weather later. Mom said she'd prepared a special lunch, though she wouldn't reveal what it was going to be. All I could gather was, it was definitely not Czech so Tom could enjoy something very different. As a family we'd decided long ago to not give each other presents which was always a relief, so we just relaxed while Dad dug out an old CD, *The Phil Spector Christmas Album* to set the mood and had the three of us singing along to all the well-known songs.

To make sure that we would have room for Mom's cooking, Dad and I just had a small breakfast before we set the table. Dad insisted that we would all have wine with the meal and put out several glasses at each place. He then handed over a small pile of cards. "These came addressed to you personally, Ethan, so we thought they could wait until today. They're not in any order, we just put them in a pile as they arrived. Just be grateful they're all cards and not the usual bills that always come at Christmas."

I opened the first one and said, "Dad you were almost right, this one's from Bill and Geoffrey and they've enclosed a photo too."

"Is that Bill Bailey you're talking about? Who's Geoffrey?"

"His husband, they were among the first to get married in May 2004 when Massachusetts was one of the first States to pass the legislation. They do look very happy, don't they?"

Dad agreed. The next card was from Michaela with her bold

signature which seemed only to be expected. "I think this little squiggle must be her boyfriend Job something. I only met him once and thought he was horrible. When we were introduced and I held out my hand to shake his, he refused until Michaela barked at him, 'For goodness' sake Job, he's gay, not a leper.' He's a first-year student at some evangelical college so apparently, I'm due for eternal damnation. His handshake was so limp and brief, I wondered what she saw in him."

"Perhaps you should've said firmly 'Jesus would have embraced me.' Most evangelicals are appalling hypocrites in my view and wouldn't recognise a Christian act if it bit them on the ass, hard."

When I opened the next card, it was a brilliant collage of Edinburgh's prominent buildings surmounted with the city's name in swirly writing and signed by all the Brown family individually. I didn't recognise the writing on the next envelope, but the card was signed "With love from Hudson and Randall" and XXXs and showed an almost naked Santa looking in a mirror, trying on a woman's bikini while an aghast Mrs Santa watched him from the door and the reindeer laughing in the background. Dad chuckled. There were lovely cards from Steph and Ed and the final one I saw had Harry's distinctive writing on the envelope.

"I wonder why he's sent a separate card?" I said as I opened the envelope to slide out a standard Christmas card and had to close it rapidly when I saw the photo contents and blushed furiously much to Dad's great amusement.

"How many guesses do I have?" He pretended to ponder before saying, "Is it perhaps a selfie of Harry's genitalia?"

At that moment, of course, Mom came in from the kitchen. "Oh, that's sounds lovely. Can I have a look?"

"Noooo. Of course not."

"Well, from what Heather's told me, you're not above showing your bits around their home."

"What? That's really not fair. I was fast asleep."

"I doubt if Harry was moving when he took the photo you've now got in your sweaty hands." Then they both burst out laughing.

I smiled. "I'm going to report the pair of you for child abuse." And joined in the joke.

Mom said gently, "If what's in the photo is anything like as attractive as the rest of him, which your father and I have glimpsed as he flits to and from your room to the bathroom, I'm sure it's well worth drooling over in the privacy of your room. Why don't you just put it under your pillow with the t-shirt?" And gave me a kiss and a hug.

The morning had somehow passed when it was time for me to fetch Tom and I got to his apartment just after eleven thirty. When I pressed the buzzer, he let me in and was at his door to welcome me. Once inside we kissed and murmured, "Mmmmy Chrmmmms." Before we let go of each other and grinned. "Ethan, it's really good to see you. I'm so happy to be spending today with you and your parents. Do you want to sit for a few minutes before we go? Would you like a cup of tea?"

"Actually, I'd love a cup, thank you." While the kettle boiled, we just held hands and kissed.

Tom had been listening to some lovely music which was new to me so, at a pause for breath, I asked him what it was. "Jakub Jan Ryba's *Czech Christmas Mass*. I think every church in the Republic performs it or plays it on Christmas Day."

"I must ask Dad if we have it at home."

While he made the tea he said, "The Urquell has it on a loop, so it's on non-stop for a few days before today unless customers ask for something different because they've got so fed up with it." He chuckled and set down the cups before continuing, "We have a couple of short pieces by Linek too, but they can request the usual Dvořák, Suk, Smetana, Janáček, Martinů, Novák etc. etc. Mostly though they just want Rusalka yearning for her prince to be naked in her arms, as I do now." And he pulled me in for a long kiss before we grinned at each other and drank our tea.

"Okay, Tom perhaps it's time to go." He switched off the music before going to the bathroom to fetch a large bouquet.

"This is for your mother. I know you said no gifts, but I really cannot accept your parents' hospitality without a small gesture of thanks."

"I think she'll be delighted. These are magnificent."

Chapter 48

As I opened the front door there was a loud fanfare. Tom laughed and said "What a welcome, Janáček's *Sinfonietta*."

Mom and Dad came to greet him and Mom gasped at the bouquet. "Thank you Tomáš," she said with a broad smile. "These are fantastic. I'll find a suitable vase."

"Hello Tomáš. Welcome to our home. Merry Christmas."

"Thank you, sir. Merry Christmas to you and Mrs Liddell. I'm really delighted to be here."

"Tomáš, while you are under this roof, it's Jonathan and Monica. While Monica puts the final touches to the meal, Ethan, would you please give Tomáš the grand tour before we have an apéritif."

Tom looked around, rather as Harry had done, and similarly took in the display of Christmas cards (my parents never had a Christmas tree), piles of books, the family photographs, the paintings, and told Dad what a wonderful home he and Monica had created. His eye was drawn to the collection of CDs and DVDs and was impressed by the range. "There is another lot in Ethan's room which he sings along to." I took his hand and we went upstairs for the "'grand tour", which took all of three minutes if that, before I opened the door to my room.

"So this is the stage for your dreams?" I ushered him in and he gazed at the posters, more piles of books and the shelf of CDs and DVDs above the desk where I did my homework. He sighed wistfully and I thought of what must be going through his mind, about what he was missing in his own life. I couldn't say anything because of the promise to Dad, so I just hugged and kissed him again. Dad had found Julius Fučík's "Entry of the gladiators" which made us both laugh.

Tom whispered, "And what of the performance you were going to tell me about then?"

"Welcome to the theatre of dreams, sir. Please take a seat in the stalls, sir." Pointing to the bed. "Many apologies for the lack of armrests, but as you know, in this area of the Natick metropolis, such niceties are rare. Make yourself comfortable, sir, because this epic production means it will be several hours before the interval and refreshments are available." Tom started to laugh. "When the curtains go up *(make appropriate gestures with the hands)* there will be a lush woodland glade where Oberon, the fairy king, and his four fairy aides-de-camp (emphasis on the last word, note!) are staring in wonderment at a mortal in their midst. Oberon, by virtue of the juice from a magic flower, is blind to the truth and is destined to fall in love with the first creature he sees, which is this Bottom the weaver transformed into an ass (a bit like Shrek's Donkey)." Tom laughed out loud at this. "Oberon dismisses the fairies, but of course they stay to see what happens next, when…"

"Ethan, Tomáš, almost time for lunch," came Dad's voice.

"We'll take a break and come back after these notices from our sponsors."

"Always leave them on a cliff hanger," chortled Tom.

"Coming now," I shouted.

"I hope *that* will definitely happen later," said Tom as he cupped my balls with one hand and felt my stiffening cock through my jeans with the other.

"If you keep on, I shall have to have another shower, so let's

184

go." We kissed before I led the way hoping my erection wouldn't show. Fortunately, I hadn't tucked in my shirt tails when dressing so there was some cover as we descended.

"What would like, Tomáš? Ethan? You can have one too. Monica?"

"Just a dry sherry please."

Tom asked for a vodka and tonic so, not knowing what else to do, I said I'd have the same and Dad said he'd join us. "Okay. I'll just change the music as well." The opening of Tchaikovsky's first symphony, *Winter Daydreams*, started to play while Dad put ice cubes in glasses, slices of lime, and from what I could see, a large measure of Absolut vodka. After we had our drinks and sat down, Tom and I on the sofa, he and Dad chatted about life at Wilberforce and how he was managing with all the demands of the IB programme as well as the cafe work. Tom confessed that it was a bit of struggle, but he hoped to do some catching up in the mornings before his shifts started. Dad said he should come to see him if he felt he was falling behind so that the school might offer some more support. He told Tom that he was too good a student to give up on. I had a horrible feeling that Tom was going to burst into tears, but was relieved when he appeared to pull himself together and the moment passed. While we sipped our drinks, we could hear Mom talking to herself which Dad and I knew was a good sign that it was all coming together in her very capable hands. As we finished our drinks, Mom called out for us to get seated and brought in a tureen. Dad asked Tom if he was happy with red wine though white was available.

"Oh, thank you, Jonathan, but I do prefer red with almost everything."

"Well, I hope you'll like this one." And produced a bottle of Barolo and poured.

The first course was one of Mom's specials, carrot and orange soup, it was light and delicious. It was followed by beef wellington, which was a new recipe for Mom, beautiful crunchy roast potatoes and broccoli. There was onion sauce too which I liked, particularly on the broccoli. Silence reigned while we enjoyed it all, the wine was very rich and smooth as far as I could tell, but it was another first for me.

"Mom that was fantastic."

"First class," agreed Tom, and Dad gave her a big kiss.

"Shall we have a brief pause before the cheese?" suggested Dad. Tom and I helped stack the now empty plates and helped clear the table and sat back on the sofa while Dad refilled our glasses. The music segued into *The Nutcracker*. When we agreed that we could carry on, Mom brought out a lovely selection of cheeses, crackers and pickles and Dad asked if anyone wanted a glass of port. Dad must have thought I looked a bit dubious, so he said that I had read enough classic literature to know that gentlemen, and the unlikely odd lady if she were still around, always had port with the cheese course and the decanter should be passed to the left. We didn't have a port decanter anyway, so Dad just filled our glasses! All I could recall from literature was the usual unruly behaviour by this stage when the so-called gentlemen discussed politics or war or whores (I think) and smoked cigars or pipes, the ladies having sensibly withdrawn to the withdrawing room with their crocheting. But it was Christmas and we could get merry — Mom had a glass too.

We were feeling quite mellow by this stage when there was a message on my phone. It was from Harry and I read it out. "He says that Ruth and he are bored shi… very bored and can they come over. His mother will drive as she's stone cold sober and can they bring Catherine?"

My parents immediately said, "Of course" and Mom immediately went to make sure there was enough coffee. We started on the cheese but only Dad had any of the pickles. Tom and I looked at each other but neither of us knew what they were other than the obvious onions and little gherkins.

Chapter 49

About fifteen minutes later the sound of a car arriving caused Mom to ask me to greet the guests. The first person I saw was Heather who gave me a hug, a kiss and a big smile. "Merry Christmas, Ethan. I don't think you've actually met Catherine, Patrick's mother." And she turned to a beautiful elegant woman who reminded me of someone I felt I knew but couldn't place.

"Hello, Ethan, merry Christmas. I've heard a lot about you. All good. Hugo and I loved your performance and you must call me Catherine."

"Thank you. Please come in. It's a real pleasure to meet you." They went into the house and before, I could say anything, Harry had put his arms around me, clamped his mouth onto mine and sought my tongue. When he let go, he said, "I've missed you." And kissed me again.

"I've missed you too. Hello beautiful," I said to Ruth and kissed her before hugging her. "Merry Christmas to you both. Come in."

I was in time to see Heather present Dad with a box which contained a bottle of Highland Park as a small gift for allowing them to intrude on our meal. Dad's eyes gleamed, I thought, and he was profusely grateful. Tom was introduced to Heather (who he knew anyway) and Catherine, when I suddenly realised who Catherine reminded me of.

I blurted out, "You're just like Michelle Obama."

Catherine laughed. "You're really sweet and kind to say so.

I'm very flattered." Mom asked if everyone would like coffee, but then noticed Harry and Ruth by the dining table and the cheese board.

"Would you like some cheese?"

Both replied, "Oooh yes please." To Heather's obvious horror.

"You've just had an enormous meal."

"Yes, but Mum, this selection looks fantastic," said Harry.

Mom brought in some fresh plates and knives and just said, "Please help yourselves."

Tom and I decided to have some more cheese too. Dad offered us another glass of port which was lovely. Heather and Catherine declined the cheese, but Catherine did ask if she could have a glass of delicious port! Harry gave Ruth his glass to have a sip, but she drank most of it, unseen by Heather thank goodness, so Dad refilled it without saying anything.

Mom told Heather and Catherine that she'd found a wonderful delicatessen in Boston that sold a variety of European cheeses, and as an experiment, had thought to try them out. "When they're finished, I'll bring in the cake to round off the meal and give you that cup of coffee at last. Heather, did you have a traditional Christmas pudding, which is something I saw online?"

"Yes, but I cheated and made a very quick version rather than preparing one a couple of months ago and feeding it alcohol regularly."

Harry, with a mouth full of cheese and crackers, chipped in with that it had been great nonetheless. The sight of the pudding, lit with the blue flame of the burning brandy, had been a real treat and a reminder of home.

"Well then, shall we clear the cheese away and let Mom bring in the cake?" I offered, and a few minutes later the table was pristine again and Mom brought in two cakes, a fruit one and a pecan pie, two of her specialities. Dad brought in a tray with plates, cutlery, cups and saucers and asked who would like which or a slice of both. There was ice cream, home-made too, or plain cream if preferred. Everyone wanted to have both with ice cream so that made it much easier. There was silence while we enjoyed Mom's baking and sipped the coffee. Dad suggested that a digestif was available if wanted, but there was no taker except himself, so he got a measure of brandy.

The conversation turned to New Year's Eve and it appeared that the Browns were expecting all the usual crew plus parents and a few others.

"Not the boring old university gargoyles that were at our home today thank goodness," said Harry scathingly. "Obviously that's not you and Hugo, Catherine. One of them had a biblical beard through which he mumbled that he wanted to study ancient Greek and Aramaic so he could make yet another translation of the bible, as if Christianity needed another schism, and one of the other eggheads couldn't be understood. I didn't know if the noises he made were even English. I don't know why my father collects these people except as an act of charity. It's not surprising that they had nowhere else to go for Christmas." Ruth nodded her agreement.

"Harry, that's very unkind," said Heather. "Back in Edinburgh, Angus does the same thing and we've had to entertain university people who are Scots with impenetrable accents," she said to everyone else's amusement.

Harry got more expansive again (the port?). "Yes, when Gordon McWilliam, one of Hamish's student friends gets a bit tipsy, his Aberdonian twang gets so thick, he's as impenetrable as his hair. We call him 'the beast' because he's so hairy. If it weren't for his beard, he'd have to shave at least three times a day. Hamish swears that Gordon's kept in a cage in Edinburgh Zoo and is only let out during the day when heavily tranquilised."

At the mention of hairiness, Tom squeezed my hand and we grinned at each other while joining in the laughter at Harry's tale. He continued, "Actually he tranquilises himself with beer at C C Bloom's quite frequently." To blank looks, he added, "It's one of Edinburgh's main gay bars."

When Catherine had stopped laughing, she remarked, "It's that sense of humour that has certainly helped bring about a change in Patrick. He escaped and ran away to Sam's in case you were wondering, so Hugo and I were happy to accept Heather and Angus' invitation. Your daily car rides seem to have made him alive to aspects of life that don't involve football. He smiles and laughs a lot more. He tells his father things you've said but he won't tell me. Hugo of course does repeat it to me, but Patrick thinks I don't know these words. Hugo and I heard much, much worse when we were growing up in a cruel, racist America facing abuse and discrimination. That odious orange man in the White House is now stirring up racism and I'm very worried it's all going to get really bad, and who knows where we'll be by the end of his presidency. Sorry, I didn't intend to go into all that now and spoil the evening. But thank you, Harry and Ruth. Patrick has definitely mellowed under your influence, so please don't give up."

Heather turned to Tom and asked whether he would be free to come for Hogmanay.

"I'm very sorry, I'd love to but I can't. The holiday period is very busy at the cafe, so all the staff will be on to cope and I do need the money. I'll only have one evening off between tomorrow and New Year's Eve."

At this I saw Harry smile at me, raise his eyebrows slightly and let his eyes slide over towards Tom, before looking back at me quizzically. I think I got the message — he was proposing that we should "see" Tom on his evening off! I raised my eyebrows with a very slight shrug not knowing if that would be possible. Harry also shifted in his chair with a slight "oomph" and I understood he had an erection at the thought. Tom was obviously unaware of this, and explained that the cafe was due to remain open until two a.m., or until the very last customer had left whichever was the later. His colleagues had told him that every year there was always one man, not necessarily the same one, who didn't take the hints, chairs upended, floors swept, etc. but just sat morosely nursing a drink or three. He'd come to be part of the noisy, celebratory crowd but evidently didn't have anyone at home. He said it was like the scene in a film, the title of which he couldn't remember, where the hero sang, *'Set 'em up Joe, here's a story'*, Frank Sinatra or Fred Astaire?

Heather said, "I'm sorry to hear that, Tom. You would've been very welcome."

Her phone rang at that moment, and after a brief word from the other end, she announced, "I think we can go home now and leave our hosts to enjoy the rest of Christmas in peace. That was Angus. All the guests have gone and the arguments about university politics have ended. Only Hugo's there, and it sounds from the slight slurring, as if they've hit the whisky, Catherine." They both chuckled. "Thank you, Monica, Jonathan, so much for letting us invade you, but Ruth and Harry were understandably bored and Catherine and I wished we were elsewhere."

Mom laughed and said it had not been any trouble and what a pleasure it had been to meet Catherine. They hugged and Dad shook hands while Ruth and Harry got hugs too. Ruth gave Tom and I a kiss and Harry whispered to me, "Have a good night." Kissed me and winked. He also whispered something to Tom and kissed him too before they went, waving as they got in the car and drove away.

Chapter 50

We settled back in our seats and there was a brief silence before Dad realised that the music had stopped, so the room filled with Ravel's *Mother Goose suite*; very restful. "I think Catherine's quite right to be worried about the increase in racism, spurred on by that 'odious orange man in the White House' as she put it, and what may happen next," said Dad. "Would you boys like a digestif now, so we can drink to hopefully better times ahead?"

Tom and I looked at each other and said, "Yes please." In unison. Mom said she would like one too, so Dad got four brandy glasses and gave us each a good measure. We stood, clinked glasses, and said, "To better times." Followed by Tom and I clinking glasses again. "Naz drovie." Mom asked if Tom and I would like anything else to eat, though the unexpected guests hadn't left much. There was cheese, some more fruit cake, the pecan pie having been completely demolished, and there was ice cream too. Otherwise, she could rustle up some sandwiches having discovered some ham she'd forgotten she'd bought and there were eggs and tomatoes and pasta as well. I said that we were very happy as we were.

Actually, I wanted to kiss Tom more than anything else and toy with his chest hair and other "attractions", but how do you say that to your parents? So I started a conversation about the Browns' Christmas guests which had caused their party to rather disintegrate and Harry's funny description of his father's colleagues.

"No wonder you got the phone message, Ethan," said Mom. "And it was lovely to meet Catherine. You were quite right about the resemblance to Michelle Obama. I'm looking forward to meeting Hugo and Patrick too. Do you know what Catherine was referring to when she mentioned Harry's teasing of Patrick and the unrepeatable words?"

Of course I knew, Patrick had told us some time ago about Harry's unrequited desire in that direction. "Yes, Mom, I do, but do you really want to know? I think when you meet Patrick at the Browns' Hogmanay party, you'll understand exactly what Harry wants to do to him if the circumstances were ever right. Which they'll never be according to Patrick."

"That tells me all I need. Thank you, Ethan." And she laughed as Dad did too.

"I'm just glad Heather didn't mention anything about our rehearsals, Dad." As soon as I'd said it, I wished I'd kept my big mouth shut as that immediately alerted Tom.

"What rehearsals, Ethan? Are you in another play?"

"No." I sighed. "It's just that Heather asked me to sing a few songs at Hogmanay, accompanied by Dad."

"I've never heard you sing. I'm sure you do it beautifully."

Of course, I now felt obliged to offer a sample, so I asked Dad to accompany me in Howard Blake's "Walking in the air". "Tom, do you know the cartoon film *The Snowman*? It's now nearly forty years old?" Tom shook his head. "Basically, it's about a British boy who builds a snowman who comes alive. After a few adventures, the snowman flies with the boy to the North Pole where they meet a lot of other snowmen and women, and Santa. They dance until the first streaks of dawn oblige them to return. The boy goes back to bed, but in the morning when he races down to the garden to check on the magical snowman, sadly he's melted. While they are flying north over land and sea, this song is heard. Originally it was sung by Peter Auty who was a thirteen-year-old choirboy; he's now about fifty and a very well-established operatic tenor. He never got a credit on the film."

Dad was ready, so I took a deep breath, smiled at Tom and Mom and sang. Tom was really delighted, and both he and Mom hugged me. Dad said I'd never done it better and gave me a hug too. Dad looked at his watch and asked if, as it was just on the hour, we'd mind him switching on the tv so he could catch up with the news. He always watched the BBC twenty-four-hour news service as he didn't trust any of the American news programmes to deliver the truth. I think the only occasional exceptions were CBC and CNN. Those famous neutral tones just told us that, following in Rudolf and company's hoof steps pulling Santa's sleigh, the Four Horsemen of the Apocalypse who never had a day off, ensured suffering in some way had to be spread to every nook and cranny in the world, Christmas notwithstanding.

When we'd heard enough to put an end to conversation, he turned it off and we settled back with the remains of our brandies to mask our relief that we were safe. To cover the silence, he sorted out some music and found something I didn't recognise. "What's this, Dad?"

"Rimsky-Korsakov, *Christmas Eve Suite*. It's a fun piece." I could feel Tom next to me getting a little restless so, having seen that all the debris from the meal had been cleared away and just the glasses needed washing, I asked if it would be okay if we went to my room and had an early night as Tom had to go to work the next day. Mom and Dad said that would be okay and wished us, "Good night." Hugs and kisses all round.

Chapter 51

Once in my room, Tom just grabbed me, kissed me hard and said, "You don't know how much I've been waiting for this moment to be alone with you, hold you, touch you, kiss you, undress you and make love to you." And proceeded to do just that. When we were naked, we let our hands, lips and tongues go everywhere, and of course, it had been two months since this had last happened in his home. Tom paused for a moment to say that he was aware that he owed me a fuck and would I please let him have it now as he had so been looking forward to this moment and it had been too long. We kissed deeply and I let my hands wander again through that lovely hairy chest. My mouth then closed in on his nipples, he moaned in pleasure, then carrying on to rim him eliciting further sounds of delight, moving round to his balls and then cock which I covered in kisses and licks before taking him in my mouth and slowly started to suck. Tom began to pant slightly as I got going, he grasped my shoulders, quick breaths, before moving his hands to my head as he gradually came closer to orgasm. I decided not to speed up but just plunged his cock deeper into my mouth with each thrust which made him writhe ecstatically, groaning "OMG" and "fuck" as he tried to hold on as long as he could before finally shooting his load.

We kissed, before I was able to ask him which way round he would prefer.

"I want you to look at me and keep your mouth on mine."

"Okay." I gently led him to the bed and he stretched out

while I opened the drawer in the nightstand to get the tube of lube and a condom…

Tom shifted the pillow and suddenly said, "What's this?" And extracted Harry's Urquhart's t-shirt and the Christmas card. So I had to explain about the t-shirt and why it was still under my pillow. He opened the card and the photograph of Harry's genitals fell out. Tom chuckled. "He's really important to you isn't he? As you are to him. When he left, Harry whispered to me to please look after you as you're very precious to him. But you are to me too, Ethan." Tom gathered me into his arms and said, "Have you ever seen the film *The Sea Hawk* with Erroll Flynn?"

"No, but I know some of the Korngold fantastic score."

"Well, I see Harry as a sea hawk, a sort of buccaneer pirate serving you as his monarch. Harry's ship passes others in the night as ships do, but his insatiable curiosity means he has to board them to find out what jewels and golden treasures are in their hold. He is always faithful (in his eyes) to you. I know that Harry wants to have sex with me and with that other lovely boy that came to the cafe."

"Josh?"

"Yes, Josh, but he and I are merely sideshows, passing fancies, Harry really only wants you."

"So where are you in this?"

"I'm an Earl of Leicester figure, who also wants you, desires you, to be mine."

"I'm glad you didn't say Earl of Essex."

"Well, if you were a lot older, wore lots of poisonous make-up and a fright wig, you might just be worth losing my head over."

"You are funny and so wonderful, I could cry."

"Please don't do that. I just want you to make love to me,

now. Be *my* monarch tonight." We kissed — how we kissed then, holding each other's heads and letting our tongues find each other before I lubed my fingers to push up into him and then my sheathed cock. When I entered him, he took in a deep breath, and once I was all in, our mouths were glued together while I took hold of his wrists and we began to move together. For me it was a fantastic moment to know that I was making love to someone who loved me and I didn't want it to end. Of course, this thought drove me to start moving faster until the inevitable result. I stayed inside him until I felt I should slide out and we lay in each other's arms again, kissing while I ran my hands up and down his chest which made him laugh.

We slept until I was awoken by Tom making moves to penetrate me. He whispered, "I'm sorry, but I really can't miss this opportunity of being naked in your bed without possessing your body again."

I whispered back that he should carry on. And he did. I happily handed him a condom and gel and gave myself up to him and his urgent hunger. An hour later he wanted to do it again, so I gave him another condom but he wanted to fellate me too so, first, he gently washed my cock with tissues dipped in the glass of water I always have by my bed. While he held my hands and kissed me, I found myself murmuring his name alternating with Harry's between the kisses and moanings; exploding in his eager mouth felt exquisite. Eventually we settled into an exhausted sleep.

I was woken by someone kissing me. It was Tom, dressed, and from his scent, freshly showered. "Hello, Happy St Stephen's Day," he said. "Your parents are already up and having breakfast. How are you feeling? Do you have a hangover after vodka, wine, port and brandy?"

I sat up feeling surprisingly okay. "I'm fine thank you, and thank you for last night. I can't say whether I feel like a king because I've only acted one and he was a fairy." We both laughed. "I'd better get up. Have you had breakfast?"

"No, I told your parents I'd wait for you."

"Okay. I'll have a shower." I threw back the sheet and comforter and Tom wanted to caress me, but I felt a move in my bowel which made a rapid move necessary. So I said to wait as I had to go to the bathroom now and have a shower.

Afterwards, when I was dry, he tried to lavish kisses on my cock and balls while I tried to put on my boxers and then let me get dressed. When we got downstairs my parents and I exchanged hugs and kisses and Tom and I got glasses of juice, bowls of cereal and mugs of fresh coffee. I asked Dad to put on Korngold's *Sea Hawk* music which surprised him, but he kindly obliged without question other than a raised eyebrow! Tom and I smirked at each other.

Chapter 52

Mom asked Tom if he would like a cooked breakfast and offered poached eggs on toast. He said that that would be perfect. I said I would have the same please. When Mom saw the way Tom wolfed it down, she asked, "What do you normally have for breakfast, Tom?"

"Um… um… usually just a cup of coffee and a slice of toast, Monica."

"With?"

"That's it. If I'm on an early shift and I get to the cafe early enough, there may be an unsold pastry from the day before which, of course, is stale and unsellable. If the kitchen staff haven't arrived, I can make myself a sandwich because, at the Urquell, sandwiches are all made to order, none is sold ready-made and wrapped. They won't miss a couple of slices of bread and a few slices of salami or cheese. That takes me through until the light lunch that is available. If I'm on the late shift, a meal is provided, anything from the menu."

"I see. Too many 'ifs', Tom." Mom went out and I heard the front door close. Dad put on Ravel's *Introduction and allegro* one of my very favourite pieces.

We finished breakfast, had a second cup of coffee and rinsed the crockery before loading the dishwasher before Mom returned with a couple of bags from the supermarket. "Tom, this is for you to take home. Just a few basic supplies. You cannot live such a hand-to-mouth existence. You've got to eat properly if you're going to keep up with your studies and get to university."

Tom was in floods of tears and hugged Mom while she put her arms around him and held him until he recovered himself. "Thank you, thank you. Thank you all for your hospitality which I can never repay." He looked at Mom, Dad and me with still rather damp eyes.

"Come on, Tom, I'll take you home before whatever's in the bags melt." I said to end the awkwardness. We got our coats, picked up the shopping and went out to the car.

On the drive I thought it best to let Tom know about Harry's intentions, how he'd reacted when he'd mentioned his one night off. Harry had sort of implied that he had it in mind to come to the apartment with me and possibly have sex as a threesome. That brought a delighted grin to Tom's slightly tear streaked face. "That would be incredible."

When we got to Tom's place, we grabbed a bag each and made our way to the apartment. Tom cried a bit more, I held him until he had dried his eyes and blown his nose. We went into the kitchen area and between us unpacked Mom's cornucopia of milk, butter, cheese, ham, eggs, various fruit, bread, tins of soup, beans and other stuff not to mention a couple of tubes of lube and condoms! I did wonder if he was going to cry again but he didn't. He kissed me ardently and I felt him undoing my belt and unzipping my jeans. "Please let me do this, Ethan. I just want you so much." He pushed down my jeans and boxers before kneeling and gazing at my very erect cock and balls before leaning in to take each ball in his mouth, rolling it around and moving on to the other. He used his hands to retract my foreskin, kissing and licking my cock before plunging his mouth down to almost swallow it and nearly gagging. All of this was very arousing and I could only react by gripping his shoulders, before holding his

201

ears as he brought me to orgasm. "Oh, Ethan, thank you. That was wonderful." He licked his lips. "My brunch." We laughed. He stood and we kissed lingeringly again. Tom stooped to pull my boxers and jeans up and even did up the zip. I re-buckled my belt. We grinned at each other and kissed again. "Please thank your parents for their incredible generosity and thank you, Ethan, for an unforgettable night."

"For a passing ship, you certainly found my hold, hoard of jewels and golden treasure," I replied to more laughs from both of us.

He showed me to the door and sighed. "I must get ready for my shift in a couple of hours, but some school work first, trying not to dream of you."

At home I told Mom and Dad how grateful Tom was for their generous support but not of his practical thanks kneeling on the kitchen floor!

Chapter 53

I sent a message to Harry telling him that Tom would be happy to "entertain" us on his evening off on Tuesday and got a suitably exuberant reply. I told him I'd pick him up en route to the cafe and we could meet Tom there to take him to his apartment. Tom had seemed happy with this arrangement, so we fixed on three p.m. when his shift ended. When I told Mom that Harry and I were going to visit Tom to wish him happy Hogmanay in advance because of his working hours, Mom gave me a list of groceries to buy on the way to keep Tom's supplies topped up. That wasn't a problem in itself, but I didn't want to say anything to Harry because of the need to keep it confidential.

When Harry jumped in, I asked if he had any experience of threesomes and how did the participants sort things out. He told me that he hadn't ever been so involved, but he thought that his brother's gay friends, Gordon and Alasdair, had once tried to get him drunk before taking him back to their room in the university with the intention of... Hamish had put a stop to it he said, slightly regretfully, I thought. Harry had heard of "spit roasting" where someone had a cock put in either end as it were and so was stuffed that way. It had been reported as an activity indulged in by heterosexual professional soccer players with women they had picked up for the purpose! He had in mind "sandwiching" where, if you had A, B and C, then A could fuck B while B could fuck C simultaneously. Then C could fuck A but that didn't seem very satisfactory either as a threesome. "Alternatively," he continued, "if A fucked B while C sucked B and then A and C changed places, followed by A being in the middle of B and C and finally C being the filling between A and B, then all three would be better satisfied having been fucked and sucked by the other two. It may take a little time to allow for those fucking or being sucked to have a rest or at least clean themselves, but..." As a thought struck him. "...Of course, condoms would help there. Does that make sense to you?"

"I think so." We arrived at the car park and went to collect Tom who was serving a couple of customers before handing over to a colleague who I recognised and greeted. When Tom was ready, we piled back in the car and were at Tom's a few minutes later. Rather self-consciously I followed them in carrying the shopping, and when we were in the apartment, I took it through to the kitchen area. "This is from my mom, Tom."

"Thank you very much and please tell her again how grateful I am."

"I shall." Harry, of course, did not know what was going on and looked puzzled, but I just shook my head at him and waved my hand to indicate explanations would follow. Tom offered to make us some tea before, what he said, was going to be an essential shower. We told him not to bother about the tea, we would sit and wait for him. He put on some music for us and disappeared into the bathroom.

"Please don't ask about the shopping, Harry. It's a confidential matter."

"Okay." He looked at me, winked and said, "Well then, shall we just get stripped to meet and greet our host when he emerges?" We grinned at each other and that is exactly what we did.

Chapter 54

Tom emerged with a towel wrapped round his waist while he dried his hair with another. He stopped when he saw us waiting and was momentarily speechless until Harry stepped forward and took away his towels, took his head between his hands and kissed him. I came round them and kissed his neck before running my hands around him to push my fingers through his chest hair tweaking his nipples. Harry and I changed places so I could carry on kissing Tom's face while Harry gradually moved down his back and eventually got to rim him which made Tom gasp and shudder slightly. As Harry stood up to find the tube of lube and condom he had carefully placed in reach while we stripped, my mouth moved across Tom's chest sucking his nipples which now stood out and traced the line of hair down to the bush where I nuzzled his pubes making him react as if tickled while I grasped his hips. While kissing Tom's neck, Harry applied the lube to his fingers and Tom's hole, and from the reaction, was pushing a finger if not two into him causing Tom to groan and shake. I got my mouth round Tom's balls and was gently stroking his penis and slowly pulling down his foreskin when I heard Harry ripping open the condom sachet and whispering, "Tom, please bend your knees slightly." Harry's breathing told me his cock was slowly penetrating Tom, so I started to suck taking him in as deep as I could manage before going back up to the glans before plunging down again. The noises from Tom of pain, of pleasure, of whatever was going through his mind were incredibly exciting.

He grabbed my shoulders as I gradually speeded up and I could feel through the movement of his hips that Harry's thrusts, having got his cock in up to the hilt, were speeding up too. Tom whimpered, panted, moaned and groaned as he neared his orgasm and he arched back as both Harry and I held him firmly in our grasp, Harry round the waist and chest and me his hips until both Tom and Harry ejaculated almost simultaneously. It took several minutes before the heavy breathing subsided sufficiently and for Harry to be able to slide out, me to stand up, and Tom able to put his arms around us. "That was amazing. Thank you." And we all grinned at each other.

After a couple of minutes silence, Harry said, "Tom, we haven't finished with you yet."

"What do you mean?"

"When we're ready to go, Ethan and I will change places."

"Oh!"

"Let's just relax for a moment and I'll just get rid of the condom and wash my cock." And he went to the bathroom. Tom and I sat on the sofa and kissed and played with each other until we were both erect. Harry grabbed us by an arm each and pulled us to our feet. We started kissing as before and I could hear Harry murmuring something about Tom's chest as he ran his fingers through the hair while they kissed passionately. I decided that I wouldn't rim Tom, but I did apply more lube to him and a lot to myself after putting on a condom and found I could penetrate him more easily following Harry. Harry had been exploring Tom's balls and cock with his tongue and from his noises Tom was enjoying the attention. As he felt me penetrating him, he reached round to grab my ass and pull me in so that I was completely in him. I was sure he must feel my balls banging against him. My arms were round his body so that I could play with his nipples and then let my fingers trace the outline of his eyes, nose and mouth where he sucked my fingers while Harry sucked him. As I moved to start my thrusts, he let go of my ass slightly and that gave me the freedom to start getting faster as my arms grasped him round the chest again. Tom and I got noisier, the oohs and aahs and other sounds, definitely went from *piano* to *forte* as our orgasms slowly built and I could feel him strain and want to buck as Harry really got him going, until Tom suddenly arched back and we both came with loud gasps of relief. This time both Tom and I went to wash ourselves and he let me dry him, so I gently towelled his cock and ass and he my now unsheathed cock. We had a lingering kiss before joining Harry.

Tom offered tea which, this time, we gratefully accepted.

As we sipped, Tom asked inevitably, "What happens now?"

Before Harry could answer, I said, "One of us will have to be the sandwich filling and I think it should be Harry, and you, Tom should fuck him first."

When we were ready to make a move, I kissed Harry while Tom decided to let his tongue run down Harry's back and cleft before rimming him.

Harry whispered, "Why?"

"Because that's what you wanted," I whispered back, playing with his nipples with my fingers and then my mouth. He ran his fingers through my hair when I began playing with his balls and then gently pulled on his cock. Harry started making appreciative noises as I guessed Tom was trying to push his tongue into him and then felt the lube being applied. Harry got hold of my ears, groaned and bit his lower lip as I presume Tom had inserted his fingers and lubed himself. As Tom also got a condom before starting to penetrate, Harry let go of my ears and let me give attention to his now throbbing cock. I held onto

Harry's hips and his reaction told me that Tom was fully inside him. He'd wrapped his arms around Harry's chest and was really making the most of it. While I had Harry's cock in my mouth letting my tongue feel every wrinkle of his foreskin which I knew he liked, he was reacting ever more noisily to Tom who was making each thrust count, partially withdrawing slowly and then thrusting hard again. I could hear Tom panting too and muttering, "Oh yes, oh yes," as he built to his climax, so I knew I had to suck harder to get Harry closer to the point where he and Tom might come together. Harry seemed to be getting to a frenzy when he flung back his head with a shout of "Yes" as he and Tom shot their loads together. My taste-buds were greeted with that wonderful flavour of Harry's cum. I kept his cock in my mouth until his throbbing stopped and I could let him go. The three of us hugged and kissed each other, laughing at the same time.

Chapter 55

When we had disentangled ourselves, Tom went to find some suitable music while we had a few moments to recover. Harry looked at me and then ran his hands over my chest and ass before holding my cock and balls. When hopefully Tom was out of earshot, Harry whispered, "You're wrong, Ethan. That was really great, but this is what I want." And fondled me before kissing my cock and getting me erect in the process.

I held him, squeezing his balls slightly, smiled and said, "I think you've still got enough in there." Harry kissed me before turning to Tom and kissed him. The three of us hugged until Harry pushed his ass towards my erection, so I bent down to kiss it and pulled his cheeks apart so I could run my tongue between those beautiful muscular globes to find that puckered rose and try to force it open a little to get my tongue in there before anything else happened. Before applying lube, I looked up to see Harry and Tom enjoying a passionate kiss while Harry pushed his hands through Tom's chest hair. He then gently pushed down on Tom's shoulders so he could employ his eager mouth more fruitfully elsewhere! I put on a condom before using lube on a couple of fingers, on his anus and my cock and pushed into him. He reacted by pushing hard against me so my fingers were completely in. I remembered that first time when he told me to crook a finger, so I did it and got what was almost a howl, but he stopped me from withdrawing immediately. He calmed which meant I could slip my fingers out very slowly and then penetrate him until I was in as far as I could go, but perhaps that wasn't enough, as he reached behind him, grabbed my ass and really thrust himself back onto me with a great gasp. After that I tried to copy Tom's slow thrust method which did seem to have excited Harry. I could just about hear Tom making a real meal of blowing Harry and Harry's punctured breathing and panting told me he must be very close, so I tried going a little faster and could feel I was very close too and was soon rewarded by another shout of "Yes" as he and I came almost simultaneously.

Another pause while Harry and I went to wash ourselves though it did cross my mind that it would have been a pleasure to soap him myself. He may have caught my wistful look as I watched him clean his ass and cock, as he smiled with his eyes and mouth before gathering me into his arms. He just murmured something in my ears which I didn't catch, but whatever it was, I felt sure it was "sweet nothings" and hoped he was telling me how much he loved me. Back in the main room it dawned on me rather belatedly that it was my turn to be the sandwich filling and the bread was the two people who made up my sex life to date and I didn't know how that would turn out. My thoughts suddenly brought a Cole Porter song from *Kiss me, Kate* to mind. I realised I was the "Dick" between Tom and Harry and I let out a laugh. Of course they wanted to know what was so amusing, but trying to explain, rather ruined the joke and neither of them had heard of Ann Miller!

Chapter 56

The pair of them began to kiss me all over, moving up and down, gradually moving round me or turning me round so I closed my eyes and let them get on with it. It meant that I could never be sure who was sucking me or trying to shove a tongue up my ass until they stopped when they'd decided. From his touch I realised that Harry would fuck me while Tom sucked and they were being very gentle about it. It seemed that they were handling me like a priceless heirloom, but that ceased once lube had been tenderly applied on one side and my foreskin slowly pushed back on the other. The dual assault began in earnest. Harry played with my nipples, kissing the back of my neck while thrusting slowly at first and Tom's tongue was relishing licking my cock while he played with my balls. It was incredibly exciting and my mind was reeling with the sensations. I was aware of my breathing in short gasps, and initially not knowing what to do with my hands, settled on holding on to Tom's hair, before doing what Harry had done to me, reaching round to push his ass into me as I pushed down onto him. That made him draw in his breath as he speeded up. Tom responded too and their joint actions made me start to shout "Oh yes, oh yes" as I got to orgasm and I felt Harry cum a couple of seconds later. I held Tom's head as I subsided and he licked me, Harry just lay his head between my shoulders while he recovered, his arms around me.

No one said anything for a couple of minutes. Harry was the first to let go and stand up, removing his condom, and once Tom allowed my cock out of his mouth, I helped him up and locked my mouth onto his in a deep kiss. When my breathing was more or less back to normal, I went to the bathroom to wash, Tom and Harry followed. Harry washed himself too, but it was while the three of us were at the sink and I looked in the mirror and saw Tom on one side of me and Harry on the other, three totally naked teenagers, I couldn't help it and laughed out loud again and sang a couple of bars of "Tom, Dick and Harry, Tom, Harry and Dick" much to their confusion. I didn't try to explain.

Three people trying to kiss each other simultaneously doesn't really work but we gave it a good shot before Tom started to apply the lube while Harry licked, kissed and gently nipped my nipples as his mouth trailed down to my cock and balls. He sucked each of my balls which sent a shiver down me before using his tongue to move my foreskin back and then lavish my cock with licks and kisses which made me arch back in ecstasy. Tom had put a lot of lube on his sheathed cock, as well as on his fingers which he inserted. This made me moan but he extracted them very slowly before penetrating, and like Harry, put his hands on my chest, playing with my nipples and kissing the back of my neck. He started to move in and out and the combination of the two of them was just as exciting as before. In the midst I suddenly thought again of how fantastic it was to have the two people in my life finding pleasure in having sex with me but then I was aware that Tom's noises indicated he couldn't hold on much longer and Harry was taking his time seemingly examining every millimetre of my cock with his tongue. I think Tom was too far along to slow down and with a great gasp he exploded inside me. Harry took this as a sign he shouldn't dally any longer and began to let me plunge my cock into his throat before pulling back until only the glans was in his mouth and then plunging again. Tom slipped out and left us to it but it didn't take long before I could sense my orgasm building. Harry really sucked hard each time I plunged and I tried to hold on as long as possible thinking this was what Harry wanted, but eventually, I had to let go. With a shudder when I thought my legs would crumble, Harry held me up while I pumped cum into his welcoming mouth. I had my hands on his shoulders bending over him, while he kept my cock in his mouth and his nose in my pubes. He didn't resist or make any move other than to keep licking presumably in case anything further oozed out. We stayed like that until a gentle cough from Tom broke my reverie. Tom, now dressed, grinned at us and told us that he'd put the kettle on and was making us some more tea as he was sure we all needed another cup. Harry and I laughed, thanked him and moved to the bathroom for a wash before getting dressed too.

Chapter 57

There was another silence while we sipped our tea, but it was a companionable silence where nothing needed to be said. Harry broke the mood by clutching his stomach and saying, "God I'm hungry. Tom, is there a decent pizzeria nearby please? My treat."

"Yes, there's one only a couple of blocks away. One of my friends from school works there sometimes. I'll send a message to see if he's on tonight." A few minutes later the reply came through. "Yes, Zeke's working. He says it's not very busy at the moment, so he'll be delighted to see us." We finished our tea and set off.

I felt hungry too and Tom said his stomach was rumbling, so a pizza seemed the right way to stop that. When we arrived, a beautiful young black man greeted Tom with a big hug. "Long time, no see." And gave him a kiss.

"Hi, Zeke. This is Ethan and this is Harry."

"Hi, welcome. Any friend of Tom's is a friend to be shared!" He winked at us and tried a leer which didn't quite work; he just looked even more attractive. "I've reserved a table for you though there aren't many other customers." And he led the way to a table away from the door. "Are you Ethan Liddell, our geography teacher's son? He's a wonderful man. I'd like to hug him but I can't very well do that at school, so can I hug you to pass it on to your father?"

"Of course. He'll be very pleased." Zeke hugged me and held me close enough to let me realise he was erect through his uniform trousers and apron.

As we hugged, he whispered, "You're beautiful." And grinned.

"Can I have a hug too?" said Harry.

"Yeah. Come here." From Harry's face I could tell he'd felt Zeke's erection too.

Zeke said to Tom, "Have you spent the day with these guys?" Tom nodded. "Wow, I'm so envious. Well, I expect to be told every, and I mean every, detail when we next get together. Okay guys, what would you like?"

A female voice suddenly called out, "Ezekiel? Where are you?"

"Just taking an order, Giovanna. Be with you in a sec." He lowered his voice. "Giovanna's about as Italian as Michelle Obama, but this is meant to be an Italian place so all the managers have Italian names for public consumption." We laughed and ordered a large pizza with lots of toppings and lemonades. Zeke went off and we all admired the V shape of his body and evident muscularity of his ass.

Harry, of course, turned to Tom and asked, "Well? Is he, and have you?"

"Yes, on both counts. We've been very good friends for a couple of years, but getting together has been really difficult. His parents are very religious and mine are impossible, so it was only when I got my own place that we could really get it on. If you think he looks good now, the naked version is mouth-watering and he's very athletic in bed. I've been to Zeke's place a couple of times and it's very strange to see pictures of blonde, blue-eyed crucified Jesuses and Scandinavian looking Madonnas on the walls. The oddest picture is of St Sebastian, the one with the arrows — he has an incredible body but strikes a really gay pose

215

with pursed lips like he's going to kiss you. It could easily be from a homo magazine. His parents don't seem to be bothered by that nonsense, but their view of gayness, like other matters, is completely anti even though Jesus never says a word on the subject. The church they attend is evangelical to an extreme."

At that moment Zeke arrived with a fantastic large pizza. "I asked the chef for a blow-out version as it was for really good friends, so you've got some of every possible topping the place has got." He grinned at us. "Enjoy." And we admired his ass again and just managed not to drool too obviously!

Chapter 58

When we got back to Tom's, we wished him a happy New Year and looked forward to seeing him early in 2019. Harry and I got a hug, a long tender kiss each, and heartfelt thanks before he opened the block door. We got in the car, and before I started the engine, I turned to him and asked, "Would you come home with me and stay the night? Not for sex, but I'd like just to have your arms round me."

He smiled, kissed me gently and replied, "Of course. I'll just let Mom and Dad know what's happening."

When we got home, I asked if it would be okay if Harry stayed the night, and as expected, there was no objection. "Dad, I have something for you. Can you please stand up." I put my arms round him and said, "This is from Zeke — I don't know his family name. He can't do it in school, but he thinks you're the greatest."

"That's very nice. How do you... oh, of course, through Tomáš. Where did you meet him?"

"The three of us went to a pizzeria where Zeke works, so we've eaten well as he got the chef to give us a special one loaded with toppings."

Dad laughed and shook his head. "Zeke's a delightful young man. He and Tomáš have broken a few female hearts among the senior girls at Wilberforce, but I haven't noticed any similar effect among the senior male students to date that is. Zeke's problem is his parents who the school thinks hold him back because of their religion. He probably only works to get away from their strict outlook. I know I've said this before, but they're the sort of Christians who wouldn't recognise a Christian act if it bit them hard on the ass. They may have faith and hope, but charity's been left very high and dry. The level of hypocrisy is incredible. So now let me be charitable. Would you boys like a drink?" And he waved at the array of bottles on the sideboard.

"Could I please have a dram with a couple of ice cubes? It's how my father has it."

"Of course. Ethan?"

"Just a small glass of wine if there's a bottle open, please."

"Coming up. Monica, would you like a nightcap, darling?"

"No thanks. I'm going to have an early night. Good night you two. I'll see you when you come up, Jonathan." We each got a kiss and a hug.

"Oh, Mom, before I forget, Tom said many thanks for the top-up shopping." She smiled, blew me a kiss and gave me a wave before disappearing upstairs.

Dad switched on the TV for the BBC news service, so we watched that in silence while sipping our drinks, Dad having joined Harry in a dram.

We raised glasses in a toast, Dad said, "Bottoms up." I said, "Naz drovie." And Harry said, "Slàinte mhath." The main news items seemed to be mostly about the horrors of the war in Syria and the solo cross-Antarctica trek by a Briton which took fifty-six days.

Harry and I decided that we had seen enough and said good night to Dad before going up to my room. We both were quite tired, perhaps the afternoon's exertions were responsible. We got undressed, went to the bathroom for a last piss and collapsed on the bed. We had a long goodnight kiss before I snuggled into Harry's arms and fell asleep while he gently kissed my neck.

Chapter 59

I awoke to find a familiar mouth on mine and a familiar hand familiarly caressing my bodily extremities, but I didn't open my eyes, just stretched and let this familiar person's hands explore me. When the familiar hand returned to my cock and balls, I opened my eyes one by one and found Harry, up, showered and dressed, sitting beside me. "Hello, handsome. How's the magic wand this morning?" He smiled and kissed me again. "I thought I should examine it to see if there's any lasting damage." He pushed back the sheet and comforter and started to gently masturbate me. It crossed my mind to protest, but decided very quickly it would involve too much effort and just lay back to enjoy his attentions. I stroked his face and hair as he worked on me. I felt too lazy to even make any attempt to sit up, and as he was dressed, I couldn't touch him intimately anyway. Harry was evidently intent on getting me to cum fairly quickly as he suddenly put on more speed. I started moaning and writhing until at the very last moment he lowered his head and enclosed my penis with his mouth.

I sat up and grasped his head as he tried to extract the last drop. "That's not fair if I can't check your wand too."

"Ethan, nothing in life is fair and you were in exactly the right position to be exploited." He kissed me and then my cock and he sat continuing to hold it. "It was great watching your facial contortions. I'm just sorry I couldn't see your face as you shot, but Ethan, are you going to get up anytime soon?"

I heard faintly Dad's choice of morning music, Prokofiev's *Romeo and Juliet*, the balcony scene, and smiled up at Harry. "Why should I, my own Romeo? You're here with me, albeit dressed for some reason, not shaved however." Feeling his chin where the very slight redness of his beard could be felt.

He replied, "I think I'll get away with another day of not shaving as I think you will too. Now, unless you're going to convince me that you're some sort of superman, you're going to have to get up, if only to fart, have a piss and shit, brush your teeth, get dressed, have breakfast and drive me home."

"You're such a romantic."

"I'd love to spend the day rolling around your bed, naked, playing with you, but my parents expect me to help sort out the house for the Hogmanay bash, move furniture, help sort out crockery and cutlery, make sure the spare room is ready for Hamish, who arrives tomorrow, don't forget. Ruth and I were planning to make an apple-pie bed for him, but that's much easier with an old-fashioned sheets and blankets arrangement." Of course to delay him more, especially with him still holding on to my cock, I got him to explain an apple-pie bed even though I knew perfectly well what it was.

It couldn't last of course, so I got out of bed, stood in front of him and kissed those so kissable lips. Harry looked up at me, felt my scrotum, grinned and said, "I've had one protein shake, but your tanks seem to have some fuel left." And stroked my cock as it stiffened. He leant forward and started to fellate me.

I held on to his head as he grasped my ass while he sucked furiously. My breaths got shorter and shorter as my legs shook, and "Ohhhhhh… ahhhhh… ahhhhhhhhhh." As I shot into that warm, wet wonderful mouth.

"Well, that was another great protein shake from your

redoubtable wand, Mr Oberon Potter. Just remember to take care with your magic juices. Don't ever rub them on your eyes before deciding on ass or arse so you don't become a latter-day Alex Portnoy."

"Who's Alex Portnoy?"

"Ethan, on your parents' bookshelf there's a copy of Philip Roth's book *Portnoy's Complaint*. Young Portnoy is a serial wanker. He manages to squirt some cum into his eye while watching himself cum and it stung badly. His other notable feat was to emulate what it felt like, in his imagination anyway, to screw a woman, so he used a slice of liver from the refrigerator and wanked into that. He then put the liver back in the fridge and his mother fried it for the family dinner."

"Whaaat?"

"It's all protein, Ethan, for goodness' sake." Harry suddenly grinned.

"What now?"

"You should ask Hudson whether he likes liver. Don't you dare say you didn't know Hudson was Jewish. One word and I'll unscrew your cock and throw it in the nearest bin. Or, better yet, I'll circumcise you myself with my teeth. There can't be a nice well-brought up Jewish boy anywhere who hasn't read, or knows about, the book. Speaking of which, reminds me of a really lovely Jewish boy at Urquhart's called Dennis Feigenblatt who was… hmmmmm." And he seemed to go off into a reverie thinking about this Dennis, not to mention getting a noticeable bulge in his pants. Harry caught me staring. "What's the matter?"

"Do you realise that Dennis Figleaf, I do know that much German, is the only one of your school friends you've ever mentioned? Was he one of your kissed frogs? Did you ever discover what was under Dennis Figleaf's figleaf? Luscious fruit dangling from a neatly rounded bough perhaps?"

"Ethan, curiosity killed the cat, so keep your claws in. Actually, I feel rather bad for not having kept in touch more. He meant a lot to me until you came along and swept him from my mind. The only problem with Dennis was that it was 'hands off' from Friday evening to Saturday evening, and after a week of school, that was exactly when we should have been getting hands and mouths on each other. Hmmmmm." And he closed his eyes, dreamily.

"Was that the eleventh commandment, Harry? Thou shall not have sex on the seventh day, or did Jesus say it somewhere obscure while trekking round Palestine and the Gospel writers didn't catch it?"

"Don't blaspheme, Ethan. It doesn't suit you." But then he laughed. "Actually, the eleventh commandment is don't get caught with your pants down in a compromising situation, and you're still not wearing anything. Are you ever going to make a move? Your magic wand's been tested, is certainly in working order and that very tasty thorough cleansing and polishing should sort you out for a while."

"Why can't I do a tasty maintenance job on your wand then?"

"While you slept, my personal elves took care of me in the shower, so my wand is beautifully clean and polished and back in its box."

"Don't you mean back in its boxers?"

"Ha ha, Ethan, don't ever try stand up or at least get a better scriptwriter. If you don't get a move on, I'll tell your mum you want some liver for breakfast. I'm sure I saw some in the kitchen."

"Okay, okay. You win, you bastard." And I went off to the

bathroom and almost deliberately farted.

All of a sudden, the strains of sumptuous music and soprano voices could be heard. "Are those sirens belatedly calling us to breakfast on the rocks?"

"It's Dad being not so subtle again. You're in the right ballpark time wise just about, but it's not Debussy's "Sirènes", it's Richard Strauss, the final trio and duet from *Der Rosenkavalier* where the teenage lovers are eventually left alone to kiss before leaving a disreputable tavern."

"But they're all women. It's not about a load of dykes, is it?"

"That's a totally unacceptable thing to say. Do I have to throw your comments to Stuart back in your face? If I didn't know better, I'd call you a lesbianophobic philistine. Alexander Henry MacInnes-Brown you should be horse-whipped — regularly."

"Promises, promises." But he did look rather shamefaced.

I sighed very sadly.

Chapter 60

"Morning, Mum and Dad. Thanks for the music, Dad. Wouldn't the prelude have been better?"

"At seventeen you'd have been okay, but Harry wouldn't have passed muster as a mid-thirties female seductress, not even in the dark with the light behind him."

"But the elderly and ugly bit would match." Harry aimed a punch but missed. "Sorry it's so late, I just didn't want to get up this morning, but this herald of the dawn eventually got me up."

Mom replied, rather dryly I thought, "Some *dawn* herald. Do you know what time it is, Ethan? Do you want breakfast or lunch?"

"Sorry, Mom. I'll just have juice, cereal and coffee please but I'll get it. What can I get for you, Harry?"

He chuckled and asked for the same, but added, "Actually, Monica, Ethan mentioned fancying liver. Do you have any?"

"Liver? For breakfast? No there isn't any but I can get some. Is there something amusing you that you haven't told us about, Ethan?" said Mom as I tried very hard not to laugh.

"No, Mom." But I'm sure she saw my shoulders shake.

Dad intervened. "Monica, they're winding each other up." And made a slight jerking off gesture.

"Oh, I see. Portnoy rides again!"

While we had our breakfast Dad changed the music so that the sound of a solo piano could be clearly heard. "Oh, thank you, Jonathan, that's one piece I really do know," said Harry to my surprise. "'Farewell to Stromness' is something Dad puts on occasionally when he's thinking about his parents who are buried just outside the town. I never knew them and hadn't realised the music's significance until Ruth and I asked our parents about theirs." He turned to me. "It was a follow up to what Bill's father said, but it's too long a tale to bore you with now," he said to my parents.

I drove Harry home and we had a long hug and kiss in the car before he got out. "I'll never be able to eat liver again you know," I told him.

We both laughed before he waved and said, "I'll see you on New Year's Eve with all the crew. Perhaps we can get to kiss and fuck Patrick."

"You never give up do you?"

"One day, Ethan, one day he'll realise the error of his ways. Anyway, what was your nasty comment about me being 'elderly and ugly' about?"

"Sorry, that was just a quote from a Gilbert and Sullivan opera and I was trying to top Dad in the musical quotes game."

He sighed, shook his head in disbelief, blew me a kiss and disappeared indoors. Apart from momentarily feeling sorry for Patrick, my thoughts suddenly filled with the thought of that cum covered liver. I shuddered and went home trying to remember the words of the songs I was going to sing, but "liver" kept coming to mind.

Chapter 61

Once home in my room, in my mind I went through the possibilities of songs that Dad and I could use on NYE. Something was needed for our hosts, to thank them for the party. One of my favourite Scottish songs was the "Eriskay Love Lilt" which was a definite possibility, as was Burns' "My Luve is Like a Red, Red Rose". Neither was very long. I thought about the French chansons, but there the possibilities were endless. It did cross my mind to repeat the Françoise Hardy "Tous les garçons et les filles" with both sets of words, French and English, which the Browns might like, or perhaps "Les feuilles mortes". Dad seemed very keen that we should include the *Carmen* Act II aria, but despite him saying I could do it, I was really not sure my voice was big enough. I'd forgotten to ask if they insisted on "Auld lang syne" to round things off but realised, of course, that that would be at midnight long after my contribution, but I'd better learn the words anyway to do it properly.

My nerves got worse as NYE got closer. Dad and I had a couple of rehearsals on the thirtieth of December but had agreed to leave the thirty-first free. The night of the thirtieth was very difficult and I just tossed and turned, but I must have slept some of the time because, when I did open my eyes, it was broad daylight. I told Mom I didn't want any breakfast but she insisted that I should eat something, so I managed a boiled egg and a cup of coffee before going back to bed to try and sleep a bit more.

There were a couple of messages from Steph and Ed saying

they'd missed seeing me for a while and were looking forward to catching up that evening. I was glad not to hear from Harry as I was sure he would be equally on edge and we would just make each other more nervous. In any case, I told myself, the Brown family would be talking non-stop to Hamish about the six months that had passed since they had last actually seen each other. Of course I wondered what they may have said about me and that got my nerves jangling again. Eventually I did calm down and slept for a couple of hours in the afternoon.

Mom woke me up with a cup of tea and biscuits. She sat on the bed and told me Heather had told her, with help from Angus and the children, she'd prepared a lavish buffet. She stroked my chin and commented that I should take care shaving because the last thing I should worry about was cutting myself. "Okay, Mom, I'll be extra careful."

"Have you thought about what you're going to wear?"

"Yes, Mom, that's all sorted. I'll shave and shower now if you and Dad are finished in the bathroom."

She hugged me and kissed me on the forehead. "You'll be brilliant, I know you will."

I laughed. "Thanks, Mom, I know I can always rely on you and Dad." She left me to gather my resolve so, after a couple of minutes, with a big sigh, I got up and went to get myself ready.

There was still some time to spare before we set off, so I googled "Hogmanay" to find out what might be expected. I finished up more confused than ever, as it seemed that the Scottish diaspora had varying "traditions" depending on where they were, and in England at least, couldn't get the final words of Burns poem right at all, insisting on "...*for the sake of auld lang syne*" when "...*the sake of...*" was superfluous and never actually appears in the poem. The crossing of hands should only be done for the *final* chorus, — ie with the verse, "*And there's a hand my trusty freir! And gie's a hand o'thine…*"; too many tended to rush into it at the *first* chorus not thinking about the actual words.

There were also varying ideas about first-footing and whether a party shouldn't begin until *after* midnight when a tall dark haired male person crossed the threshold with symbols of warmth, food and prosperity plus whisky of course! The legend was that a blonde man might be a Viking and slaughter everyone once the door was opened. I was in two minds about contacting Harry, but decided that that it was up to the Browns to adapt Scottish traditions as they saw fit. Too much had already been put in place.

Because of my nerves, Dad insisted that he drive us to Wampanoag Drive. So Mom sat with me in the back, she holding my slightly trembling hands. I suppose it was inevitable that there was no space to park near the house. A couple of other households were having NYE parties as well so, with all the extra cars that involved, we were quite a way along the road before Dad could stop. As we walked back Dad handed me the car keys and said, "You'll probably be spending the night with Harry after the party. Your Mom and I will get ourselves home, possibly with the Svobodas depending on whether Jaroslav or Margita is relatively the more sober!"

"Thanks, Dad." And I gave him and Mom a hug.

Chapter 62

We could hear the sound of several parties as we made our way but number five seemed to be bursting. The house was completely lit up and we could see the Christmas cards and decorations through the main windows. At the door, which was slightly ajar, we went in with Mom and Dad ahead of me and we were greeted with the wondrous sight of what must be the MacInnes tartan on the Brown family. The pattern of blues, greens and black with thin red, pale blue and yellow stripes was beautiful to see. Heather and Ruth in white blouses, long skirts with plaid sashes, held in place with large brooches, presumably the clan badge with an inscription in Gaelic, and the three men resplendent in full Highland dress. They looked incredible to me who had only ever seen pictures, but here was the living, breathing reality. Angus and Heather immediately came over to greet us and I got a very warm welcome hug and kiss from Heather and a manly handshake from Angus with a, "You're aye welcome, Ethan." Before Ruth hugged me round the waist so I kissed the top of her head.

Someone grabbed my shoulders before pulling me in for another hug and then stood back still with his hands on my shoulders. "Och, ye must be Ethan. Ah've haird so much about ye for the past six months, so it's a real pleasure to finally meet ye and welcome ye to the family. Ah'm Hamish." The familiar piercing blue eyes gazed into mine as the familiar features, albeit with a trim red beard and framed by slightly longer hair, held me.

"I'm delighted to meet you too. You and Harry certainly do look alike, but you do sound more Scottish."

He laughed. "Aye, well ah haven't escaped the confines of Edinburgh, so it's nay surprising." He looked at me searchingly before saying, "Ah can see now why Harry would be attracted to ye, but what the hell do ye see in Harry?"

"Bastard," came from Harry and pushed him out of the way before kissing me, putting his arms round me.

"Ouch, your sporran's sticking into me."

He grinned before nudging Hamish and pointing to a gaily wrapped box on the side table.

"Hamish."

"Och aye, yes, ah nearly forgot in all the excitement. Ethan, here's a wee gift from Edinburgh which the family would like ye to accept in friendship with all our best wishes."

"Thank you very much. This is very unexpected."

"Ethan, from the emails and photos ye've been an incredible friend to Harry and Ruth and this trifle is the least ye deserve." Of course I blushed at such sentiments, and didn't know what to do next.

Dad said softly, "Why don't you open it?"

"Oh yes, of course." I carefully unpicked the package, whatever it was had been really beautifully and neatly wrapped. Under a couple of layers of tissue paper there was a tartan tie and a clan badge. Hamish explained that the tie in several shades of blue with faint white stripes was the Clan Liddell tartan, apparently registered as recently as 2009, and the amazing emblazoned shield was the clan emblem. I was suddenly aware that the whole Brown family was standing round smiling at me. "Oh, thank you, thank you all, this is really wonderful."

"Shall I look after that, Ethan?" said Mom and I happily

admired the design again before handing her the tie and badge, for her to stow away pro tem, in her handbag.

We followed the family into the main party area and a quick glance showed that everyone was already here, the gang with partners, their parents and Laurent and Yves of course. Everyone seemed to have a glass of something in their hand so Angus quickly made sure that Mom and Dad had something too. I declined a drink because, after that greeting which had made me forget temporarily why we were here, my butterflies were starting to flutter. I think Harry realised and came to hold my hand and whispered words of encouragement. It was very sweet of him, but then Angus hit his glass with something to get attention and asked the crowd to find a somewhere to sit. He nodded to Dad who went to the piano and he settled himself while I tried to calm myself and Harry went off to stand next to Hamish who put his arm round him.

Chapter 63

When I felt a little calmer, I started to speak which got everyone quiet. "The first two songs are Scottish and are a thank you to our hosts for their generous hospitality and friendship. The first is 'O my luve is like a red, red rose' a poem by Robert Burns whose birthday will be celebrated round the world on the twenty-fifth of January, his two hundred and sixtieth anniversary. I gave a little wave to Dad, took a deep breath and sang. My voice wavered a tiny bit at first but I managed to get through all four verses ending more confidently. Everyone applauded politely. "The next song is 'The Eriskay Love Lilt'. I hope you'll forgive my murdering the Gaelic bits."

"Aye, laddie yer'll nae ge a Glesga kiss fer a'," suddenly came from Angus which brought forth a shout of laughter from Hamish and Harry, barely suppressed giggles from Ruth and Heather and bemused looks from everyone else, though Mom and Dad were laughing quietly I noticed.

I could only say, "Thank you very much." And nodded to Dad who had recovered himself. Another deep breath and off we went. I thought this went a little better if anything and my voice carried more. Again, polite applause, perhaps more enthusiastic. "The next song is 'Les feuilles mortes' which you'll probably know as 'Autumn Leaves' when we get to the main tune." Dad was ready, another deep breath and off. There was a distinct murmur of appreciation when that well-known tune started and I finished more confidently to quite a lot more enthusiasm.

"You'll be pleased to note that this next item is the last so you can get back to the party. It's a more dramatic piece, an opera aria from *Carmen* by Georges Bizet. The hero, Don José, has just been released from three months in prison for letting Carmen escape in Act I. She had flirted with him, throwing him a flower which he had put in his jacket by his heart. In Act III she foretells her fate in the cards and in Act IV he does kill her viciously in a paroxysm of jealous rage, but in Act II she's ready to reward him with the night of passion she'd promised. He's had three months to dream about it, but he's realised he wants more, much more, he wants *her*, body and soul." I plucked a flower out of a vase on the piano. "He has kept the flower, or what remains of it, but it's kept its scent and this is what he pours out…" I closed my eyes and tried to imagine myself in Lillas Pastia's inn with a young very sexy woman, heaving breasts, my passion for her barely contained and eventually declaring throatily "Carmen" followed by the rising phrase "Je t'aime" and then the final diminuendo chords. I was unaware then that my hands were clenched tightly together, having crushed the flower, and I was trembling with all the unleashed emotions. There was a brief silence when Dad played those last chords before there was an eruption of cheers and applause. I opened my eyes and first spotted Mom crying before Dad hugged me saying I'd never sung it better. Everyone crowded round to congratulate me and I couldn't help noticing that the girls were dabbing their eyes. It seemed that I'd actually managed to sing an opera aria to a crowd of people and conveyed the emotions that I was experiencing.

Fortunately, after a few minutes of hubbub including a very vocal, "Magnifique. Merci beaucoup," from Laurent and Yves, Heather was able to move people in a different way by declaring that the buffet was open. Ruth hugged me and told me I was the best, Hamish followed suit leaving me alone with Harry.

He just kissed me for what seemed like hours before saying softly, "Je t'aime, aussi, Ethan. Je t'aimerai toujours."

Chapter 64

A couple of polite coughs made us stop. Of course I blushed immediately which got a smile from someone's parents who were holding loaded plates from the buffet. Harry grabbed my hand and led me through to the dining room where an incredible spread was all laid out. I wasn't very hungry as my stomach was still in some turmoil despite the singing being now behind me. However, Hamish seemed to have appointed himself as maître d' and insisted on piling up a plate for me. "Can't have our star waste away." And gave me a lovely smile that was so like Harry's.

He hadn't wasted any time on exerting his considerable charm on Steph, Sam and Rosita I noticed and it hadn't gone down too well with their beaux. I overheard him say at one point something like, "Ye're all so attractive, how can ah possibly entertain all of ye in the few days ah'm heer?"

Harry, needless to say, thought this was not on, so he said to Ed, Jan and Patrick, loud enough for Hamish and the girls to hear, "Would you like to see a picture of Helen, Hamish's girlfriend? Don't you think she's beautiful? We're hoping to hear about an engagement soon." And showed them his phone. Actually, she really was fantastically good looking. Hamish did not rise to the bait and just laughed, as did the girls who were just enjoying the party and the flattering attention of a very handsome, engaging young man who would soon be back across the ocean.

I managed to eat a few of the goodies on my plate and shared them with Harry. His attention was suddenly drawn across the room and he groaned, "Oh no! What the f… Hamish must have brought Dad's bagpipes. I'd hoped never to hear the bloody things again." He gave me a quick kiss and said, "Sorry, Ethan, you may want to block your ears with cheese. I think it's almost time for a performance like the von Trapp Family in Salzburg."

Angus started to tune and a space was cleared for Heather, Ruth, Hamish and Harry in the middle of the room. Angus announced, "Aye. A foursome reel." And it was wonderful to watch the intricate steps as they danced. Sitting on the floor as I was, of course, gave an excellent view of the way Hamish's and Harry's kilts swung as they danced with very brief glimpses of their naked bums excitingly revealing that nothing was worn under the kilt! It was over all too quickly but Hamish and Harry then gathered up the girls, Ed and me for an eightsome reel. Heather had excused herself because something or other needed her in the kitchen, Jan and Patrick having refused absolutely to be involved. Hamish explained what we needed to do. He organised us into pairs; Ed and Rosita, Harry and Steph, himself and Sam and Ruth and me. It wasn't particularly complicated, but it was exhausting and seemed to go on forever while each person took a turn in the middle.

The reel was followed with something called "Strip the Willow" which demanded attention as to the weaving in and out of the dancers. Hamish, Harry and Ruth seemed to be the only ones not out of breath by the end. I thought no wonder the Highlanders were so fit! We were given a few moments to recover before Angus announced that the last one would be a "Gay Gordons" and encouraged the other guests to join in. Hamish and Ruth quickly demonstrated the relatively simple steps. Harry whispered that he and I should be partnered but I whispered back that that really would be a dreadful cliché — we giggled and got in position. Ruth and I, Harry with Heather, while Hamish partnered Catherine. I gathered that Hugo was preparing to first foot. I think everyone really enjoyed it, even Jan and Patrick took part with Steph and Sam. I saw Mom and Dad grinning away, as most of the people joined in where possible which made it a bit difficult as the house was not a ballroom. Lots of applause and chatter greeted the end. Heather invited everyone to please help themselves to the remains of the buffet, and after "Auld Lang Syne", to please find a glass of something as we were fast approaching midnight.

A few minutes later we were all gathered in a rather rough ring when we were told that tradition and the actual words required us to wait for the final verse to cross arms with our neighbours, so the family spread themselves around so we could all follow their example. Of course as virtually all the guests were American, very few knew any of the poem other than the opening words, but in the spirit of the occasion, joined in enthusiastically and crossed arms at the right point and moved in and out of the circle.

Then there was a bit of a scramble to get hold of a drink as Angus switched on the television to get the accurate moment of the first stroke of midnight. Hugo suddenly reappeared having evidently spent a while in the bathroom. Harry and I looked at each other now puzzled by who the first footer would be as no one else who was tall and dark had gone out. However, we couldn't worry about it as the last seconds ticked by and it was midnight. Everyone kissed their partner as the front door bell sounded with the first chime. Hamish and Ruth went to answer it.

Chapter 65

When the kissing and cheering had just about stopped, Hamish and Ruth appeared with two youngsters who were holding hands. There was a pause in the general noise when Hamish announced loudly, "Ladies and gentlemen, please welcome our first footers, Grant Peters and Logan Summers." There was a burst of hi's, welcomes, happy new years as Hamish continued, "Aye, they've kindly brought the traditional symbols of warmth, wealth and nourishment as well as a miniature of Scotch, so we're all set for the year to come." Laughter and smiles. "They're sixteen and rodeo champions from Alberta, Canada and last summer were kidnapped and threatened with being murdered." One of them muttered something to Hamish who continued, "Apologies, ah've been corrected. They are *local* rodeo champions from South Alberta and Montana." There was an appreciable buzz in the room when Hamish invited the boys to explain the events that had brought them to Natick.

They stepped into the room still holding hands when Grant, who was about five foot ten, light brown hair and clear blue eyes, started to relate their adventures. Their families owned neighbouring ranches separated by some dense woodland either side of a stream which was the natural boundary of the properties. They'd both discovered deer which initially looked as if they had been attacked and mauled by a cougar, breaking fences in the attempt to escape. Grant had been on his horse called Thunder when he got to the woodland and dismounted before following a track when he met Logan doing the same thing. Logan (who was about the same height, but had a slightly more athletic build, long, lustrous black hair in a pony tail, and very dark almost black eyes) chimed in that he and Grant attended the same school, but because of their rivalry at the local rodeos, had not been friendly.

However, they'd agreed to combine forces, both armed with loaded rifles in case they actually met a cougar, and continued down the track when they were surprised by a group of thugs who tied them up, back-to-back, and made horrible threats. Grant came back in to say that they'd realised that their captors were part of a scheme to strong-arm their parents into selling most of their ranches for oil prospecting. The big problem was that neither ranch had been doing too well and the money offered was really very good.

The thugs thought that the deliberately savaged deer had not been sufficient incentive to sell, but their dead bodies, again made to look like cougar victims, would be the final straw. Using a storm as a cover, they'd set fire to a couple of guest cabins where, in better days, people escaping the cities and modern life for a while, could get fresh air, campfire cook outs, be taught to ride, use lassos and rope calves, which is what he and Logan did during vacations, hence the rodeos.

They were terrified that they were about to die, when his sister Lila, a crack shot and also a rodeo star, had suddenly appeared. Thunder, having got anxious had galloped back to the ranch house alerting everyone that something was very wrong. He'd brought her to where he'd been left. She'd followed the track and had overheard enough to take action. She'd shot one of the thugs in the foot, and after having their shotguns restored, they'd marched the gang back towards Grant's ranch. However, en route, a real cougar in the woods had made her presence felt, no doubt attracted by the smell of fresh blood. It took several well aimed shots near her head to cause her to disappear. One of the gang, an oil company man, tried to escape, but with both of them on Thunder's back and Logan ready with his lasso, they chased after him and caught him. They were handed over to the police, the injured one to paramedics.

These "adventures" had got into the public domain and the resulting publicity had made both ranches profitable again through bookings for the cabins and camping areas. The boys looked at each other, smiled and Grant said, "We discovered through our mutual support in that ordeal, we had a lot more in common than just being neighbours and rodeo rivals, so you could say we're sort of together now."

Logan added that an established author called Dylan James had offered to write a book detailing the whole thing. He'd proposed to call the novel *Thunder* because *he* had been the real hero.

"Dylan James?" said Harry "We've got several of his books on the shelves back in Edinburgh. Ruth and I have read them. Of course, he lives in Canada, so it's not really that surprising he would be interested in using your incredible tale."

Logan nudged Grant with his phone which prompted him to ask, "As we live in rather isolated places, parties like this one are very rare, so please, would it be okay if we took photos to send to our families to prove where we are? It's difficult enough for us to even have a cup of coffee as neither of us is old enough to drive and anyway it's a long drive to the nearest town. Even if Logan and I met at the border stream with flasks, it means a horse ride of about fifteen minutes at full gallop. What passes for our social life centres round school, but no after school activities unless someone's in town to take us home. Of course, there are the rodeos but we're always surrounded by other people when not in the competition."

Everyone was very happy to co-operate and organised themselves to fit into a group picture and then in family groups. Grant and Logan were delighted, especially with all the Browns in one with all that tartan, kilts, MacInnes clan badges, garters and sgian dubhs carefully displayed. They were insistent that Harry and I pose together and also separately for some reason.

Chapter 66

Inevitably someone asked if they had any photos of their ranches so we could have some idea of what they'd told us about. Logan asked Angus if he and Grant could be given his email address and they could get in touch with home to forward some suitable stuff which could then be easily seen on a laptop or PC screen; the screens on their phones would be too small.

Logan added rather drily, "Anyway Grant's phone only has five hundred pictures of Thunder and not one of me." Angus was happy to oblige so the boys immediately telephoned their parents with the request. While we waited for the response, Heather encouraged everyone to help finish off the buffet. When she asked the boys, they shook their heads and thanked her. Logan told her that his grandmother, with whom they were staying as she knew, had made sure they had had a big meal to get them through the night.

Obviously, Logan's remark about photos of Thunder had not been well received by Grant who riposted, "That's not quite true, Logan. I do have one photo of you, but it's not one I can show to these people, is it?" Logan was silenced. "I just needed something useful that I could blackmail you about!"

At that moment Angus announced that material from Grant's parents had arrived, so a crowd gathered around Angus's big screen PC and he got Grant to come and say what was what. The first pictures were of the ranch which drew a few gasps. "Are those the Rockies in the background?" someone asked.

"Yes. The view is something that Logan's and my family really do treasure and why we were so adamant about not giving up the ranches." Then there were pictures of the ranch house, Grant's parents and sister Lila toting a rifle and looking very attractive, as the murmurs of Hamish, Ed, Jan and Patrick indicated! Grant explained that Lila had a problem with finding a boyfriend because, when any prospective beau found out where she lived, the distances involved were seen as insurmountable unless he had a motor vehicle and was prepared to drive for hours. The screen showed what was presumably Grant's room with an amazing display of medals and trophies along one wall. We then moved on to rodeos and there were various exclamations at some of the scenes showing Grant astride Thunder waving his lasso and the frightened calf he was going to rope. The last shots were of Lila in a shooting competition and clutching her gold medals.

Logan had held back while the Peters family archive was being displayed and stood with me at the rear of the crowd, but he did hold my hand until Angus called out, "Logan lad, where are you? Your stuff is here and it appears to be all videos."

When he got to the front, Logan explained that his grandmother had given her son a video camera to record family life for her as she was moving to Massachusetts. Again, we had sweeping views of the ranch, and the distant Rockies, but this was followed by shots of the inside of the ranch house with Logan's collection of trophies and medals to the fore. Logan's mother came into view waving at the camera, but as her colouring was so different to his, he explained that she was German and he looked exactly like his father.

The next videos were of Logan at work round the ranch, often shirtless, revealing beautifully well-defined musculature. It was very apparent that Logan had no idea he was being filmed as his mouth dropped open in amazement and he blushed furiously.

From his breathing, I was aware that Harry was really enjoying those semi-nude scenes! The rodeo ones were incredible showing so much more than Grant's photographs. The concentration of boy and horse, as they waited like coiled springs for the calf to be released, was mesmerising as was the twirling of the lasso as it snaked whip-like towards the terrified animal.

However, the most revealing video showed a medal ceremony where Logan had come second to Grant. Logan was all congratulatory smiles, but as Grant seemingly stepped down without really acknowledging him, the smile was replaced momentarily by evident longing. It was only a split second because he immediately went back to his glorious smile as the camera came towards him. The final video was of Logan on his horse Montana waving to the camera, riding into a superb sunset behind the Rockies. "Sorry about that. My dad loves Hollywood films, as you can see from that dreadful schmaltzy scene." That got quite a laugh.

Both the boys were profusely thanked by the hosts and guests for giving them that insight. A few of the parents also made their excuses and called it a night, so the press of people did thin out a little. Angus, ever the thoughtful host, pointed out that the time was approaching two o'clock when Alberta would be celebrating New Year. He asked the boys if, as a special treat and they were in a private house, they would like an alcoholic drink. They looked at each other for a minute or two before Grant said, "As we're at a Scottish party, could we please try some real scotch?"

"Aye, of course. With a drop of water or a couple of ice cubes?"

"Whatever you recommend."

"Okay. I'll be back shortly. Does anyone else who is not driving want a dram of spiritual uplift?" As there were several others happy to be uplifted, it was a few minutes before Angus could return with the boys' drinks.

I couldn't help but overhear Grant whisper to Logan that he'd noticed that brief look and asked how long he'd felt like that, as he had convinced himself that they'd not liked each other at all and had, more or less, ignored each other at school. Logan just sighed and smiled before saying that it had been a while but the horrors of the "cougar hunt" had sorted it out for the pair of them.

They turned to Heather, Ruth and Hamish, and Grant said, "Thank you again for inviting us. This party is amazing for both of us. As we've explained, such gatherings are rare at home because of the isolation of the ranches."

Logan added, "It was so different to be able to sit in a genuine cafe, where you met us, and your invitation for us to be first footers (when that was explained) was an opportunity we couldn't possibly have refused. We're only in Natick because our parents considered that we really needed a break and Granny was delighted to be able to accommodate us. Even being able to share a bed has meant a lot." And he squeezed Grant's hand.

Grant commented that the cafe staff had been particularly welcoming, and they'd wondered whether the waiter had noticed them holding hands as he was hovering, constantly asking if they'd wanted more coffee or anything. When he'd shown Heather and Ruth to share the table because the rest of the place was full, they'd been delighted to start chatting and that was how their tale had all spilled out.

"We've been thoroughly spoiled while we've been in Natick. Do you know Tomáš at the Urquell cafe?" Of course this was greeted with a lot of laughter.

Harry told them, "The Urquell is our main meeting place in town, so we all know Tom."

Chapter 67

Angus handed the boys their whiskies and the television programme announced that it was two o'clock and listed the states that were now celebrating. The Canadian provinces weren't mentioned, but we all raised glasses to wish all Albertans wherever they were, a happy new year. Of course then both boys' phones rang almost immediately. Grant managed to keep his exchanges with his parents and sister fairly brief, but did say what a wonderful time he and Logan were having and hoped that the photos taken earlier had shown that.

Logan tried to keep his conversation short, but it soon became obvious that his father just wanted to talk. Logan managed to tell his father that he was enjoying his first taste of genuine scotch. "No, not Canadian Club, this is the real thing, it's…" Angus showed him the bottle. "…It's Highland Park, twelve years old when bottled and is distilled in Orkney. Sorry, Dad, if I could pour some down the phone I would, you know that."

After some more talk Logan said, "I can't ask questions like that, Dad." He put down his whisky, looked up at Harry who was standing next to him and sighed. "Dad wants to know if Scots wear anything under the kilt." Harry grabbed Logan's free hand and put it under his kilt. I didn't know where Logan's hand went, but his eyebrows rose, he swallowed hard and said, "Dad, I've just had proof that Scots go commando! Is the dagger real please? He wants to know now." Harry drew his sgian dhub from its sheath and very lightly put its point into one of Logan's fingers. "Ow! That's sharp. Yes, Dad it's very real, but I don't think it's used for scalping redcoats if that's your next question. You've seen too many old movies. Yes, please put Mom on. Hi, Mom." And then he spoke in German. From learning the words to some Lieder, I understood a little of the exchange. He assured her that all was well and they were having a great time and enjoying a small glass of whisky. Of course whisky is whisky in any language which prompted Angus to pour a bit more into Logan's and Grant's glasses. "We'll be safe getting back to Grandma's," he said in English.

I waved at him, so he paused while I said, "Neither of you can go around Natick reeking of whisky at sixteen. I'll drive you there when you're ready."

"Thank you very much," they chorused, before Logan said to his mother, "It's okay, Mom, we've been offered a lift and the driver is completely sober… She wishes everyone a very happy new year." Everyone clinked glasses and wished them a happy new year in return. "Tschüss Mutti. Ich liebe Dich."

Most of the rest of the parents took that as a good point to drink up and make their adieus so there were a lot of hugs, kisses and handshakes, and when everything had quietened, Heather asked whether anyone left would like coffee, tea or even soup. Then she suddenly said, "Oh my God! I almost forgot." She hastened to the kitchen and appeared a few minutes later with a large dish of home-made hot sausage rolls which had been left in the oven on a very low heat for quite a while apparently. The remaining guests were delighted even though the treats had to be left to cool down for a few minutes.

Grant and Logan having slowly sipped their whiskies and nibbled a couple of sausage rolls, decided they should go back to

Grandma's and did a tour of those left to wish them all a great 2019 and expressed the hope that perhaps some of them might come to Alberta, the ranches, horses etc., were waiting. They said the same to their hosts with special appreciation for Angus (whisky), Heather (food), Ruth (for the invitation), Hamish (for being his charming self) and Harry who said he would see them off.

At the front door Logan excused himself to go to the bathroom and I set off to where Dad had parked the car. Harry told me later that the moment Grant and he were alone, Grant had his hands under his kilt and had then quickly put his head underneath and given his cock a suck. It had been so sudden that he'd almost cum but hadn't. When Logan got back, they were the picture of innocence which he was sure Logan didn't believe!

Chapter 68

The car was a bit further away than I'd remembered, but the road was almost entirely clear of vehicles now which meant I was unlikely to meet a drunk reveller on or off the road. When I got back to the house, I wondered if the boys had enjoyed kissing Harry farewell. They got in, Grant in the back and Logan as shotgun. "What's the address please?" Logan told me the street name. Fortunately, I knew where Grandma lived, or at least roughly, where. As we set off Grant leant forward and kissed the back of my neck and started to undo the top buttons on my shirt so he could put his hand behind my t-shirt and play with my nipples. Logan began undoing the other shirt buttons and tried to tug my shirt and t-shirt out from the prison of my trousers.

Grant paused his kissing to ask, "How often do you and Harry have sex then? Ruth told us that you and he are always in each other's beds and have you had sex with Tomáš as well?"

Trying to drive with this dual attack was difficult especially as I was erect due to their attentions. I was very grateful that the roads were so empty. Logan somehow managed to undo my belt and top button of my trousers so the shirt and t-shirt came adrift allowing him to run his hands over my body. I was able to gasp out that Harry and I had sex as often as possible and yes, I had had sex with Tom, but they were the only two.

Logan's grandmother lived out on the western edge of town and I managed to get us there despite a couple of wrong turns. They told me that Heather had given them the first footers' gifts of coal, shortbread, British ten pence piece and miniature of whisky because they hadn't any idea of what she'd meant, and also money for a taxi to take them to Wampanoag Drive. Ruth had filled them in about Harry and me because she had seen that they were holding hands and may appreciate meeting two other gays. Logan's wonderful black hair had been instrumental in them being asked to be first footers. A call had confirmed that Hamish and Angus fully supported the idea especially when told of the meeting in the Urquell and the incredible tale of their kidnapping ordeal and its happy outcome.

Between them I was told that Ruth had shown them on her phone pictures of Harry and me naked which had made them really want to experience "the real thing". I realised that the only possible occasion when I could have been seen naked like that was the morning after the night before when Heather had brought in my washed and ironed clothes, so Ruth must have crept in behind her. And that bastard Harry had never said anything!

When we finally arrived in Grandma's road, Grant suggested I park in a less well-lit place. He said that his father had the same model car on the ranch and he was being taught to drive it by one of the ranch hands, Jackson, who was a walking warning against smoking as his nicotine breath was sheer poison. Grant couldn't understand how Jackson's wife could permit him to kiss her! "Sorry, that's beside the point," he said. "This model allows you to fold down the back seat to create a sort of station wagon, so shall we do that and then would you please get in the back, Ethan."

I undid my seatbelt and got in to find the seat down and Grant in the far corner with his jeans round his ankles. He pulled me across to him, bent down to kiss me before planting his knees either side of my head. He then put a hand under my head and pushed himself forward so his cock was right in front of my lips.

At the same time, Logan had got in behind me, unzipped and pulled my trousers and boxers down to my ankles and proceeded to lick my balls before fellating me. Grant pushed himself into my mouth and I immediately obliged, willingly letting my hands wander up and down his tight ass and taut slim body as I sucked. He moaned pleasurably as I was doing too, I realised. All too soon his short breaths told me he was about to orgasm and Logan was getting me close to orgasm as well. A few more thrusts of his cock in my mouth, he came and very shortly afterwards I did too, Logan evidently liking the flavour!

Grant shuffled down my body kissing me. Logan moved up on my other side, and looking at Grant, they undid the rest of my shirt and pushed up my t-shirt to expose me completely. The pair of them started to kiss my body and play with my nipples again. Grant then moved to replace Logan as he had evidently noticed I was getting another erection. He nudged Logan, who I suspected didn't really need prompting, but he immediately undid and lowered his jeans and underpants, placed his knees either side of my head, hand under my head. I needed no encouragement to take him in my mouth and happily confirmed what had been seen in the home videos, exploring his rather better muscled body. When I grabbed his ass and tried to push a finger in, he groaned, I hoped ecstatically. He seemed to be pushing down wanting more. I regretted not having any lube and I wasn't in a position to use spittle as the cowboys in *Brokeback Mountain* had done.

After Grant got his reward, a very short while later I got mine as Logan's creamy load hit my grateful taste buds after much gasping (on his part) and moaning (on mine). After Logan dismounted, I sat up and stretched a bit, feeling very uncomfortable. The three of us grinned at each other before a joint kiss. Grant got out of the car fairly easily while Logan somehow managed to pull up his pants before clambering over me and then helping me to move with my trousers still round my ankles. Once out of the car I pulled up my boxers and trousers, tucked in my t-shirt and now re-buttoned my shirt. I was grateful it had been a comparatively mild evening and not blowing a gale or snowing a blizzard, as New England had faced in previous new years.

Grant and Logan now had their arms round each other. "Well, Toto, I don't think we're in Alberta any more," said Logan with another grin.

We all laughed. Grant asked, "Is there any chance we could meet you and Harry before we have to go home on Sunday? We're due back in school on Monday, so Saturday would be the only day really."

"Here, put your contact details in my phone. If Harry is okay, and I can't see him not being, I'll be in touch and come to collect you." More kissing.

"Happy 2019 to you both — it's been quite a start!" And I watched them disappear into a house a little further down the road where it was rather more brightly lit, but not before Logan turned and blew me a kiss, which I pretended to catch and put in my mouth. He laughed out loud.

Chapter 69

When I got back to Wampanoag Drive, I was very happy to see that I could now park right outside the house. The front door was slightly ajar, obviously a departing guest hadn't closed it properly. I opened the living room door to find the gang, Laurent, Yves and the MacInnes-Browns all evidently waiting for me. "Hello all. Have I missed anything?" was my rather lame response to the silence that had greeted me. The laughter that followed was amazing.

Heather stepped forward and said, "Ethan you may wish to tidy yourself up." There was a mirror on the wall and I saw my hair was a total mess, only one shirt tail was tucked in and the buttons were not in the right holes. I wanted to swear but the continuing laughter rather stopped me.

Laurent stepped forward and gave me a bear hug. "Mon petit. We couldn't leave without wishing you a personal Bonne Année." And gave me a lingering kiss with tongue. He still held me while apparently savouring the taste like a wine expert. "Hmmm. Yves what do you think of this?"

Yves then hugged me, kissed me, again with tongue, and did the same. "Oui. Après les aventures canadiennes avec les jeunes hommes, definitely a Jackson-Triggs, I would say. Very young, very nouveau. What do you think about the after tastes?"

"Cheval et cuir, n'est-ce pas?"

I thought I knew where this was going, but managed to say "What's a Jackson-Triggs please?"

"Ah, the best Canadian wine maker with excellent wines from Ontario and British Columbia. Highly recommended, Angus and Heather. However, this may be their newest one, just on the market, called 'Le Tonnere de l'Alberta" — The Thunder of Alberta'." Of course everyone had another laugh at my expense. Laurent and Yves having waited patiently, apparently just for this moment, gave me another kiss, but on the forehead this time, hugged me and waved to the crowd as they left with a loud, "Bonne Année".

I had to assure everyone I was perfectly okay and that I was sorry if I had caused anyone to worry. Of course I then had to go to the bathroom to properly dress myself. When I emerged Heather offered me a cup of tea which was very gratefully accepted. Before I could take a sip, however, Harry grabbed me, kissed me and really plunged his tongue in my mouth. When he let me go, he turned to our friends and said, evidently in all seriousness, "Those French poseurs are real frauds. I couldn't taste any horse or leather." Even I had to laugh especially when he added "The 'cuir' perhaps."

On the drive back I'd thought there might be some teasing about the length of time it had taken to take the boys home, but perhaps the worst example was from Hamish, of all people, who suggested that, "Perhaps some mutual exploration had been enjoyed with a view to semen-ting US-Canada relations!" Harry guffawed, Ruth shrieked, Angus chortled in his bass-baritone way, and everyone else laughed a lot. I just refused to say anything about my absence, though my dishevelment must have indicated very clearly what had happened.

Needless to say I was very touched that everyone had stayed so long in order to make sure I was unharmed, but I was left in no doubt that there had been speculation about the boys' intentions as several had noted in particular Logan's staring at me, standing so close and possibly even his holding my hand. However, after all the assurances I was safe and sound, that did seem to be the signal to my friends, it was time to go. They all thanked the hosts and gave me a hug or a kiss or both before getting their coats. Rosita and Ed said, "Hasta luego." Steph and Jan, "Dobru noc."

The last one to come to me was Patrick who hugged me and whispered very quietly, "Shall we make Harry jealous? I want revenge."

I whispered back, "Okay." So he held me right up against him and kissed me but no tongue. I could feel the soft bulge of his genitals and he must have been aware of my raging erection. There was no way he couldn't have been aware of it. We both moaned gently as his powerful arms seemed to crush me.

When we parted, he put his hands on my shoulders, gave a fleeting glance down at my bulging trousers, smiled and whispered, "I'm very flattered." And gave me another very quick kiss before saying in his normal football captain voice, "Well, I think that's my 0.0001% for 2019 all used up now so, team, are we ready to head out?", and as in all the books and films involving football coaches, he gave me a hearty smack on the butt. He gathered up Sam who blew me a kiss before they all left laughing out loud as they had heard about that first drive to school all those months ago.

Chapter 70

Silence. The Browns settled back into their seats, Angus and Heather with their arms around each other, no doubt somewhat relieved at the quiet. Harry appeared to be seething with a fixed expression that certainly didn't indicate his usual contentment or bode well. After a minute I felt I should make a move too, so went across to Angus with an outstretched hand to say goodbye. Before I could open my mouth, Harry said, "Not so fast. You can't go yet, Liddell, you've got a lot of explaining to do." He had never called me by my family name.

"I don't have to explain anything, and who do you think you're talking to? We're not in some fancy school in Edinburgh now." I saw his eyes open wider and I think there was a very faint smile too playing about his lips.

It came to me very belatedly, how could I have been so blind and stupid, not to have seen that Harry liked to be challenged, and of course, the biggest challenge of all had been Patrick, none of the other encounters had come close, so Patrick's "revenge" in front of the gang, having put up with those months of teasing which he had tolerated with good humour, had been the biggest slap in the face by kissing *me*.

Harry checked his phone in his sporran and said, "Dad, could I please have a couple of malts with ice because Liddell and I need to celebrate Hawaiian new year shortly."

Angus, with a barely disguised laugh. "Aye, of course." Went to get the drinks while I was equally determined not to be told what to do.

"No, thank you. I've celebrated enough!" I gave Ruth a kiss, she was almost asleep, shook Hamish's hand saying it had been a real pleasure to meet him.

He didn't let go, but said quietly, "Don't let the bastard off the hook, he gets away with far too much." And winked at me.

I hugged Heather and she returned it with a kiss and a laugh saying, "Thank you, Ethan, for making this a truly memorable Hogmanay, and in particular for your lovely singing."

Angus added, "Aye lad, we were surprised by the Bizet and had thought you'd chose something from Mozart or possibly Donizetti."

"Come along Tweety Pie Liddell… please," came from the stairs where Harry was cradling the very generous drinks from Angus. (Thumbs up from Hamish.) After that "please" I decided to relent a little and made my way to the stairs. Harry still looked a bit grim however.

"If I'm Tweety Pie, doesn't that make you Sylvester? You are aware that Tweety always wins, and in any case, if we're actually going to toast Hawaii, it is still New Year's Eve there and in Germany that is called Sylvester."

"Oh, is that little nugget something you picked up from Logan?"

"No. You patronising…"

"Don't hold back on our account, Ethan. Give him both barrels," came from Hamish as Angus and Heather laughed.

"Not all Americans are as ignorant as you snotty Brits seem to think." Our voices had gradually risen through this exchange and Hamish and his parents had evidently found it very amusing as a quick glance had proved. Ruth, thank goodness, had fallen asleep.

Chapter 71

We got to Harry's bedroom door, but as he was still carefully holding on to the whisky, he curtly nodded to me to open it. When inside he carefully placed the glasses on a nightstand next to a tube of lube I noticed.

I was going to say, "Like a good scout, always prepared." When Harry just lunged for me, wrapped his arms round me and silenced me with a kiss that had me gasping for breath when he eventually let go. "I've been wanting to do that since eight o'clock when you arrived." (He'd obviously forgotten the loving kiss after listening to my squalling.) He switched on his computer so that we could keep track of the time as Hawaiian midnight approached. "Please help me take off this outfit, it feels more like a straitjacket until the moment I can hold you naked." I kissed him while he slipped off the jacket and undid the waistcoat and carefully hung them up. I was admiring the workmanship as Harry undid the belt and slipped it though the loops at the back of the kilt. "Can you please undo the chain that holds the sporran?" He gave me one of his glorious smiles while he pulled at the leather straps that held his kilt in place and let out a sigh as he unwrapped it so I could see the length of wool cloth that was involved and the amazing pleating that preserved the pattern of the tartan. He put the kilt on its hanger and then undid his bowtie before getting me to unbutton his shirt and remove his cufflinks, which I saw were in the shape of the MacInnes clan badge, while we kissed again. He had to sit down to unlace and take off his special shoes before undoing the garters and put them, with his sgian dhubh, in a special bag.

Finally, he was naked and looked at me quizzically. "Well, what about you, if we're going to celebrate Hawaiian style?" We each took a sip of whisky before I unbuckled my belt and unzipped, letting my trousers fall and pushed down my boxers to rest round my ankles while Harry started to unbutton my shirt but had to stop while I took out my cufflinks. While we paused, I bent down to untie my shoelaces and kicked off the shoes, trousers and boxers. We gazed into each other's eyes while he pushed my shirt off my shoulders, letting it fall to the floor and tugged up my t-shirt. I raised my arms as he pulled it up over my head and dropped it on top of the shirt. He grinned and said, "At least it's a white one and not battleship grey." Before kissing me. I took my socks off so we were finally totally naked and could embrace properly.

We lay on the bed and kissed after each sip of whisky. After a few minutes Harry raised himself on one elbow, fixed me with a stare and said, "Well?"

"Well, what?"

"What was it like being kissed by Patrick?"

"I don't think I should tell you. I don't want to inflame your jealousy even more."

Harry laughed. "Oh, Ethan, I got that he was deliberately trying to provoke me to get revenge for all the teasing, but that was only a momentary reaction. But did you enjoy it? The pair of you did seem to be making a meal of it."

I let him wait while I considered my answer.

"Hmmm, what can I say?"

"Ethan, I'm sorry for what I said downstairs. I deserved your rebuke. but please speak to me, tell me."

I relented. "Okay, his kiss was wonderful, but there was absolutely no tongue nor any movement in his groin, not a twitch of any kind, but he was certainly aware of my reaction."

"I think we were all aware of your reaction, Ethan." Silence.

"Will you tell me what happened with the Albertans then?"

"Do I have to?"

"Well, if it helps, the moment you went off to get the car and Logan was in the lavatory, Grant had his hands up my kilt in a flash and was feeling everything before he put his head under and started to suck me, but it could only be for a couple of seconds before Logan joined us. But it was very exciting and I almost came. That boy certainly needs and wants an injection of fresh, hot, home-made Scottish produce in both ends. Speaking of which, I think you could do with some too. Ethan, please, please forgive me and just get on top." And he reached for a condom and the tube of lube.

I grinned at him and straddled him. "All I can say about the boys is that they were desperate for sex."

"They didn't…?"

"No, it was all oral. If you think about what they said about the isolation of their ranches and the difficulties about time to be alone together, their assault wasn't surprising I suppose. They both wanted to be sucked off and both wanted to have me too and feel my body, so it took a bit longer than just taking them home. It was incredibly uncomfortable in the back of the car despite folding down the back seat, I can tell you. I just presumed that they were reluctant to take advantage of Grandma's generosity and couldn't invite me to their room. But I was able to let my hands roam over their lovely taut bodies. As you saw on those video clips Logan is very nicely built."

Harry murmured agreement while putting on the condom

and applying lube to me and himself. "When Logan was in my mouth he reacted very positively when I tried to push a finger into him, as you are doing to me now, so I know what he wants."

Harry held me by the waist and raised me to let me guide his sheathed cock to enter me slowly. "By the way, the boys want to meet us on Saturday before they fly home on Sunday," I managed to gasp out as I settled back on Harry before he began to thrust quite vigorously. It was going to be quite a bumpy ride! I thought about quoting Bette Davis, but decided against.

Chapter 72

"So was that your hot, fresh cock-a-leekie then?" We grinned at each other once our breathing had calmed.

"Hmmm, hmmm, you're getting cocky, smartarse." And we kissed as he held me on top of him. "Are you going to give me a sample of something special from New England in return?" He let go of me while he slid out, took a mouthful of whisky and then tried to suck my cock which caused me to almost scream in agony as it stung. "I've wanted to try that since I read some time ago that whisky is a natural disinfectant. Why do you think that in cowboy films they can pass around a bottle of Scotch without having to wipe the neck between swigs?"

"You really are a total bastard. Will I ever recover?"

"Oh yes, because once I get us lubed up, you are going to be able to do whatever you want to me." He stretched out that lovely body, but all I really wanted to do was let my hands wander over it.

Harry looked contemplative and when I asked why, he said, "Do you know that, other than that wonderful time with you and Tom a few days ago, since I have known you, it has been the longest time that I've been celibate."

"What do you mean by celibate? Do you understand what it means, and might I say, it's not for want of trying, is it?"

"Well, yes of course I understand what true celibacy is, but you know what I mean?"

"No, I do not, and you know perfectly well that I don't. You were the first and only one until Tom. Oh, Harry, I wish I could make love to you all day, every day. I just love *you*."

Chapter 73

He put out his arms to gather me in to him, kissed me and his hands stroked my back as he pretended to nibble my nose. "Ethan, I love you too, but what are you going to do with the queue?"

"What queue?"

"The line of guys who are waiting to use their hands and mouth on you and for you to do the same to them. You can't not be aware of your appeal? There's Logan and Grant to start with, then Tom who would welcome you at any time, Zeke, Josh, Hudson, Randall, and God forbid you should ever be that desperate, Laurent and Yves. And those are only the ones I know of. Goodness knows who else at John Eliot has yet to make themselves known, and there are gays everywhere, in Natick too. Whatever it may seem like, only a tiny minority of the population is gay, perhaps three per cent, though Hamish has told me that on his excursions to CC Bloom's with Gordon and Alasdair, it seems as if at least half of Edinburgh's adult male population is there at the same time! I'm not saying you should go out of your way to have sex with everyone, but as you said about Josh after the chat with your father, you shouldn't turn down the opportunities to make friends though, with some, you may well be just kissing frogs. You may go to the college or university where Tom or Josh, for example, will go this year. Having contacts in place can only be an advantage. Perhaps, preferably, you'll find a way of coming to Edinburgh, which is where I want to be in eighteen months' time, and if you were to be with me, 'my cup would runneth over'." He kissed me. "Ethan, you are my one and only prince, please, please don't forget that, whatever I may do or say."

Harry then put the gel on his arsehole before applying it to my cock which stiffened as his hands gently moved up and down the shaft, moving my foreskin up and down which nearly got me to cum. I had to get him to pause for a moment or two before I could put on a condom and with gel slowly penetrate him. When I was inside, I decided it was time for a couple of essential matters to be sorted. "Harry"

"Yes?"

I sensed his body stiffen as if wary.

"When will you be eighteen, please?"

He relaxed. "I thought for a moment you were going to ask awkward questions about my past. Ethan, that really is a closed book. Dennis helped me through a rather bad time at school, which is why he is... was special., but to answer you, it's actually next month on..."

"Don't tell me, I bet it's the fourteenth. Being you, it couldn't be otherwise."

"Yes, you're right." He laughed. "And Hamish's is a week later. Ruth will be sixteen in May. So when will you be eighteen?"

"You beat me by two days."

Harry started to move underneath me. "Is there anything else?"

"Yes. Do you remember the first night we spent together?"

"As if it were yesterday."

"You wanted to keep a mystique about your other name. Alexander Henry something. What's the something please?"

Harry grinned as he grabbed hold of my ass and pushed me

into him. "Why don't you guess? And see if you can find the name before you fill the rubber with hot, fresh New England chowder."

We got moving slowly. "Angus, Hamish."

"You're close."

"James, Andrew, Alasdair, Alexander, Gordon, William, Robert the Bruce."

"No, no, no."

"Charles Rennie MacIntosh… Miss Jean Brodie… Marcia Blaine… Flora Macdonald." We were speeding up and I was getting more breathless and panting with each thrust. "Magnus… Columba… Iona… Skye… Mull… Clyde… Moray… Fraser… Darling… Macbeth… Macduff… Porter … Duncan… Douglas… Dou… aaaaaah." I just couldn't hold on any longer. I collapsed onto Harry who just wrapped his arms tightly around me again and we lay there, silent other than my deep breaths which gradually got calmer, but I could feel him shaking with laughter.

"What name were you going to say before ejaculation so rudely interrupted you?" he managed to whisper.

"Dougal" I managed to whisper back.

Harry lifted my head, kissed me, grinned and said, "Close enough. It's Dugald, not Dougal, not some long-haired dog from the *Magic Roundabout*, but at least you didn't say Jabberwocky."

"I wouldn't ever — not to your face. Anyway, you're more of a 'frumious Bandersnatch'."

We giggled, he bared his teeth before licking my face all over followed by lavishing kisses. "Alexander Henry Dugald MacInnes-Brown! It's a bit of a mouthful isn't it, which is why I normally shorten it. Hamish is just Hamish Dugald which is a combination of our grandfathers' first names."

"I think it's lovely and it does suit you."

"But in Gaelic it means black stranger. I thought I was going to die laughing when you said Miss Jean Brodie."

"I was getting desperate."

"Aye, that you were, but I love you for trying. In fact, I just love you. Please don't ever change."

There was a knock on the door. It opened slightly and Hamish's voice told us that Hawaiian New Year would arrive in just under five minutes if were still interested in celebrating it and did we need anything. "Thanks, Hamish. I think we're probably done celebrating New Year, but we'll toast the Hawaiians anyway with the whisky we've got left. Are you off to bed?"

"Aye, Mum and Dad are coming up now too. Ruth was put to bed a wee while ago. I'll see you both at lunch or tea or whenever. Good night or perhaps, good morning."

We chorused back, "Good morning." The door closed. The computer clock showed that it was the Hawaiian hour so, as we clinked glasses, the same thought occurred to us, we toasted "Kissing frogs", laughed and kissed at length before snuggling down.

Harry whispered in my ear, "Tomorrow is another day, my Prince."

"And it's only a day away *my* Prince," I replied.

To be continued.

Books read for inspiration
(most still on my bookshelf)

André Aciman — *Call me by your Name/Call me by Your Name**

Arvin Ahmadi — *How It All Blew Up*

Becky Albertalli — *Simon vs the Homo Sapiens Agenda/Love, Simon**

Becky Albertalli & Adam Silvera — *What if it's us*

S W Ballenger — *A Gay Polyester High School Romance; A Gay Polyester High School Romance 2*

E F Benson — *Mapp and Lucia (Six volumes)*

Philippe Besson — *Lie with Me*

John Boyne — *The Heart's Invisible Furies*

Joe Brewer-Lennon — *The Diary of Andy Angus — The Lost Year*

Stephen Chbosky — *The Perks of Being a Wallflower*

Val Emmich/Steven Levenson/Ben J Pasek/Justin Paul — *Dear Evan Hansen/Dear Evan Hansen**

Jonny Garza Villa — *Fifteen Hundred Miles from the Sun*

Mark Gatiss — *The Vesuvius Club; The Devil in Amber; Black Butterfly*

Sophie Gonzalez — *Only Mostly Devastated*

John Green & David Levithan — *Will Grayson, Will Grayson*

Simon James Green — *Noah Could Never; Noah Can't Even;*

	Alex in Wonderland; Heartbreak Boys; Life of Riley:Beginner's Luck; You're the One that I Want
Alexis Hall	*Boyfriend Material*
Brent Hartinger	*Geography Club*
William Hussey	*Hideous Beauty; The Outrage*
Dylan James	*Thunder; Frankenstein Builds a Boyfriend; Drag Queens, Emo Teens & Big Dreams; Gay Love and Other Fairy Tales; Gay Love and Other Christmas Magic*
Tomasz Jedrowski	*Swimming in the Dark*
Bill Konigsberg	*Openly Straight; Honestly, Ben; The Porcupine of Truth; Out of the Pocket; The Music of What Happens; The Bridge*
Felyx Lawson	*L.I.F.E.*
George Lester	*Boy Queen*
David Levithan	*Boy Meets Boy; Two Boys Kissing*
Kenneth Logan	*True Letters from a Fictional Life*
Adam Macqueen	*Beneath the Streets*
Vitor Martins	*Here the Whole Time*
Armistead Maupin	*Tales of the City (nine volumes); Maybe the Moon; The Night Listener; Logical Family*
Marco May	*Abhorrence*
Calum McSwiggan	*Eat, Gay, Love*
Justin Myers	*The Last Romeo; The Magnificent Sons*
Charles Nelson	*The Boy who Picked the Bullets Up*
L C Rosen	*Camp; Jack of Hearts*
Philip Roth	*Portnoy's Complaint*
Benjamin Alire	*Aristotle and Dante Discover the Secrets*

Sáenz	*of the Universe*
William Shakespeare	*A Midsummer Night's Dream; The Taming of the Shrew/ Kiss Me, Kate**
Muriel Spark	*The Prime of Miss Jean Brodie*
Phil Stamper	*The Gravity of Us; As Far as You'll Take Me*
Kevin van Whye	*Date Me, Bryson Keller*

* Film or stage musical or both.

Some authors have written (a lot) more than shown.